P9-CEM-101

Praise for *AUTOFOCUS*

"Maude felt like someone I knew—a girl so easy to root for— and her story captured me completely. *Autofocus* hit all the right notes, leaving me satisfied and smiling."
—**TRISH DOLLER,** author of *Where the Stars Still Shine*

"*Autofocus* is a beautifully told story about friendship, family, and finding yourself. My heart ached for Maude so much that I couldn't stop turning pages."
—**LAUREN MORRILL,** author of *The Trouble with Destiny*

"*Autofocus* is a beautifully written story that takes you on an emotional ride, touching on the complexities of adoptees and family, distance and friendship, first love and first heartbreak."
—**ERIC SMITH,** author of *Inked* and contributor to BookRiot

Praise for *THE NIGHT WE SAID YES*

"Lauren Gibaldi so cleverly weaves the past and the present to tell an authentic, spontaneous story of friendship, romance, and all the gray areas in between. With the turn of each page, you'll be so glad you said yes to *The Night We Said Yes!*"
—**JULIE MURPHY,** *New York Times* bestselling author of *Side Effects May Vary* and *Dumplin'*

"Irresistibly sweet and full of heart, Matt and Ella's romance charmed me twice." —**JESSICA MARTINEZ,** author of *Kiss Kill Vanish* and *The Vow*

"You'll wish you could step into the pages and go along for the ride. Suspenseful, romantic, and just plain fun. Say yes to this book!" —**TARA ALTEBRANDO,** author of *The Best Night of Your (Pathetic) Life*

"This is a story for anyone who's ever wanted to give first love a second chance." —**MELISSA WALKER,** author of *Ashes to Ashes* and *Lovestruck Summer*

"*The Night We Said Yes* captures the flutter and heartache of first love. This book is a first kiss and a first touch. It is a promise of a night filled with the thrill (and fear) of so many possibilities." —**JENNY TORRES SANCHEZ,** author of *The Downside of Being Charlie* and *Death, Dickinson, and the Demented Life of Frenchie Garcia*

"*The Night We Said Yes* is filled with brilliant insights about what it's like to be young and alive. You haven't met Lauren Gibaldi, but she already knows you." —**DC PIERSON,** author of *Crap Kingdom* and *The Boy Who Couldn't Sleep and Never Had To*

"Effectively captures intense, all-consuming teen attraction." —**SLJ**

"Gibaldi's special debut will make readers ruminate on first chances, first loves, and those big, life-altering decisions. Fun to read, and the love story embedded within—along with a boatload of awesome characters—will appeal to lovers of all genres." —**ROMANTIC TIMES**

"A story of friendship and romance, music and trespassing, and ultimately pursuing your own dream and your heart's desire. For fans of books like *Nick & Norah's Infinite Playlist.*" —**ALA BOOKLIST**

"Speaks to the power of friendship and the importance of nurturing relationships." —**VOYA**

"A light but meaningful summer romance." —**KIRKUS REVIEWS**

AUTOFOCUS

Also by Lauren Gibaldi
The Night We Said Yes
Matt's Story (e-novella)

auto focus

LAUREN GIBALDI

HARPER TEEN

An Imprint of HarperCollinsPublishers

To Leila.
To every version of yourself that you are now,
and every version you'll become—I love you now,
and I'll love you always.

HarperTeen is an imprint of HarperCollins Publishers.

Autofocus
Copyright © 2016 by Lauren Gibaldi
All rights reserved. Printed in the United States of America.
No part of this book may be used or reproduced in any manner
whatsoever without written permission except in the case of
brief quotations embodied in critical articles and reviews.
For information address HarperCollins Children's Books,
a division of HarperCollins Publishers,
195 Broadway, New York, NY 10007.
www.epicreads.com

Library of Congress Cataloging-in-Publication Data

Names: Gibaldi, Lauren, author.
Title: Autofocus / Lauren Gibaldi.
Description: First edition. | New York : HarperTeen, 2016. | Summary: "A senior
    photography project gives Maude the perfect opportunity to search for more
    information about her birth mother—but she may not like what she finds"
    — Provided by publisher.
Identifiers: LCCN 2015046352 | ISBN 9780062302236 (hardback)
Subjects: | CYAC: Adoption—Fiction. | Photography—Fiction. | Family
    secrets—Fiction. | Birth mothers—Fiction. | BISAC: JUVENILE FICTION /
    Love & Romance. | JUVENILE FICTION / Social Issues / Dating & Sex. |
    JUVENILE FICTION / Girls & Women.
Classification: LCC PZ7.1.G498 Au 2016 | DDC [Fic]—dc23 LC record available
    at http://lccn.loc.gov/2015046352

Typography by Michelle Gengaro
16 17 18 19 20 CG/RRDH 10 9 8 7 6 5 4 3 2 1

First Edition

ONE

FAMILY.

The word is big, bold, and blue on the whiteboard, underlined three times.

"Family," Ms. Webber, my photography teacher, says aloud, rolling the marker between her palms. "What does it mean to you? Who is in your family? How would you define family?" She looks around the classroom. "For your next photography assignment, I want to see your version of family."

I shift in my seat, the squeaking of the chair sounding as loud as a siren. I look around and see everyone nodding and starting to jot down notes. My paper is blank; I'm not sure what family means. Not really.

"When's it due?" Celine asks from the other side of the

room, pencil tapping on the table.

Ms. Webber answers, "December, so you have two months, but it's part of your final portfolio, so you'll be balancing daily classwork and other projects as well. This is your first long-term project, and I really want you to focus on it." She turns around and I swear she looks right at me. "I want you to impress me with it."

I breathe in deep and can't help but wonder if she knows how much this terrifies me.

"Okay, for the remainder of today's class, I want you to start planning your photos and how you'll present them—exhibit style, online, physical portfolio, et cetera. Go ahead and use the computers, or walk around for inspiration," she says.

As soon as she's done, chairs scrape the floor as they're pushed out, conversations start, and I'm still here, in my seat, frozen. Because I have no idea what I'm supposed to do, what I'm supposed to focus on.

I sit for a few more minutes, then start to get self-conscious. I don't want to look like I'm lost, so I head over to the editing bay—what we call the row of computers where we edit our photos—and look for the latest picture I'm working on for another assignment. It's a photo of a bike, left alone on the side of the road. It looks like it's been there a while, chain rusted and weather worn, and becoming part of the ground. I can lose myself in this project now, then figure out the family assignment later. I pull up Photoshop and get to work, changing the exposure and making the photo a little lighter, hoping to give it a more fantastical feel.

"So what do you think of the assignment?" Celine asks, sitting down next to me. Her slick dark hair is pulled into a low bun and I'm suddenly conscious of the frizz escaping my ponytail.

"I don't know yet," I admit, looking back to my computer. I've been in-class friends with Celine for three years, since starting photography my freshman year, but only this year, after my best friend, Treena, left for college, have we become closer. She knows why the subject makes me uncomfortable—I told her all about it over pizza after we had an assignment about secrets. Not that my adoption is a secret; it's just not something I reveal every day to people.

"You're gonna do it on your parents, right?"

"Yeah, of course," I say, clicking the mouse absentmindedly. "I mean, they *are* my family."

"I know, I know," she says, swishing her hand. "I was just wondering if you ever thought about, you know, your *real* parents."

Real parents. The words affect me more than they should.

Truth is, yes, *of course* I have. How could I not? I always wondered who the people were who gave me this frizzy hair, this bumpy nose. This penchant for biting my nails, and lactose intolerance. But I guess I never thought of them as family. Just, more as people who were part of my life long ago that I don't know or remember.

But I don't say all that. Instead I say, "A little, I guess" and leave it be. Because how can I describe the numerous Google searches without sounding just a little bit crazy? Treena understood, but that's because I've never kept anything from her, and she went through it all with me. But I don't want to go back there. "What about you?" I ask, changing the subject. "How are you going to fit in all seven hundred family members?" Unlike me, Celine has a *large* family of four siblings and numerous aunts and uncles and cousins.

"Ha," she says, opening up her own photo to edit. I look over and see a picture of a dog, and though it sounds simple, the lighting is really great and the dog's eyes shine. "I think I'll just focus on my parents and brothers and sisters. They're family enough. Did I tell you, my little brother tried to eat my last portfolio project? Like, I found it . . . in his mouth."

"Oh god. I can't imagine it tastes good."

"Mmmmm, photo paper." Celine chuckles and adjusts the lighting on her picture a little bit more. She's a better photographer and Photoshopper than me, by a lot. Sometimes I wish I had her talent. "Anyway, I'm going to Java Jump after school, want to join?"

"Yeah, maybe." I turn back to my computer screen and work on my photo some more. I don't know if I'm making it any better or worse; I'm just changing it to keep myself busy.

So when the bell finally rings, I quickly pack up my bag and start to head out.

"Maude." I look up and Ms. Webber is standing by her desk, smiling. "Can you come here for a second?" My heart thumps as I mentally retrace all of my assignments, wondering if I turned something in late. Celine gives me a devilish grin and gestures toward our teacher. She's used to being called up and reprimanded. Me . . . not so much.

When I get to her desk, she looks at the room, then back to me. I look around and see that most of the people have cleared out, except for a few still on the computers. We have a tendency to stay here during other classes. If she thinks we need it, Ms. Webber gives us an excused pass.

"I wanted to ask you if you've thought about the family assignment."

"A bit." I hate lying to her because she's nice and she's always here for us. She's younger than most of the other teachers, with bright red hair, brown glasses, and a stare that penetrates you until you confess all of your secrets.

She nods. "Look, I know this must be a harder assignment for you, but I also think it'll challenge you in ways other students won't understand. I think, because of that, it will make you a better photographer."

"You think?" I ask, a bit skeptical.

"Definitely. I just want you to know that I'm here, in case you have any questions."

"Thanks," I say, awkwardly adjusting my books in my

hands. "I don't really know where to start."

"You'll figure it out," she says with the conviction only a teacher who's seen it all can have. And, I don't know, I kind of believe her. "I also wanted to ask, have you started looking into colleges yet?"

"Not yet. I've looked at some pamphlets, but I haven't made any decisions. I think I might want to major in photography, but I don't know," I admit, because I do, but is that the right step to take? It's such a huge decision.

"Well, that's up to you, but if you *do* decide on that, I can definitely recommend a few colleges."

"It's not a bad major? Like, I could eventually get a job, or something?"

She nods. "I did, right?" She smiles. "You should do what makes you happy and what you have a talent for."

I smile back and thank her, then leave the classroom and head out to lunch. The rest of the day glides by, and I barely notice; I'm too wrapped up in my thoughts. After the final bell, I walk home. I don't live far, a few blocks, and I hope the walk can help clear my mind. Of the project. Of the future. Two girls from my trigonometry class wave to me, and as I wave back, a burst of fall air blows leaves across my feet. And the breeze feels good. It feels like a breath of something new.

◇◇◇◇

When I get home, I find a stack of college flyers in the mailbox. They've been coming in daily since junior year started.

Inside, I toss the mail on the kitchen counter and head

to my room. My laptop is already open, and I stare at it, thinking about photography class and my assignment and what Ms. Webber said. I walk over to my desk, wiggle my mouse, and Google "Claire Fullman."

It's one of the two bigger things I know about my birth mother—her name. It was a semi-open adoption, and my parents met her once, so they've given me that much information, along with whatever else they remembered—she was short and had dark, wavy hair (like mine). They'd planned to send her updates as I grew up, but then she died when I was born due to some sort of complication.

That's the second thing I know about her.

Once again, my search comes up with absolutely nothing. A few Facebook pages, a wedding photographer, white pages information, all for people very much alive. She lived before everyone documented their lives online, as my mom tried to explain the first time I unsuccessfully looked for her, but it's still frustrating. How can someone leave no footprint at all? How can a person have no impact? I try adding "Tallahassee" to the query, which is where I was born, but again come up with nothing. I add "Florida State University" because I know she went there, but again, nothing. I shouldn't be upset—I've done this dozens of times—but I still sigh and shut my computer, wishing my past was tangible.

I look up and see the photo pinned to my corkboard, showing my parents and me at my tenth birthday party.

They took me and a few friends ice-skating. In the picture my face is flushed from the cold, and my knees are red from ice burn, but I'm so happy. I'm squeezing my mom, and she's laughing because I'm taller than her in the skates.

I could do that. I could just take pictures of us, the three of us, together. Because they are family—they're my family. They're who raised me and helped me become, well, me. And I love them, of course.

But part of me knows that just showing them isn't enough. That I can show so much more if I try. I just don't know how to try.

My fingers twitch and I know I need to take my mind off this, get away from it for now. I might as well join Celine at Java Jump. I grab my camera from my bag and throw the strap over my neck. I feel more complete with it, like it was begging for me to pick it up.

I grab my keys and head out, wanting to make the most of the changing weather. I take a left out of my street, cross over the train tracks, and head north toward the shopping center on the corner. Cars pass, birds fly overhead, and the sun begins to consider setting. I love this time of evening.

Shouts and laughter tell me that there are kids playing at the nearby park. I stop and see parents sitting on the benches talking, no doubt comparing stories and woes. They're having their own, real-life conversations as a world of activity takes place right in front of them. There, spies are murdering dragons, princesses are being rescued by superheroes, and the evil villains are always captured no matter what. I lean against a post, just outside the sandy playground that holds a slide, swing set, monkey bars, and seesaw.

"Hi, Maude," one of the mothers says to me, and I smile and wave in response. I've babysat her daughter before. In fact, I've babysat a lot of the kids here. It's both a curse and comfort of living in a small suburb—we've all lived here forever, so we all know one another.

A little girl with bright red pigtails—the woman's daughter—is sitting at the top of the slide, contemplating her descent. She has a finger in her mouth, and a hand clutching the railing. My fingers twitch again, so I point my camera up and slowly adjust the lens to focus in on her, blurring the trees and houses behind her. I get absorbed in her world, feeling her worries, her pains, as I capture the moment. Everything looks so much better through the viewfinder. Easier and clearer.

She takes the finger out of her mouth and grabs the other bar. No one is behind her. She has all the time in the world. I click, showing her slow resolve. Then, with a slight push, she slowly totters down the slide, slipping, slipping, slipping until she gets to the bottom with a laugh of excitement. I shoot everything, the determination in her face, the change from fear to joy, the cry of happiness at the end. I get it all. She throws her arms in the air and her mom materializes beside her, picking her up. She gives the girl a kiss on the cheek and then helps her back up the stairs in case she wants to go again. And she does. Five more times. I'll give them the photos later—her mom loves when I capture her daughter having fun.

After a few minutes, I realize I've stopped taking pictures and am just watching. That was me at one time, scared and giddy, confused and determined. The slide was the biggest problem to me. And my mom was always there to kiss my cheek and tell me I did a great job, even when I didn't quite make it down.

I think back to my search and wonder—would it have been the same with my birth mother? Would she have taken me to the park and helped me face my fears? Would I have turned out the same, had my life been with her? Would I be me?

I twist my camera's lens, thinking. I know I don't want a different life, but that doesn't keep me from wondering.

I push off the post and head to Java Jump. Celine will be waiting, and though I know she won't have answers, she might, at least, have distractions.

TWO

I open the door and see Celine right away. Her back straight and tall, she's chatting with the barista at the counter. She has her large, black-rimmed glasses on, and once again I am envious of the way style and cuteness come so easy to her.

"Hey," I say when I get to the counter. The barista—a guy a bit older than us with sandy-brown hair and similar glasses—does the hello nod, and looks back at Celine. She smiles at me and says, "Oh, hey" very casually. I suddenly wonder if she invited me here just to be nice, and didn't actually intend for me to come. A blush crosses my face, and I make a gesture toward the end of the line.

I am an idiot sometimes.

After a few seconds, she comes over to me. "Hey, sorry!"

"No, sorry for interrupting," I say, waving my hand.

"Oh, don't worry about it. He's a friend of my older brother. Cute, isn't he? He just started working here, so, you know, excuse to get more coffee or whatever," she says with a smile. And it's in that moment that I miss Treena. Like me, she hasn't had a boyfriend. We used to talk about the whole world of flirting, and how we weren't very good at it.

"Very cute," I say instead, and she grins.

We get iced coffee and sit in the corner, where she has a good view of the counter. I feel my phone vibrate and see it's my mom asking where I am. I text her back a quick explanation, and then tune in to Celine.

"So I've been thinking about my project."

"Yeah?" I say, taking a sip of my drink.

"I think I'm going to do that thing where I re-create photos of my brothers and sisters and me. You know, like, find old ones and have us pose the same way again. Kind of showing how we've grown and stuff. So the whole family-changes-but-not-really angle. What do you think?"

I think of the photo I was looking at earlier of the ice-skating rink and answer, "I think it's a really cute idea. I've seen it done before, but not in class. I think it'll be fun."

"What about you?" she asks, looking me over casually, then back down at her drink. "Any thoughts after class?"

"Tons, really, but none that amount to anything. Family to me means my parents. But there's an entire other side that feels like it would make the project incomplete if I didn't include it."

Celine nods, and suddenly, a song comes on that Treena and I used to sing along to all the time on the way to school—like, annoyingly loud. Naturally, I smile and start moving my head to the beat of the song. My mind goes to her, now at Florida State University, being the college girl. And then I realize the connection. "Oh my gosh."

"What?" Celine asks.

"Sorry, hold on a second," I say, not wanting to stop my thoughts from coming. I let the idea rush over me, and tell her, "I just had the best idea. I can't believe I hadn't thought of it before."

"What?" she asks.

"I was adopted in Tallahassee. Treena's in college in Tallahassee."

"So you're gonna go visit her?" she asks, swirling her straw around her drink.

"Yeah," I muse. "I mean, I'll try to. Maybe I can go up there and find something on my birth mother."

"That's pretty cool," she says. "Have you tried Googling her?"

"Yeah, of course, but nothing. But maybe if I'm up there . . ."

"You can find something in person," she says, eyeing me, then looking briefly over at the guy back at the counter. Celine's a good friend, but my best friend is a phone call away.

I hold my thoughts for a little longer and Celine tells

me about her plans for the weekend, and this movie she saw about vampires that was very explicit. I listen, but really my mind is going as fast as it can.

After a while, I finally make my excuse to leave. "Hey, my mom's waiting for me. Talk later?"

"Yeah, of course," Celine says. "Let me know what you decide for your project. I'm gonna go talk up the barista," she says, wiggling her eyebrows. "Baristo? I don't know."

"'Guy at the counter' works well, too." I smile.

My phone is in my hands the minute I'm outside.

It rings for an excruciating second before Treena picks up.

"MAUDE!" she literally yells into the phone, and I count down until she launches into her typical second sentence. "AHH! When are you visiting?"

"That's actually why I'm calling," I say. Just hearing her voice makes me feel better, more me and less a floating buoy with no one to cling on to.

"WHAT! Oh my gosh, details," she continues, and I laugh at her excitement. It's always there. She's always turned up a few degrees more than everyone else, and it makes everything with her an adventure; I mean, even going to the library.

"Okay, well, it's not set in stone or anything, and I haven't even asked my parents yet, but I have an idea that I want to run by you first."

"Yes, please," she says, and I can hear wind in the background. She's outside like me, probably walking to or from class as I walk home. We're in different areas, but our lives are still parallel.

"So I have to do this photography project on family," I begin, then tell her about my idea of looking for my birth mother.

"Wow. That's really cool," she says when I'm done, more gently than normal, and I know she's worried. I know she's thinking about what this all means.

"This won't be like last time," I tell her, referring to the time that I just started calling people with the last name of Fullman who lived in Tallahassee. I was fourteen and angry and she helped me put the phone down. She was always good at that—being there for me through the hard stuff, but stopping me when it was time.

"No, I know, that was a million years ago." She pauses. "I'm all in, and I'm totally going to help you, you know that. . . ."

"But . . ."

She hesitates again, then sighs. "Okay, I love you, and that's the only reason why I'm saying this."

"I know what you're going to say. You're worried."

"You've been down this road before. I'm just afraid you won't find anything again."

I sigh, disheartened, as she states my fear out loud. "I know." I nod, even though she can't see. "It's totally a possibility. But I think there's something there, I really do. I don't know, I want to try."

"I know, I get it. And I think you should, I'm just—"

"Playing mom?" I joke, referring to how she always took the role of mom when we would play house growing up. How she kind of turned out that way, always watching over her friends, always there to take care of me when needed.

"You love it," she says, and I laugh.

"I do. And I can't wait to see you!"

"I KNOW! Oh my god, it's going to be so much fun. I can't wait to show you around! And show you off! And everything!" Treena says. And I smile. Because, yeah, she knows when to stop me or caution me. But like the time she sat in the car with me the first day I got my license, she's also always there to hold my hand and take my mind off things when I'm ready to go.

And I'm ready.

THREE

When I get home, my mom is in the living room, sitting on the floor, submerged in a sea of essays. Her glasses are on and her purple pen is in her hand, meaning she's in grading mode.

"I was wondering when you'd come home. I was about to send out a search party," she says sarcastically.

"I was gone for an hour, and only spoke to seven strangers," I deadpan, taking my shoes off.

"Did you tell them where you lived? They need to know such things," she says, and I smile, thinking up my retort. "I texted you, you know, after you responded to my last text." I pull my phone out and do, in fact, see a message from her. It probably came when I was on the phone with Treena.

"Sorry," I say, realizing she was at least a bit worried. "I was taking photos for class, and then talked to Tree for a bit."

"Oh, how is she? Still loving FSU?" my mom asks, finally looking up.

"Very much so." I open my mouth and then close it, not ready to ask about Tallahassee. That's a big conversation, not one for the entryway. "Grading?" I ask, nodding toward her pile.

"Yes," she sighs, taking off her glasses and pointing to a paper. "This one actually has a hyperlink on it. A blue, bold, underlined word. They didn't even try to disguise the fact that they were copying and pasting. If you're going to cheat, at least be creative."

"Wow," I laugh. "That's really bad."

"Never hang out with any of these kids. Never," she says, and I nod, grateful that she doesn't teach twelfth-grade English at my school. I'd rather not know the victims of her purple pen.

"How do you know I don't already?" I ask, taking off to my room.

"Funny. Dinner in ten minutes!" she yells as I leave.

"Okay," I yell back, then flop on my bed. I feel uneasy, knowing what I'm about to ask her. It's not like my mom's ever been secretive about my adoption, but I also don't know how she'll react to me hunting for details. She knows about my previous attempts, but for some reason this feels so much bigger. I'm stepping away from my computer and actually scouring for information on my own, in person, in another place. It's all been so fast, this whole afternoon, deciding this. I don't even know if it's the right thing to do.

Do I ask my parents if I can go look for a woman who gave me up seventeen years ago? I could find out everything I've ever wanted to know about her, right when I need it the most, when I'm about to pick a college and start a new chapter in my life. But that would mean maybe hurting my parents. How would they feel about me focusing my senior project on someone I've never met?

I go to my dresser and pull out the blue box in the very back. It has a few silly notes from Treena I don't want my mom reading, my journal, and there, at the bottom, the only picture of my birth mother I have. She gave it to my parents when she met them. It's from her high school graduation. She's wearing a black cap and gown and smiling at the camera. It's obviously posed, so I can't tell how she was actually feeling at the moment, but still. It's always surreal looking at her—in a way, at me.

The little girl on the slide earlier flashes in my mind, and I wonder once again—would that have been me with my birth mother? Probably not—before I was born, she was already planning on putting me up for adoption. But if she hadn't died and had decided to keep me, how different would my life have been? It's not just the photography assignment that's making me question it—it's everything. It's college. It's life.

It's this deep yearning I've always felt in the pit of my

stomach to know *more* about the other life I could have had, the mother I never knew. And this is the opportunity to explore that. If blood makes a person, am I more her than my real parents? Or maybe blood is just blood.

"Dinner!" my dad calls, and I know what I'm going to do.

"Your dad cooked. Be forewarned," my mom says when I walk into our very tidy kitchen. My dad is a bit of a neat freak, and he ensures the kitchen is perpetually straightened. Even now, there's not even a splatter of sauce on the granite counters.

"It's just pasta. I can't get pasta wrong, honey," my dad says while putting plates on the table.

"Hi, Dad." I give him a hug before sitting down.

"Hey, Maude. Good day at school?"

"It was okay," I say. I put my fork into the pasta and twirl it around. Over and over again.

"Not bad, honey," my mom says after taking a bite. My dad gives her a pleased look.

"And you sound so surprised," he says, passing the premade frozen and thawed garlic bread around.

"I might make you cook every night," she says, picking up a piece of bread.

"Let's not go that far," he says, laughing. They both look at me when I don't join in on making fun of Dad, which is a normal ritual.

"Everything okay?" Dad asks, putting some pasta into his mouth. He has the straightest, best teeth out of everyone

I know, which is probably why he's a dentist. I'm convinced it's a requirement for the job.

"Yep, all good," I say. I make a show of eating the pasta and smiling.

"I saw you received more college brochures in the mail. Narrowing down your list yet?" Dad asks, adjusting his glasses.

"Um, not yet," I admit.

"Well, let us know if you want to visit any of the schools," Dad continues. "We can make a weekend trip of it."

"Mmmm," I answer, nodding and smiling. "Actually, I was wondering . . ." I pause, heart thumping in my chest. "What if I go check out Florida State next week during fall break?"

My mom looks at my dad and I grab my napkin and twist it around on my lap.

"That's a great idea!" my dad says eagerly. "Perhaps on the weekend? We can drive up there together."

"I mean, what if I go up there . . . alone. And stay with Treena."

"Oh," Dad says, putting down his utensils. Automatically I feel bad.

"I don't know if I want you driving that far without us," my mom muses, also playing with a napkin.

"It's only four hours from Orlando to there, and Treena has been begging me to visit ever since she moved. I mean, I'd love to go with you guys, but maybe it'll be fun to really experience the college life." I stop as my mother raises her eyebrows. "Okay, not like that. God, it's Treena. She'll probably be studying the entire time."

"I do like Treena," my mom says. "I bet she'd never put hyperlinks in her essays. I don't know, though."

"I'd also like to," I say, faltering, "go there because I'd like to see where I was adopted."

There is silence for what seems like minutes.

"It's for my senior photography project, and . . ."

"Oh," my mom says, and I don't dare meet her eyes.

"Sorry," I say instead.

"No, it's okay. It's only normal . . ." she continues.

"Looks like you've given this a lot of thought," Dad says, a bit louder than necessary.

"What . . . have you asked Treena yet?" my mom asks, still not looking up.

"Yeah, she's excited," I say.

"When will you leave?"

"Sunday? Then come back in a few days. . . ."

"A few days? How long do you plan to stay out there?"

"Not long. It's fall break. I have time."

Mom sighs and picks up her fork again. "We'll see."

So all I say is "Okay," and I go back to eating my pasta in silence. I want to fight, I want to state my case, but not now. It's not the time.

◇◇◇◇

After dinner, I go up to my room and open my trigonometry textbook and work out some problems. I like math because, unlike life, there are concrete answers you can always find if you work hard enough.

I'm into my seventh problem when I hear a knock on my open door and look up to see my mom standing there. She seems small, worried. "Hey." I sit up on my bed, a silent invitation to come in.

"I've been thinking about what you asked at dinner . . ." she starts, her sentence drifting off at the end. She sits on the bed with me, playing with her hands as she speaks. "We've never been secretive with you about the adoption, you know that. We want you to know as much as we do. And the thing is, you do. There really isn't anything more to know."

I nod my head. "I know. I just . . . maybe there's something out there? Something that we missed or weren't told. Something from my birth mother's family, or—"

"Honey, you tried before. There are hundreds of people with her last name, and we can't access your adoption files until you turn eighteen in August. And the last address we were aware of, the one from when you were born, was Return to Sender."

"Right," I say. "Maybe we can try again?"

"Maude, it was seventeen years ago. And you tried again a few years back, remember? Honestly, I don't think you are going to find anything new."

I do; I just don't admit it. It hurt seeing the Return to Sender stamp on the letter, even though I was expecting it. My parents tried, I tried. That family moved on. But knowing they're still out there, maybe, gives me hope.

"But maybe going there will help. I can see, I don't know, her high school?"

She opens her mouth, and then shakes her head. "*If you find out where she went to school, what then?*"

"Maybe I can find her friends . . . or family from there?"

She nods, staying silent, which unnerves me. My mom is usually so much more talkative than this, so much wittier, and sarcastic. I know this is hurting her, and I hate that I'm doing it, but I still want to know. "I won't stop you from doing it. I didn't stop you in the past, and I won't now, because I'd love for you to have all your questions answered. I'm just afraid you'll be disappointed. I know what you know. I know her name was Claire Fullman. She grew up in Tallahassee, and went to Florida State University."

"That's it."

"That's it," she says, turning to me. Her eyes are serious, leveled. I brace myself. "Your dad and I only met her the one time, when she agreed to give us you through the adoption agency. She was really nice. She knew what she was doing was hard, but she wanted you in good hands, and she knew hers weren't the best. I don't know anything about her personal life, just that she wanted you to be cared for."

"Did she know she'd have . . . complications?"

"I don't think at first, but she was aware later on. We were told she had a preexisting heart condition, and labor was too much for her. We only knew because the doctors wanted to test you, to see if you carried that gene, too.

24

Thankfully, you don't."

"Yeah . . ." I say. "But did she know she was sick when she decided to give me up? Or do you think if she *wasn't* sick . . ."

"I think she decided before she knew. But you never know. You never know if there's more going on with someone; we see only what's on the outside. And though she was nice, she didn't completely let us in or anything. She didn't have to." She stops, then begins again. "Maude, I wish I could tell you more, I really do. But that's all I know." I know she's being truthful. She's always been open and honest with me.

"Okay," I say simply, not sure what's left to discuss.

She looks down, and then back up at me, and I see it. I get it. It's in the tears gathering in the corners of her eyes. And I don't know how to tell her that she'll always be my mom, no matter what. The words don't come, so instead I hug her, and when I feel her chin on my head, she says, "Okay, you can go." My heart fills with joy as she talks. "But you have to check in every day, keep me updated, and come home immediately if anything goes wrong."

"Of course," I say, smiling and containing the excitement and fear bubbling in my throat. I'm going. This is real.

"And Treena's okay with you staying with her?"

"Absolutely," I say, already planning the call in my head. Already knowing how she'll react. But before I go there, before I get too excited, I ask, "What does Dad say about all of this?" My dad doesn't let on his feelings toward my birth mother–based inquiries, and I'm never sure if it's because he doesn't care about the subject much, or because it pains him to talk about it. Does it hurt him that they couldn't have a child of their own?

"Not much." She shrugs. "I told him I was going to let you go, and he grumbled. But you know your dad. No matter what you decide, he'll be worried about you."

"I'm going to grow up one of these days."

"Don't tell him that," she whispers, and I smile. "When you get to Tallahassee, start at the school's registrar. Maybe they'll have a lead. They probably won't be the easiest to work with, but you're sweet. Hopefully they'll be nice and not DMV mean."

"The registrar. I wouldn't have thought of that." I give her another hug.

"Okay, go call Treena, like I know you are dying to."

I laugh as she gets up to leave, then grab my phone.

◇◇◇◇

"MAUDE!" she yells, again, when she answers.

"I'm coming!" I say back excitedly.

"NO!" she yells.

"YES! I'm coming! Ahhh!"

"Ahhh! Okay, when? Now?" she asks, excitement oozing out of the phone, and I can't help but laugh, because it's how I feel, too. I'm glowing, in awe of everything. How my mom is letting me go. How *good* it feels to know that, to realize I'm actually doing it. I might see a part of me I've never known. And, also, I get to see my best friend. "Oh my god, tell me!"

Treena continues, mashing the five words into one, so it sounds more like *ohmygodtellme*.

Just hearing her voice is making me think of last year and all our trips to the ice-cream place across from the high school, our lazy pool days during the summer at her house, and how she always smells of her vanilla body spray. The time we stayed up all night watching as many episodes of *Degrassi: The Next Generation* as possible. I didn't realize how much I miss her. It's getting me even more excited for my trip.

"Next week, during fall break."

"Perfect! You're going to love it here. Everyone is awesome." I then hear her say, "Yes, you're awesome, too."

"Oh, sorry, is there someone there?"

"No, it's just Trey being a dork."

"Trey . . . ? Who's Trey?" I ask.

"A guy in my hall." Then off the phone again: "Yes, I'll tell her you're extremely handsome." I hear a shuffle, then she's back. "Sorry, anyway, I'm so excited to show you around, and for you to meet everyone, and to just get *us* time."

Hearing that—"us time"—calms me a bit. Of course Tree has new friends up there; it would be weird if she didn't. And I'm excited to meet them.

"Awesome. Well, I'll let you get back to guy-from-your-hall."

"Ha ha," she says. "Okay, well, I love my Maude and I'll see you *soon*!"

"Love my Tree," I say. I smile and hang up, ready for whatever will happen next.

◇◇◇◇

That night I update my photo blog, *Maude's Menagerie*, with a photo I took on the way home from school of a group of birds sitting on an electrical line. Ever since we started the blog last year, in Photo II class, I try to post daily, both to document my life and to challenge myself to take at least one photo a day. Some are with my DSLR camera, and others are simply phone snapshots, but they all tell a story, at least in my mind. I click the Archive link and pick a post from April, before Treena moved away. It's a picture of the two of us standing in front of the ice-cream place we used to love before it closed. Treena is laughing as ice cream drips down her hand from the heat, and I'm holding the camera out, capturing the moment. We called this a Buddy Shot. Selfies are for one person, but Buddy Shots are for two. There are so many other photos like this, the two of us being, well, us. My blog is full of them.

I wonder what pictures I'll take in Tallahassee when I visit her. I close the window and open FSU's, clicking on the map. Treena lives in Gilchrist Hall, an honors dorm at the center of campus. It overlooks a gazebo on one side, and a giant grassy knoll with a fountain on the other. Treena's told me about it—it's where she sometimes lays out and does her homework on nice days.

I imagine Treena hanging out there now, lying on the

grass with her books. Maybe having a picnic, or studying for class.

I scroll through the map, passing the squares posing as buildings, and find a giant oval that signifies both the football stadium and the registrar's office. I guess it's somewhere within the stadium, amid the locker rooms and gyms. I scroll back to Gilchrist Hall and touch the screen, making a route with my finger of the path I'll take. It's a straight walk down a sidewalk, then a curve at a traffic circle. I'm sure it's not hard to miss. My heart flutters with anticipation of what's to come.

I close my laptop, get out a notebook, and make a list of things I want to do while there.

- Spend time with Treena.
- See campus, decide if I want to go there.
- See Tallahassee sights. Capitol?
- Find out about my mother.
- Find out about myself.

I know my birth mother is not there, I know she won't magically come back to life once I step foot into the city she once knew . . . but I just feel like I might find a piece of her, a part of her I didn't know existed. And maybe, in doing that, I'll find a piece of myself, too.

FOUR

The next few days pass, and I'm constantly thinking about the project. On Friday, in photography class, I fill Celine in about the details of my trip.

"That's so cool that your mom's letting you go," she says, spinning in her chair. We're supposed to be editing photos for a quick in-class assignment, but instead are taking the time to gossip. Everyone else already left for lunch.

"Yeah, I'm really excited. I'm staying with Treena and am going to check out the campus and stuff."

"And stuff," she says, giving me an exaggerated wink.

"Not *that*," I say.

She knowingly nods and says, "If you need make-out tips, let me know. I've got you covered."

"I'm not going to be making out with anyone," I say, rolling my eyes at her. "It's not really my priority."

"Uh-huh. I bet your friend has tons of parties lined up for you."

"You don't know Treena; she's not like that. She's more of a night-at-the-library kind of girl. You know, for her sixteenth birthday, we went to see a Disney movie in the theater, and then got cake. *That's* Treena."

"She sounds like a party and a half," Celine says.

"She is." I defend her. Because to me, Treena always has been. Those are our nights. That's what I'm looking forward to. Since she's been gone, I haven't had sleepovers, and our heart-to-hearts have been rare. So I'm excited for all of that, too. To us being us again.

"So how do you plan on finding out stuff about your mom?" she asks, missing the defensiveness in my voice. "Are you going to find people who knew her?"

"Mother," I explain. "Mom for my real mom, mother for my birth mother. Um, but yeah, I'm going to try. I know she went to FSU, so it doesn't hurt to look her up, right?"

"What if people tell you some awful stuff about her? Or what if she was totally awesome?"

I straighten up and look away, tapping my fingers absent-mindedly on the computer. "I don't know," I say. What if I learn something not so great about her? Then what? I shake my head and dismiss the thought. I will deal with that if I need to.

"Well, I think it's cool that you're doing this. My life seems so boring in comparison."

"Does not," I say. "How'd it go with Starbucks guy?" I

ask, changing the subject.

"I'm playing it cool now," she says, grinning. "He has my number, he knows what to do." I'm taken again by how sure she is of herself. If only I could channel that sometimes.

The bell rings, signaling the end of lunch, which we apparently completely skipped while talking, and Celine rolls her eyes. "English. Yay," she says, all deadpan, and I smile. As I get up, I see Ms. Webber by her desk.

"Hey, go ahead," I say to Celine, and she shrugs. "I have a question for Ms. Webber."

"See ya later," she says, then leaves. I keep my computer on and walk to the front of the room.

"Maude, how's your project coming along?" Ms. Webber asks immediately.

"I'm still not totally sure what I'm going to do, but I think I have an idea. Actually . . ." I stop to take a breath. "I'm going up to Tallahassee next week during break . . . to see where I was born."

"That's terrific. Are you excited?"

"Yes, definitely. And nervous. And, I don't know . . ." I say.

"You know, FSU has a terrific photography program," she says with a wink, and I smile.

"So I've heard. I kind of wanted to check it out."

"You absolutely should."

I nod and then confess. "Ms. Webber, I . . . I'm not really sure where to start my senior project. Like, I know I'm going up there, and I know I'm going to find out about some things—maybe—about my birth mother, and maybe I'll find out more about my whole family. But . . . as for the project, I'm, well, where do I start?"

She tilts her head and crosses her arms, leaning back against the whiteboard. "How do you feel about an extra assignment?"

"I, um . . ."

"Hear me out. Do you still post on the photo blog I had everyone make last year?"

"Yeah," I say.

"Okay, post every day there. Of anything within Tallahassee. Don't even think about it—just take photos of the school, the people, the trees. Then post the photos you take during your trip, at least one a day. And I think, in not trying, you'll find things will start to click."

"Okay," I say, kind of excited about the assignment. It's not hard, it's something I typically do anyway, and maybe it'll help. Maybe it'll point me in the direction I need to go. "Okay, I'll do that."

"Great," she says, then sits down at her desk. "Good luck."

"Thank you," I say excitedly, then go back to my computer for my bag. My photo is still up on the screen waiting to be finished, the one of the girl on the slide, where she's on the cusp of pushing herself down. Will she go, or will she turn around and leave? Even if I didn't see the ending, the look in her eyes gives it away.

No matter what, she would have gone.

FIVE

"You have water, right? In case you get thirsty?" Mom asks. We've been up since early this morning, and I've just finished packing the car. I hold the three very full bottles of water up to her, and then place them in the car's cup holders.

"Do you have a map? What if you get lost?" my dad asks from the other side of the car.

"Dad. I have my phone," I say, holding up my iPhone. I put that on the passenger-side seat with my camera, in case I need it. Now it's just a matter of my parents saying good-bye.

"What if you don't get reception? I don't want you looking at your phone while you're driving," my mom says, arms crossed in front of her.

"Mom, I love you, but you gotta calm down. I set my phone to GPS mode, so it'll tell me when to turn. That way I don't have to look at the screen. And if I lose reception, which I won't, I printed out the directions just in case." I lean into the car and pick up the pieces of paper arranged on my seat and wave them in front of her. "I'm prepared."

"No answering phone calls while driving," Mom says. "And—"

"And no picking up hitchhikers," Dad adds.

"Guys, really. I have a full tank of gas. I will drive slowly. No hitchhikers. No phone. No thirst. Anything else?" They look at each other, not sure what to say next. "I'll be safe, I promise. I'll call you as soon as I get to Treena's. I've driven before, I've got this."

"But not this far alone," Mom says, and I hug her.

"I'll be fine. You gotta let me grow up. I'll be leaving for college next year anyway."

"Don't remind us," Dad says, coming close, too. I pull them both into a hug. "Be safe."

"Call us. We love you," Mom adds.

"Love you, too," I say, trying to let go, but they won't budge. "If you don't let go, I'm telling your students that you watch *The Real World*, Mom."

"So? That'll show I'm hip," she says, loosening her grip and wiping a tear from her eye.

"And that you use the word 'hip.'"

"I got it, I got it. Go."

"Okay," I say, looking at them one last time. My heart, I realize, is racing as I step into the car, turn on the ignition, and press Play on my phone's playlist. One more wave good-bye. Mom is teary-eyed. Dad is hugging her. The house is the same one I grew up in: one story, brown, white shutters, and a big citrus tree in the front yard that I used to try to climb. It's bizarre, leaving all of this behind, if only for a few days, and knowing I'll come back somehow changed.

At least, I hope I will.

I keep the windows open as I drive down the long interstate roads leading to Tallahassee. The delicious smell of curry wafts in the car, food Treena's parents forced me to pick up for her before I left. The wind rushes in, muffling the music I carefully curated for the trip: fast songs to keep me awake, but melodic ones, too, to set the perfect road trip mood. But I don't care about the lack of volume. It's this, the road, the constant movement, that feels good. Watching the houses and buildings and cars pass by as I continue on to my destination. There are signs leading to places I've never been, and might never go. But they're all out there, all options for me.

As the drive continues, I let my mind wander again to my photography project—family. When I find puzzle pieces connecting my mother's life, I wonder if I'll find bits of my own, as well. I think of developing film—actual film in a darkroom, old school—it's like one photo is done and ready and another is just starting to be exposed. It's revealing itself inch by inch. I could belong in either of them, really, and only when the second is fully developed will I know.

I've always felt a bit different from my parents—like they were on the same path and I was a few steps behind, always trying to catch up. They would say something and laugh, and it wasn't as funny to me. I don't look the same as them, either, with my frizzy near-black hair next to Mom's brown and pin-straight and Dad's blond—now graying—soft hair. And my nose looks more like our neighbor's, Lucas Feinstein's, with its bump at the top, unlike their ski-slope-perfect noses that I used to trace with my finger when I was younger.

When I was ten I had to do a family tree for class. I did mine on my parents, of course, but while I was learning about grandparents' birthdates and ethnicities that flourished on our family tree, they sat me down and said that though I wasn't biologically part of it, I'm what made it complete. They said it just like that. Like the tree, with me at the base, always had a root reserved for me.

What hurts the most is the fact that I'll never know what my birth mother was like, or if I'm anything like her. I'll never know my biological family tree, and if there was a root, somewhere, on it for me, too. But after time, and a lot of late-night talks with Treena, I realized it was easier that way. I was adopted out for a better life. Which is why I don't really know where to begin with this family project. To leave my life behind and search for one that has nothing to do with my parents. Because I love them for all they've done for me, for who they are. They never treated me like an adopted daughter; I was theirs, as if I was always meant to be that way.

I cross over the Suwannee River and remember the text Treena sent me just last night.

Sing Suwannee River song from chorus when crossing river. It's good luck!

So I turn off my music, open my mouth, and belt out the lyrics I barely remember. Good luck is what I need.

The exits become fewer and fewer until I see a big green sign welcoming students and families to the home of Florida State University. The home of football champions. I turn off the interstate, onto the exit ramp, and know it's home to plenty of other things, too.

◇◇◇◇

A few minutes later, I pull into the dorm's parking lot and see Treena standing in front of her building, waiting for me. She's bouncing on her feet and waving madly. I laugh to myself and park my car, eager to get out.

"AHHHH!" Treena yells as soon as she sees me, running through the parking lot to give me a hug. Her vanilla body spray hits me instantly and I smile. It's the same kind she's been wearing since we first bought it in seventh grade. It's a scent that means I'm home.

"I've missed you so much, Tree!" I say into her arms. We're half hugging, half jumping up and down in excitement. It's been only a few months—not even three—but it still feels like too long.

"I've missed you, too," she says. "I'm so glad your parents let you make the trip here."

"I know!"

"How many rules were you given?"

"Probably the same ones your parents gave you—no boys, drugs, murder, et cetera."

"Ugh, why do they all have to be so strict," she says sarcastically, and laughs.

It's so good to see her. She looks the same: same beautiful light brown skin, same dark eyes, same jeans, I'm pretty sure, only there's still something slightly different. Her dark hair is shorter, to her shoulder blades, and she looks fuller. She was always so bone-thin; she now has cheeks and legs. She's still wearing the purple and gold bangles she got on her family trip to India to visit her grandparents before leaving for college. She brought me back matching ones, only in blue and gold. They're in my bag, which we grab from the trunk.

"I live right there," she says, pointing to a large redbrick building dotted with white-trimmed windows.

We get my other stuff and my camera from the car, along with the cooler of food she excitedly takes. "I grumbled when my mom said she was forcing you to bring me food, but honestly, I totally miss her cooking," she says.

We take the sidewalk to the side door. Trees line the walk, and the cool breeze moves the branches. My fingers twitch to get my daily picture, but I hold out. There will be time later. She slides her FSU ID into a scanner and the door clicks open. "We'll have to find a way to get you in and out when I'm at class," she says over her shoulder as I follow her in. While the outside is grand and collegiate, the inside is exactly as I imagined—a long, off-white hallway with a lot of doors on both sides. "So, I'm on the fourth floor. At the end of this hall is the elevator. There are also stairs, but people are usually making out on them."

"Really?" I ask, thinking about what Celine said.

"Really. We have roommates, so I guess that's where some people go for privacy."

"I guess," I muse while she continues to narrate who lives in each room as we walk down the hall. While the doors are similar, they're each different in their own way. Whiteboards are taped to them, with colorful swirls and notes. Names are pasted and decorated. Some Greek letters are posted on top, for fraternities or sororities. Some have nothing at all—and I assume those are the guys' rooms. Though the doors are shut, music and laughter can be heard on and off. As we make it down the hall, I feel like I'm in a movie. It's everything that I've seen on screen, only live. In person. This is Treena's life now.

"Are there guys and girls on all floors?"

"Yeah. Here the girls are on one side of the hall," she says, pointing to the right side, "and the guys are on the other." She points to the left. "It's like they thought if they separated us by a hallway, it would be safe. But, come on. We can walk the two steps from door to door."

"Oh," I say. It surprises me how flippant she is about it. This is the same girl who was too shy to even talk to a guy up until eleventh grade, much to the delight of her parents.

I wonder what they think of her living across the hall from guys. I wonder how often she walks the two steps.

"Elevator!" she says triumphantly, and we get in. The walls inside are lined with flyers, advertising author talks, socials, clubs, and concerts. There's one for a Fourth-Floor Social and I wonder if Treena went to it. "Oh my god, remember the time we were stuck in the elevator?"

"At the mall! Because we were trying to avoid the creepy guy who worked at Macy's, so we stupidly decided on the elevator over the escalator."

"And then he had to help get us out."

"And he was still creepy in the end."

"Right? Didn't he comment on your top or something? Like, odd time to be complimenting," she says, and the doors open to her hallway. "Okay, my hallway!" She grabs my wrist, pulls me out excitedly, and then we're walking arm in arm down the way and it feels right. I lean on her shoulder. "It's the best one. Our RA—resident assistant—is so cool, she kind of lets us get away with anything. Like, the guys were having chair races down the hall and she didn't stop them."

"Chair races?" I ask.

"Pushing rolling chairs down the hall. It was noon and we were bored." She smiles and I shake my head because *This is Treena?* She seems so sure of herself, so cool about everything. I love it.

We get to her door at the end of the hall, where her name

is written in her perpetually messy handwriting, all loops and lowercases. Unlike the other rooms, her door has only one name—and I remember her telling me that her roommate dropped out after three weeks.

"MY ROOM!" she yells, and just as she opens the door, the stairwell door opens.

"TREENA!" a stocky guy yells. He's got short, cropped brown hair and is wearing a soccer jersey.

She turns and smiles. "Hey, Trey," she says, and when I turn back to her, she's blushing.

"Floor party tonight. You better stop by, okay?" he asks, and Treena nods in response.

"Uh-huh, okay," she says, grinning.

"And bring your cute friend," he says with a wink, then goes into the room across the hall from hers and, with a wave, shuts the door.

Face blazing red, I push her inside her room, and when the door is closed, I ask, "Okay, *who is that?*"

"Oh, that? Ummm." She blushes more, a full rouge covering her face. "That's Trey."

"The same Trey you were talking to when we were on the phone?" I ask.

"Uh-huh," she says casually, smiling guiltily.

"Ye who rarely talks to guys, can I get some details here?"

"Okay, okay," she says, "but first, room!" She gestures toward her room. It looks similar to her bedroom at home—colorful and clean—only about half the size. She wasn't lying when she said it was tiny. There are two beds in opposite corners, one made with a bright quilt and the other bare, and two desks separating them. Treena's has a picture of her family on it, her laptop, and a ton of papers and notebooks. There are two dressers across from the beds, and a closet between the dressers. On one dresser is a tiny TV, and next to it are piles of the rest of her bangles. On the wall is a purple-and-pink sari, adding color to the otherwise beige-and-brown room.

"It's very you." I smile.

"Oh, look!" she says, jumping on her bed to show me a bunch of photos taped to her wall. She must have had them printed out or something. They're of her turtle from back home, her parents, her sister. And there, in the middle, a bunch of us through the years, hiding, of course, the embarrassing ones.

"Oh my gosh, tell me you do not have a picture of me in pajamas," I say, pointing to the picture of us from Pajama Day at school.

"And Twin Day," she says, pointing to the one next to it. "We looked nothing alike."

"At all. But it was fun." I look at the other pictures and see some that I took for class and must have put on my blog. It makes me smile again to think she wants them in her room.

"So Trey," I say, sitting on the bed with her.

"I would have told you about him sooner, *obviously*, if there was a story to tell. But he's just the guy across the hall, you know? He's super cute and nice and *everyone* likes him," she says, exaggerating everything with her hands.

"But, okay, so I've known him since I moved in, but a couple of weeks ago, I started studying in the common area—it's down the hall, there's, like, a little TV and couches, I'll show you later," she says, and I signal for her to continue. She has a tendency to ramble sometimes. "Okay, so I was working on a problem with this guy, Bennett, from my biology class, and Trey walked by. Bennett apparently knows him from home or something, so they started talking. And then Bennett went to get a snack downstairs. Oh yeah!" She stops, changing subjects again. "We have a snack shop downstairs if you need anything. Nothing special, but it has subs and stuff."

"Okay, but more about Trey," I say, laughing.

"Okay, okay. Anyway, when he left, Trey came and sat next to me and we talked for, like, half an hour. I mean, we've talked before, of course, but this time it was just me and him, and it was more, I don't know, different. Personal? Anyway, I started doing homework out there more regularly, and he started coming by and stuff, so we've been getting closer. . . ."

"And?" I push.

"And that's it! We're not, like, engaged or anything!"

"I can't believe you have a boyfriend," I joke, leaning back on her bed.

"I do not have a boyfriend!"

"Just promise to invite me to the wedding, if I'm not the maid of honor."

"I hate you," she says, laughing. "But I'm so glad you're here."

"Me too," I say, and lean on her again. I can't deny the jealousy creeping inside me—Tree has a guy! But I push it back, because for now she's all mine.

"And you can see my room," she says, gesturing like it's a mansion worth a million dollars and not the size of a shoe box. Really, though, it's her first place on her own, without the confines of her parents. I'd feel like it was a palace, too.

"It's perfect," I say, taking everything in in one swoop. I nod toward the empty bed. "Good thing you're roommate-less," I say. "How is that, by the way?"

"It was kind of lonely at first," she admits, "but now it's okay. The floor is awesome—everyone is friends."

"How were the clubs you tried joining?" I ask. Back home she helped with our high school's newspaper for a bit, but really she stuck to her studies.

"Eh, I tried joining the Hindu Students Association, but everyone was so . . ." She waves her hand around, trying to pick the right word.

"Smart? Beautiful? Kind?" I try, describing her.

"*Indian.* They were nice enough, but so focused on school and premed, and, you know. It was like they were channeling my parents. I've been to so many Indian events growing up, I'm cool just making friends on my floor."

"Your floor meaning Trey," I joke. She used to always complain about going to events with her parents. The festivals were fun—she brought me to a Holi one where we threw powder at one another until we looked like Smurfs—but she didn't like *just* hanging out with Indians, as many of the other people did.

"Ha ha." She swats me with mock indignation.

"So, wait, what'd he say about a floor party?"

"Tonight!" she says excitedly. "There's a floor party. They're really fun—we all keep our doors open, and everyone visits each other. Our RA organizes them, so we won't, like, get in trouble for making noise. She thinks if we have parties like this, there will be less of a suicide risk."

"What? Really?" I ask.

"I guess some people get really depressed their first year, so she keeps us happy. It's nice." She shrugs.

"Jeez," I murmur.

"Yeah. So, party tonight. Everyone is excited to meet you!"

"You told everyone about me?" I ask curiously.

"Of course! You're my best friend, why wouldn't I brag that you're coming?"

"Cool," I say. I'd been kind of hoping we'd have the first night together, and she could show me around and we could plan my week. But floor party sounds fun. Floor party seems like college.

"Don't worry, everyone will love you," she says, giving me a look that makes me believe her. "Hungry?"

"Starved," I say with a nod, and we get up and leave for the downstairs snack shop.

SIX

Before going into the snack shop, I call my parents to let them know I made it by 4:00 p.m. on the dot. After confirming that yes, I arrived safely and no, we aren't partying, Treena and I eat some gummy pizza and chat about her classes (English is terrific, anthropology is not) and my project ("You'll find inspiration here easily," she says). After, we sit outside on the grassy knoll behind her dorm, leaning back on our arms, and just talk. About everything and nothing. And it's nice and normal and feels like last year.

"So you're looking for information on your mother tomorrow, right?"

"Yeah," I say, "I'm thinking of going first thing in the morning. Can you come?"

"Ugh, I have a test in the morning. If it wasn't for that—"

"No, you'd still go to class," I laugh.

"Hush," she says, even though she knows I'm right. "No, seriously, I feel bad I can't come. I'm free after the test, so can I help out then?"

"Of course." I nod. "I need you, you know that."

She looks at me and smiles, then says, "You know, if you enroll here, we could do this every day."

"I know, I know."

"Have you started applying yet? Last you said you were swimming through the endless pile of information."

"Still am, and thanks to my mom, getting more every day. I think she signed me up for every mailing list," I joke. "I don't know. I am looking at FSU. Ms. Webber said they have a great photography program." As if on cue, I spy a student taking pictures of a tree across the field. He crouches down low and angles his camera up, capturing the arc of the branches, I think.

"Oh my gosh, they do. You need to come here," she says excitedly. "We can live together. I'll even let you share my Oreos."

"You *never* let *anyone* share your Oreos."

"But for you living here . . ."

"I'm thinking about it." I grin, then nudge her. "It doesn't seem that scary, college."

She shrugs. "It is and isn't. It is at first, but the people make it better, I guess."

"Are any of your friends coming to the party tonight?" I

ask curiously. She's mentioned a few girls she's friendly with, but it still makes me kind of jealous. She has a whole friendship universe here, and I'm not part of it.

"A few. I'm excited for you to meet them." She clears her throat, then asks, "How's Celine?"

"Oh, good, you know," I say, and then realize she doesn't actually know Celine. She went to school with her, of course, but we never all hung out or anything. "She's a really good photographer," I say.

"You've said that before." She stiffens a little, then looks at her phone. "Floor party starts at eight, in twenty minutes—we should get ready."

"Sounds good." I nod, thinking that maybe how I feel about her friends is how she feels about Celine.

We walk upstairs, get back to her room, and start the process of getting ready. Treena's nervously pacing the room, and I smile because that's how she gets before any event, especially ones that involve boys.

I open my duffel bag and stare at the assortment of jeans and T-shirts I threw inside. "Um, I didn't really pack for a party," I say, wondering what else I should have brought. "I kind of assumed most of the week would be just the two of us hanging out. Plus, I don't really have a mountain of party clothes at home. When was the last time we went to a party in high school?"

"Oh, wear whatever," she says, exchanging her shorts for a pair of jeans and taking out an olive-green tank top. "We all wore pajamas at the last one. That was really comfy."

"Pajamas? Your mom would have freaked," I say. "Didn't she wear her fancy sari just to pick up schoolwork for you? When you got your wisdom teeth out?"

"Always dress to impress," Treena says, quoting her mom with an exaggerated Indian accent and the matching head bob her parents often do. They were born and raised in India, but moved to Florida after getting married. Tree and her sister were pretty much Americanized from birth, but there are still little traditions she holds, like the tiny statue of Shiva on her dresser with a candle next to it.

"I love your mom. How're your parents getting along without you?"

"Apparently Trishna is giving them a hard time."

"I haven't seen her around school a lot," I say, thinking about her little sister, who used to copy everything we would do when we were all younger.

"That's the problem. She has a new friend who's a bad influence. She skipped class the other day."

"No way!"

"Yeah, so Mom's convinced she needs to be sent to India or something."

"How many times has she threatened that?"

"Right? And it's not like it's a valid threat! I loved my visit! Anyway," Treena says, putting her bangles back on.

I copy Treena's outfit and put on a pair of jeans and a gray tank top, along with bangles. Nice and comfortable, but not quite pajamas.

Just as Treena turns on her iTunes playlist—indie music I'm not familiar with—there's a knock at the door.

"Trey!" she yells, dashing to the door.

"Oh my god." I laugh at her excitement. The same guy from earlier steps inside. He's wearing khaki shorts and a team T-shirt, and it takes me a minute to register that she actually likes this guy. He's so not the type she usually went for in high school—back then it was more band geek or mathlete.

"Yo, pregaming in my room. You in?" he asks, then notices me. "Hey again." He walks toward me and adds, "Trey" with all the self-esteem in the world. He reaches out his hand and I take it.

"Maude," I say.

"Best friend from home?" he asks, and Tree, who has not spoken yet, nods, and I think it's nice that he knows about me. This isn't just an infatuation; she really does talk to him. "Cool," he says, then looks back at me. "Pregaming in my room before the floor party. Makes them more fun," he adds with a wiggle of his eyebrows.

"Oh, okay," I say awkwardly.

"She's here for a week." Treena finally snaps to. "I'm gonna show her around."

"Cool," he says. "Gotta go—I'll see you two later." With a cocky grin, he leaves the room. When the door shuts, I turn to her.

"What's with the silence? Didn't you say you talk with him daily?"

"Shut up," she says, thawing out. "I just get, ugh, you know."

"I know." I nod. "Pregaming?" I ask, because I can guess what it means, but I'm not entirely sure.

"Drinking before the party. It's his thing."

"Have you . . . ?" I ask, raising an eyebrow as she innocently leans back on her desk chair. "*You have!*"

"Okay, once I had a drink! It kind of tasted like death."

"Uh-huh," I say, crossing my arms and staring at her like the time she crossed her arms and stared at me after I admitted to cheating on a test. It was *one* answer, and it was on my phone, so I kind of looked.

"Like you're perfect." She grins.

"You're bringing up the test again," I deadpan.

"It's my one piece of ammo, let me use it," she laughs, and I shake my head.

I guess I shouldn't be surprised—she is in college and all—but I am. Between her new crush and her first taste of alcohol, she's getting into things I never expected from her. Or maybe it's me who feels different. Like I'm left behind or something.

Music from the other side of the door begins to play, and Treena again runs to open it. The other doors start to open, too, with people filing out, leaning against doorways and walls. It's as if a light was turned on, and everyone was forced to party.

I follow Treena out, and lean against the wall with her,

right outside the door. My heart is thumping because this is it—this is what a college party is like, right? Somehow I feel both old and young at the same time, as if I'm part of it, but also playing the part. I look at Treena for something, and she grins at me, giving my hand a squeeze. "I can't wait for you to meet everyone," she says, and I nod, excited too.

There are two girls in short-shorts down the way doing handstands, with their feet barely touching the wall. Two guys are holding cups and throwing a Ping-Pong ball back and forth from one to the other. One guy has brought out his laptop and is blasting some party music. And I'm here with Treena, in the middle, watching it all unfold. My skin starts to itch, and I feel that awkwardness I usually get at school dances, where everyone is engrossed with one another, and I'm on the side with Treena having a party of our own. We were always both inside and outside the party, so I do what I always do—I reach for my camera. This can definitely convey the first day here.

I realize absently that my camera is still on the bed, and I don't want to run in and get it yet, so I use my phone instead. I snap a quick picture of the handstands, the red cups. The revelry, the open look on everyone's faces. I swing around to Treena and snap a picture of her waving to a few people walking toward us. Trey, I notice, is talking to a girl in pajama pants a few doors down.

Some girls come over and one yells, "TREENAAAAA" in a deep, sports announcer voice. I raise my eyebrows and

Treena laughs. "Guys! This is my friend Maude," she says, giggly.

"The friend from back home!" one girl shouts, and gives me a hug. She's got this wild blond hair that looks like it hasn't been washed, and rope bracelets piling on her small wrists. I smile and awkwardly hug her back, shooting Treena a confused look, but she just gives me a go-along-with-it nod.

"That's me," I say, hugging her back. When she lets go, she asks how I'm doing, like we're old friends, and it's sweet, actually.

"Oh, good. This is fun," I say. "It's my first college party."

"Isn't it great? Our floor is the best."

"So you like it here? At FSU?"

"I mean, it's fine, I guess," she says, waving her hands. "The people are great, but I'm only here because my parents said I had to go to school before joining the Peace Corps."

"That's—"

"They really need help out there, and I know I can do it." She keeps talking and I nod, impressed that she wants to do something to make the world better, when, personally, I just want to find information about my mother and take some cool pictures along the way. Her views are so much bigger, more meaningful than mine.

"I'm sure you're going to make a difference," I say, nodding my head, and kind of at a loss for what to say.

"I hope so. Hey, if you come here, you should think about joining Amnesty International. It's an amazing experience."

"Amnesty International?" I ask.

"It's this organization that fights for human rights. Like last week, we protested in front of the capitol, trying to get more financial aid to Africa's crappy schools. It's really awesome; I mean, when you go to the meetings, you meet people who are just so connected, and so passionate. It makes college worth it."

I nod, envying her knowing, her assured way with what she wants, and her future.

"That's awesome. I'll totally look it up when I start school," I say, not sure if I'll follow up on that offer, but it feels like the right thing to say.

"Great," she says, then turns around quickly when a girl with long, dark hair pulls on her arm.

"Oh! Sorry, gotta run, girl thing," she says with a wink, then takes the girl's hand and walks down the hall.

"See ya," I say, and both girls turn back to wave.

"So you're Treena's friend?" I turn abruptly to see a guy to my right. I step back, uncomfortable with his proximity. He's leaning against the wall close to me. He's got black hair and a crooked nose, and is wearing a T-shirt that simply says COLLEGE on it.

"Yeah, I'm Maude," I say, looking behind him for Treena. She's animatedly talking to a few other girls, so I look back at College guy.

"Hi," he says, grinning. "Are you here for a while?"

"Just the week. Checking out the campus . . ." I can feel

him next to me, despite us not touching, and it's making me feel awkward. I take another step back toward Treena's direction.

"I can show you around, if you'd like. I'm a tour guide."

"Oh, cool," I say, wondering if he's simply a close talker, or something more. "I might need that. I need to go to the stadium tomorrow. . . ."

"I've got a map in my room. Let's go get it. I'll show you the route," he says, touching my shoulder and leading me away. I walk automatically, until I feel someone tug on my hand.

"Um. No," Treena says, holding on to me. She turns to me. "Did he ask you to go to his room?"

"Um, yeah, a map," I admit, eyeing her questioningly. And then I get that, yeah, he wasn't just a close talker. "Ah."

"He does this to every girl," she says, throwing her arm around me and pushing me into the conversation she's having. "Just ignore him."

"Did he . . . with you?" I ask.

"Ugh, tried, but Jill here saved *me*."

"Happy to do it," a short girl with short blond hair says. "He's, like, the worst kind of guy there is—I hate that he lives on our floor. He's just always trying to make out with girls, using stupid lines like that."

"He sounds delightful," I say, shaking my head.

"Yeah, he's mostly harmless. But still, what a skeez," Treena says. "He tried it with me, offering cookies. And I love cookies."

"You do love cookies," I say, thinking about the secret

supply she used to keep hidden in her old room. The old memory brings me comfort—some things don't change, thankfully. "Well, thanks for . . . that," I say, shrugging.

"It's my job." She smiles, then turns when someone calls her name. I float back to the wall, where I was standing, and watch it all unfold some more. A person who I assume is the RA walks around, nodding. She looks older, serious, and one guy quickly hides a cup behind his back before smiling wildly at her.

It's like school, really. All the different cliques, and people in the same places pairing off. I wonder how I look among all of them. And then I remember that it's not just me I should be wondering about, but my mother, too. Did she live in this dorm? Did she lean against the wall or join the party?

Was she ever right here?

"You're Maude, right?" a guy behind me asks. He's wearing glasses and a hat. He's tall and in all black.

"Yep," I say, wary this time. After College guy, I'm just not sure.

"Like Harold and—"

"Maude. Ha, yeah, my parents love that movie," I say. "It's how I got my name." What I don't tell him is that it's because Maude loved the idea of living life to its fullest, so they thought, since I was born from death, I should be named something to do with life. It wasn't until I watched the movie in high school with Tree that I realized Maude dies at the end.

"I do, too. I'm a film major, so I watch all those old movies all the time."

"Cool!" I say, because I'm a sucker for old films. I was practically raised with them. "Like what else? I loved *Bonnie and Clyde*. Oh, and of course *Casablanca*."

"Well, I prefer newer ones," he says, "like *Scarface*."

"*Scarface*? Really?" I ask.

"It's awesome. I have the poster in my room. You have to see it."

"Mmmm, maybe some other time," I say, having learned from the last interaction.

"Well, sometime while you're here, you should come by and see my movie collection. It's epic," he says. "I have a special edition of *Harold and Maude*, too. It's got all the deleted scenes. You know they had deleted scenes back then? Awesome, right?"

"No, I didn't," I say, backing up. He could be totally innocent. Or not. I don't know.

"They found some!"

"Wow," I say, thinking that this might be his way to relate to people—through bragging about movies he likes, movies he knows about. "But hey, I have to find Treena?" I say, feeling the largeness of the party and what's going on. "I'm staying with her."

"Yeah, yeah—Treena's great. Well, stop by sometime. Room 412. Right there," he says, pointing to it. "I'm the *Scarface* room." He arches his eyebrows and I nod, not impressed with *that*. Do you really want to be known for a movie about drug dealing?

I don't see Treena in the hallway, so I double back to her room and let myself in. "Hey, Tree—" I stop short. She's sitting on her desk, with Trey in front of her, and they're in the midst of serious kissing. I gasp, then quickly walk back out, shutting the door and blushing madly. I smile to myself, wanting to high-five her. She's been kissed before, of course, but not like that, at least not that I knew of. I cover my mouth with my hand, suppressing a laugh, and just shake my head.

I take a step down the hall and realize I have no idea where to go, and no one to talk to now. I don't want to risk bumping into another annoying guy, but I also don't want to go back into Treena's room.

And I'm in a hall of people I don't know. Great.

Down the hall there's a door to the stairs. I'm hoping Treena was wrong when she said people make out there, because I'm thinking that'll be a good place to go for a while, giving Tree her space. I make my break quickly, and press on the metal door, entering silence from a world of noise.

I sit down on the concrete steps and lean against the cool wall, taking a deep breath. The music is still outside, but it's muffled now, less in my face—or ears. No one is here. Privacy.

I pull my phone from my back pocket and see that I have a message from Celine.

Maybe it is more like she said it would be, and less of what I expected. I wanted a week of me and Treena reconnecting, and finding out about my mother together. I wanted it to be like old times. But I guess things change. And I'm here, alone, in a stairwell.

I think about Treena and wonder if this is what's supposed to happen in college. If moving away means moving into a new role, a new you. My life has been so controlled, so defined, I never thought of going in a different direction. I wonder how my mother acted in college.

I fiddle with my phone and check Twitter, my blog, my email. About ten minutes go by and I text Treena. I'd rather not go up there and interrupt again. She doesn't answer, so I wait longer, letting the noise filter in. I don't really feel like going back up there to talk to people I don't know without her.

As the minutes go by, I start getting irritated. With Treena. With myself. I should have made her stay with me, not go off with him. And she should have wanted to stay with me. Why did she sneak off with him? I mean, I *know* why, but shouldn't hanging out with me be more important?

I hear footsteps coming up the stairs and consider moving—but to where? I start texting Celine again so I don't look like a loser girl hiding.

"Avoiding the party?" a voice asks me. I look over and

see the stair climber approaching. He's skinny, with curly, dark brown hair, and is holding a notebook in one hand. "Oh, sorry, thought you were someone else. Wait, you're Treena's friend, right? I saw your picture in her room; she said you were coming to visit."

"Yeah," I say, offering a clipped answer, and wondering if he's going to invite me to his room, too, just like the others. I usually don't mind talking to strangers, but right now I'm just not in the mood.

"What're you doing out here?" he asks.

"Phone," I say, waving my phone up.

"We're making that great of an impression on you so far?" he asks, and sits against the wall next to me, one step lower.

"Quite." I'm not really sure what to say next.

"You know, I've nearly slept on these stairs. I wouldn't recommend it, they're kind of uncomfortable."

I take the bait. "Why'd you nearly sleep here?"

"My roommate had a girl over, and I really didn't want to stay in there while they were . . . you know . . . um, in there."

"That's kind of where I'm at right now."

"Wait," he says, furrowing his brow. "Treena is—"

"NO!" I gasp, remembering that he knows her. "No, no, but she *is* hanging out with a guy in there."

"I see. So you're kind of room-less?"

"I guess." I'm assuming he's hinting, so I say, "And I don't want to go back to your room, before you ask."

"Whoa, okay, I wasn't offering, but now I know not to," he says, but he doesn't get up and leave. He stays there. And something about that makes me turn my head.

He's cute, actually, in a nerdy way. He's in a *Star Wars* T-shirt, a hoodie, and cargo shorts, and has worn skater sneakers on. There's something authentic about him—he looks like himself, even though I don't know who he is, unlike the others who are trying so hard to look like a better, more polished version of who they actually are. The film guy. The College guy. Trey. They're all trying so hard to be someone. Even Treena, in a way.

"Sorry. Long night," I murmur, putting my head in my hands, extremely embarrassed.

"It's okay."

"It's not. It's just . . . I'm not used to guys being so in my face? It's like every guy here wants to talk to me just because they think I'm this new shiny high school kid waiting to get laid."

He laughs and shakes his head. "Welcome to college." He puts his hand out to me. "I'm Bennett. I promise to not try to get in your pants."

I blush, but smile at his comment. "Maude. And thank you." I falter, trying to figure out how I know his name. "You're Bennett? You study with Treena and Trey, right?"

"Yeah, I live one floor up." He points in that direction. "Wait. Is it Trey?"

"Hm?" I ask.

"She's with Trey, isn't she. She gets this, like, gooey look when he's around."

I laugh. "Gooey look?"

"I don't know, you know, like . . ." He makes an exaggerated face with hands cupped and eyelashes batting.

"It *is* my best friend you're talking about," I say. "But, yeah, she's with Trey."

"I knew it. I'd be jealous if . . ." he starts, then stops. "Trey's a cool guy, have you met him yet?"

"Briefly. He asked about pregaming?" I answer, wondering what his "if" meant.

"Yeah, that's his thing," he says. "So, Treena says you're here on some sort of mission? I mean, one that I absolutely promise to not help you out on because that means I'd be nice and, therefore, trying to get into your pants."

I laugh again at him, feeling a bit shyer now, less confident. "Yeah. Um . . ." I start. She told him I was on a mission? I guess I am, but not one I really share that openly. But I'm probably not going to see him again, so why not talk. I haven't really had a chance to tonight. "I'm trying to find out about my mother."

"Is she missing . . . ?" he asks gently.

"No, no. It's nothing like that. I never met her; she died when I was born. I'm adopted," I say.

"Wow. We just met, and you're already telling me your deep secrets," he comments, and I blush. Maybe it was a bad idea.

"Not so much a secret; I've had seventeen years to get used to it," I say quickly.

"I bet, no, it's cool, sorry, I was joking," he says, backtracking as well.

"It's okay."

"So your mother?"

"So, yeah, I never knew her, so I'm trying to find out something about her."

"And your birth dad?" he asks, genuinely interested.

"Never knew him." I shrug. "He's not on my birth certificate. I have no idea who he is."

"Ah," he says, leaning forward to stretch, then relaxing back on the wall. "That's intense. Are you going to find him next?"

"You know . . . I don't know," I muse. "I hadn't thought about that. Maybe?"

"It's an idea," he says, stretching his legs out in front of him. They're long and lean. "This should be a movie or something. *Looking for Mom*, or something like that."

"Yeah," I laugh. "I guess it is all a bit . . . theatrical."

"So why Tally? I'm assuming she lived here?"

"Yep. It's the only connection I have, really. I know she went to FSU, so I'm going to the registrar to see if I can find her old professors. And then I'll go from there." I shrug. It's the only thing I have, and even though it's small, I have to keep believing in it. It's what's pushing me forward.

"Seriously. Movie. There's a film school guy on the hall

who I'm sure would film it. But don't ask him, he's kind of a weirdo."

"I met him!" I say. "For a film major, he has horrible taste in movies."

"Did he tell you about *Scarface*?"

"Yes!" I laugh.

"I hate that movie. Then again, I'm known for watching *Star Wars* more than is healthy, so I probably shouldn't talk."

"How many times have you seen it?" I ask.

"This year?"

The door bangs open and we both jump.

"*There* you are!" Treena says, coming over to us. "I was wondering where you went."

"Yeah," I say, looking up at her and seeing what I'm 99 percent sure is a hickey blooming on her neck. The sight of it kind of annoys me. "I texted you. . . ."

"You did? Crap, my phone died. I'm so sorry I lost you!" she says, and in the moment I see the nervousness in her eyes, the secret she's waiting to share, and I get it. She is sorry; she didn't mean to lose me. She was just . . . lost in the moment. She then realizes that Bennett is next to me.

"It's okay," I say, trying to smooth it out. "I had a message from Celine anyway."

"Oh," she says, her face dropping a little, then coming back. "Cool. Oh, Bennett, hi! Hey, so I was telling Trey we should all go to dinner tomorrow night! The four of us!" She sounds excited, and I wonder which Treena I'll get. This one, or the lovesick one. Whichever one, I'll be happy to have her.

"Sounds good," he says, looking up at her.

"How's the party going?" I ask.

"Okay," she says. "Ready to come back? I need my Maude with me. . . ."

I look at Bennett, and he shrugs. "Yeah, give me a second," I say, kind of preferring the quietness of the stairwell, but also wanting to be back up there with her.

"Okay." She shrugs, looking at me. I think she's trying to tell me something with her eyes, but I'm not sure what. "I'm going to go find Trey," she says, then looks back at me. "Come in in a bit, yeah?"

"Of course," I say, and it feels awkward, uncomfortable. Like there should be more said. After a second, she leaves and it's just the two of us again.

"Now, when she says 'go to dinner,' that means I'm to storm you into my bedroom, right?" he asks with a cocky grin.

"Shut up," I say, hitting him lightly and laughing.

"Is that the real reason you're here, hiding in the stairwell?"

"I'm not *hiding*," I say.

"Uh-huh."

"If you want to go enjoy the party, you can," I say, gesturing toward the door, but in truth, I really don't want him to leave. I like talking to him.

"Uh-uh. Not without you. Don't want to leave you alone to be feasted on. These guys are like zombies, you know, always coming back for more."

"Har har har." I roll my eyes.

"I'm serious," he says, mock serious.

"Well. If they're zombies . . . at least they'll like me for my brains."

He shakes his head with a smile. "I'm not laughing at that."

"You really shouldn't," I agree, sighing.

"Okay, let's go. I'll protect you," he says, standing up.

"Promise?" I look up at him. I should worry. I don't know him at all. But a guy who makes me laugh, and who's wearing a *Star Wars* T-shirt, isn't all bad, right?

"Promise," he says, offering his hand to pull me up. I grab on, unsure of what the other side may lead to.

SEVEN

MONDAY

Not much happened after Bennett and I entered the party. Trey left for some soccer thing at one of his teammate's houses, so Treena spent the rest of the night with us. It's not until the following morning when Treena gives me the details on Trey.

"So . . . something happened last night," she starts as she pulls out her shower caddy. "Trey kissed me." Her voice is bubbling with excitement and makes me wake up immediately.

"I know!" I say, sitting up in bed. "I mean, I saw, and then quickly ran away."

"You *saw*?"

"Your door was unlocked, but when I saw you two, well, that's why I went to the stairwell. I didn't want to disturb you."

"Sorry about that. I didn't mean to—"

"Tree, it's okay. I'm super happy for you," I say, and I am. I wish it hadn't all happened when I was here. But maybe I'm being selfish. This is a guy who likes her, so I want to cheer her on. I have to. "Anyway, details!"

"There aren't many! I don't know," she says, smiling and blushing. "Did you like Trey?"

"Yeah, he seems nice," I say, figuring it to be the safest response, "but we didn't talk much."

"Yeah, parties aren't great for bonding. Tonight will be better. Speaking of . . . I see you got along with Bennett really well," she says in a singsong voice, and I sigh over my warming cheeks because it's not like that. Sure, he's cute and funny, but he's not the reason I'm here. I don't need to be distracted by guys while I'm here for a more important reason.

"Yeah. He's cool. I mean, we were just talking," I explain, getting out of bed and rifling through my bag for some clothes.

"Just talking, uh-huh."

"We were!" I protest.

"Maybe *my* goal of the week will be to get you a boyfriend," she says, and I shake my head at her enthusiasm.

"How about instead of a boyfriend," I start slowly, "let's

make it our goal to do something fun each day."

"Oh, don't worry, we will. I have plans." She raises her eyebrows as she says this, and I perk up.

"Really?"

"You're going to love college," she says, and I wonder if she's right. "It's so different. I mean, we can be someone new. No one knows about high school us, not that high school us was bad. It's just . . . I was able to start over."

Perhaps for her that works, but maybe I don't want to start over. Maybe I like who I am.

"Anyway," she continues. "Tonight will be fun."

"Yeah," I say, remembering that we're having dinner with the guys. "And this morning, too," I remind her. "I'm excited to start investigating."

"Yes! Ugh, I still hate that I can't go. You'll be okay, right?"

"Of course," I say, sad, too, but understanding. She needs to take a test. I need to do this . . . and maybe I *should* do it on my own. "I'll text you immediately after."

"Can't wait." She grins, knocking her shoulder onto mine. I repeat the gesture.

"Me either," I say.

"Okay, I should get ready," she says, heading for the bathroom. I'm far too awake to go back to sleep, so I decide to start the day as well.

While Treena's in the shared bathroom down the hall, I have a second to look at her room and the person it represents. There's not much on the walls; it all seems like her, but a cleaner, tighter version.

I think of what she said, about starting over, and remember the last sleepover we had. It was a week before she left. We were having a movie night, and it was my turn to choose, so I went with *Ferris Bueller's Day Off.* With a sigh she agreed to watch Ferris and friends skip school. By the end, we wondered what it would be like to have one crazy day where we did whatever we wanted and found ourselves in both adventures and misadventures. With only my purse and camera, I'd go to the airport and board the cheapest flight, just to see where it would take me. She, on the other hand, wanted to go to another school and pretend to be someone else, just to see what it would be like not being her for once.

I guess, in a way, she's doing her Ferris Bueller adventure now, only it's lasting much longer than a day.

After getting ready, I nervously get a map from Treena.

"It's a straight shot to the stadium—just follow the sidewalk around the park, then pass the library, and keep walking until you see the biggest stadium you've ever seen."

"That big?" I ask, putting the map in the shoulder bag I usually use at school. It also has my phone, notebook, pens, a bottle of water (extra from my trip up, courtesy of my mom), and my camera.

"Gigantic. I'll be back from class by three, so I expect a full report then. And don't forget we have dinner plans tonight." She leans over to tie her Chuck Taylors.

"As if I have any other plans to get in the way," I joke.

She jumps up and gives me a hug. "Good luck. Let me know how it goes, okay?"

"Will do," I say into her hair. Then I turn around and take my first step out the door, and not just onto campus, but into my future.

◇◇◇◇

On campus, I find Treena's directions extremely simple. The sidewalks are crowded with people going to class, flipping through books and texting as they walk. Some are engaged in conversation, but not everyone, so I don't feel as alone. I pull out my camera and take a quick picture of a row of students walking forward, all looking down at their phones, and then, to contrast, a shot of a group of people walking and talking to each other. I'm thinking these might be good for my blog, to show that I'm starting my search. To show the campus, and though it surely doesn't look the way it did back then, to show a place where my mother's history is rooted.

A girl yells out, "Mrs. Donnelly!" and a woman turns around. They laugh about something, and their ease with each other reminds me to check in with my mom. I text her quickly, sending her a picture of the campus, and she responds enthusiastically. I think she's getting used to the idea of me going here for school.

I walk a few more minutes, cutting through the park behind Treena's dorm, which is pretty empty right now, as everyone is rushing off to class. There's the fountain, also empty, except for statues playing inside, and I take a picture of the fake college students doomed to spend eternity splashing in water.

I cross a busy intersection, where car horns blast as we flock sheep-like across the street, and people start thinning out. The walk is slow and quiet and I'm having fun taking in the campus. It really is beautiful, with oak trees lining the way, and buildings over a hundred years old. I can't help but wonder if my mother walked these streets, if she went into these buildings. That thought never fails to amaze me. In the distance, just as Treena said I'd see, an enormous stadium is perched atop a small incline.

It takes a while to get there, but finally I'm standing in front of an intimidatingly large iron statue of a Native American atop a horse, holding a feathered spear. Below it is a round base taller than me that says UNCONQUERED.

I walk behind it and stare up at the brick stadium reaching toward the sky. It's so intimidating, so vast. The doors are right in front of me. Heart racing, I breathe in, taking in this last moment. Inside might be information I never dreamt of having. Or, it could be nothing at all.

It's weird; I've spent a lifetime not knowing anything more than my mother's name, and today, things might change.

Air-conditioning hits me as soon as I walk in, and I'm greeted by a roped-off line in front of an information desk.

"Hi," a girl with a face full of freckles says, waving me to the desk.

"Hey." I'm suddenly nervous. I was expecting an older person to take pity on me, not someone close to my age. "Um. This is the registrar, right?"

"Yep! Can I help you with something?" she asks. She has long blond hair and bright blue eyes, with matching blue feather earrings. Before her is a computer that looks older than me.

I take a deep breath. "I was wondering if I could get some information about someone who went here a while ago."

"Um, we don't give out personal information . . ." the girl says, furrowing her forehead and looking to call up the next person in line. I look back and realize I'm still the only one here. Good.

"Right, I know, it's just . . ." I fade out. "Okay, so, seventeen years ago a girl named Claire Fullman went here. She was a freshman then. She died that year. She was also my mother." The girl's mouth drops open a little. Then, almost instantly, her face changes to that same sympathetic gaze I get every time I mention this. "I never knew her, and was adopted. I'm trying to . . . find out about her now. I'm about to start college, and I just want to know what kind of person she was, you know? I want to know something about her, because all I have right now is that she went here."

"That's it?" she asks sympathetically, and I can see that my story actually affected her, made her feel.

"Yeah," I say, shrugging. "I was just hoping for more. So I was wondering if you could possibly find her schedule from seventeen years ago, and at least let me know if any of her teachers still work here. Because maybe he or she might remember her, and then I'll have one more fact about her."

The girl bites her lip, and then asks, "What about your father?"

"I never knew him. He left, I think," I say stoically, and she lowers her head again.

She leans toward me and drops her voice to a whisper. "My cousin is adopted, too. She's doing the same thing you're doing right now, trying to find her mom. But her mom is still alive. I'm not sure which is better, really."

"Me either," I admit, knowing I've thought this same question countless times before.

"I can't image how hard it must be," she muses, absent-mindedly tapping the desk. My heart is racing, wondering if I proved something, anything. She snaps out of it and looks at me, as if coming to a decision. She whispers again. "Here's the thing, I'm not really supposed to do something like that; it's an invasion of privacy. But since she's no longer alive . . . and since you're her daughter . . . I mean, it can't hurt anyone, right?"

"Right!" I excitedly whisper back, and suddenly I love this girl.

"Right. Okay. Let me see what I can find." She types into her ancient computer, and I wait anxiously for something, anything. She frowns, types again, and asks, "Claire Full-man, right?" and I nod in response, heart pounding. She did go here? I'm not just on a wild-goose chase. "Okay, hmm, well, let's see," she says, "hold on."

She gets off her chair and picks up a piece of paper from the printer, and then puts it on the counter in front of me. There are four classes listed, four teachers listed. "Here's her schedule for, it seems, her first and only semester."

"I thought she went here for a year?" I ask, and the girl sadly shakes her head.

"Unfortunately, three of these teachers are no longer here. Some were TAs, um, teacher assistants, so they just graduated. And then one professor retired."

I nod.

"But the good news is that one professor *is* still here. It looks like she was a TA back then, and now she's a professor in the English department. She's really awesome, too—I had her last year. Do you have a map?"

My spirit lifts with every word she says—one professor is still here. One professor might know my mom. This is *amazing*. I shake the thoughts and quickly get the map out of my bag.

"Okay, we're here," she says, pointing to the stadium on the southeast corner of the map. "Professor Stark teaches in the Williams Building, all the way over here." She points to a building on the top northeast corner. "It's a bit of a walk, but just stay on the outer rim of campus, and you'll hit the back of it. Hold on," she says, typing something else in her computer. "Okay, she teaches in room 216. If she's not there, her office is room 210."

"Thank you so much" is all I can mumble out, my heart soaring with excitement and nerves. "You have no idea how much this means to me."

"I do." She shrugs. "I hope someone helps my cousin, too, you know?" she asks, and I grin at her. I back out of the room, paper and map in hand, and greet the warm sun once again. And this time I don't find the unconquered statue intimidating, but instead, empowering.

EIGHT

The Williams Building looks like every other redbrick building on campus. The only thing that sets it apart is the grouping of students loudly debating a Shakespeare play near the front door.

I go inside and head up the stairs to the second floor. A guy looks at me and instantly I feel out of place, as if he knows I'm still a high school student and not in college. I look down and continue my way up the stairs.

The building is much nicer than the dorm. The hallways are white, but the doors are old, wooden, and open, leading into well-lit classrooms. I pass a few rooms of conversation and hear people reading aloud and chatting and waiting for classes to start.

Professor Stark's classroom is the third one on the right.

I don't know if she had this classroom so many years ago, but I still feel antsy, standing here, where my mother might have once stood. Heart pounding, I take a deep breath in, close my eyes, and then open them, looking into the small window on the door.

The room is empty.

Just to be sure, I knock lightly and wait. Nothing. I turn around and look at the map for the professor's office number. When I look up it's right there, across the hall from me. I wait for a gap in students, and then walk over. Peering inside the window, I see a woman sitting at a desk, reading from a book. I knock lightly.

"Come in," she calls, and I bite my lip as I open the door. "Can I help you?" she asks, taking her glasses off. The woman—Professor Stark, I'm assuming—is older, in her forties, and wearing a tan cardigan over a white button-down shirt. She's sitting at a brown wooden desk that's covered in papers and books. A picture of the Globe Theatre is on the wall behind her. If my mom had an office, it would look just like this.

"Hi, um, are you Professor Stark?"

"I am. What can I help you with?" she asks, eyes darting back and forth between me and the book before her. Of course I'm bothering her. Of course she realizes I'm not one of her students. I must look like a baby.

"I was, um, wondering if you possibly remember my mother," I say, and her eyebrows go up. "She was a student of yours seventeen years ago, when you were a TA."

"Oh, that was a very long time ago," she says, tapping her pen on the desk.

"I know, I was just wondering if you . . . did." I stop, realizing how weird this really sounds. I suddenly feel stupid standing here, a child in a grown-up world. "I never did, I mean, I never met her, so I'm trying to find people who might have. So I can . . . learn something about her."

"Oh," Professor Stark says, and lowers her head just like the girl at the registrar did. She looks back up to me and asks, "What was her name?"

"Claire. Claire Fullman." I watch her eyes for any sort of recognition, but they're gazing across the room, and I almost wonder if the answer could be found in any of the hardback volumes piled against the walls.

"Claire . . . Fullman . . ." she muses. "Claire Fullman." She shakes her head, then looks at me sadly. My heart drops; she doesn't need to answer. "I'm sorry, the name doesn't ring a bell."

"Oh," I say, looking down.

"It was quite a long time ago. I was only in my early twenties back when I was a TA, and I had *a lot* of students. Unless she did something truly remarkable . . ." She trails off, then takes me in. "But I suppose she did. She made you, didn't she?"

I force a smile. She's trying to be nice, but it's not enough. I feel my quest slipping through my fingers as I realize that she won't have the answers I'm looking for. If not her, who? Where do I go from here? I don't want to ask my mom again. . . .

"Right. So, I'm very sorry I can't help you. I wish I could, but I don't have any records from my TA days, and like I said, I had a lot of students."

"It's okay," I say, because I don't know what else to say. I know she can feel the disappointment pouring out of me. "I knew it was a long shot."

"If I may ask, how did you find me?"

"Registrar?" I say as a question, and blush a little from admitting my way of going around things.

She nods, and I smile. "Smart girl." She stares at me again. "Did she grow up around here?" she asks, rubbing her chin with her hand.

"Yes," I answer.

"Well, there are six high schools in the county, three that are close to the college. You can start by checking them. Osceola High School is the closest."

"Oh! Thank you. I'll do that." Another shot. Another place to try. Maybe this isn't the end of it all just yet.

"You're welcome," she says, standing up and looking at the clock behind her. "If you'll excuse me, I have to teach a class in a few minutes. But it was nice meeting you . . ."

"Maude," I say.

"Yes, Maude. Good luck on your odyssey," she says with a raise of the eyebrows. Yeah, my mom would like her.

"Thank you. Thank you very much," I say, nodding.

When I step into the hallway, I lean back against the wall and watch as the students pass before me. Some walking fast, some slowly ambling on, talking to friends. And one girl telling a story so large, so vocal, with so many hand movements. I stand up straight, realizing that not only am I in a building my mother once stepped into, but also, possibly, a hallway. She was here. She was part of these walls, these floors. And maybe she's still here. Somewhere.

I get out my camera and place a trembling finger on the button. *Snap.*

One more photo for my blog. One more photo for the day.

NINE

I walk around campus for the rest of the afternoon, taking in the sights, grabbing lunch, and then navigating my way back to Treena's dorm. After snapping a few more photos (including sneaking one of a guy who looked shockingly like the guy Celine was flirting with at Starbucks to the point that I had to do a quadruple take), I find myself outside Treena's building. I've called her a few times since it hit 3:00 p.m., to no avail, so I assume she's still in class or busy. I find a bench outside and wait for her to call me back.

To pass the time, I flip through the photos I've taken so far, and decide to update my blog—first with the photo from a few minutes ago, which I label "Here," then with the photo of the Unconquered statue, with the caption "Will not be stopped." I flip through a few comments I got on my last photo, and then put my phone down.

I still don't know what to do for my project, I'm nowhere closer, so I decide, instead, to follow Ms. Webber's advice and keep taking pictures for fun. I take out my camera and change the shutter speed to hold it open longer. I place the camera on my lap and press the button, getting a long-exposure shot, blurring the people passing by, but focusing in on the static things, like the tree across from me, the ground below me, and the lamppost a few people tap as they pass. It should be a cool shot. But waiting for it to properly expose is making me even more anxious.

"Maude?"

I jerk up and see Bennett standing next to me. "Oh, hey," I say, capping my camera again and putting it back into my bag. The shutter closed just in time for me *not* to mess up the photo. "Just getting back from class?"

"Yeah, drawing."

"Oh! Are you an art major?" I ask.

"Computer animation. I've admired Pixar, like, my whole life."

"I love those movies! I babysat a kid who'd watch *Cars* over and over again."

"My kind of kid," he says, sitting on the bench, then pointing to my lap. "Cool camera."

"Thanks, it was a present."

"So you're an artist, too?"

I shrug. "I don't know if I'd call myself an artist, but it's

84

what I like to do. It's what I hope to go to school for."

"You're like a real live Peter Parker."

"I'm Spider-Man?" I ask, amused.

"Totally. Photography. Unknown parents. Quest to find them."

"So you're saying I'm a web-slinging superhero with a mysterious past and a fun hobby."

"Exactly," he says with a deadpan expression, and I laugh.

"I'll take that."

"What were you taking a picture of?" he asks.

"Just the activity of the sidewalk," I say, my leg tapping repeatedly.

"Cool," he says. "Is that why you're out here?"

"No," I sigh. "I'm waiting for Treena. She said she'd be home to let me in, but she's not answering her phone."

"What time is it? Hold on." He takes out his phone. "Oh, it's three. That's when we used to study, which turned into when she and Trey hang out. They're probably spending some time together. . . ."

"Oh! Wait, Treena? She said she'd meet me after her classes."

"Come on, I'll let you in," he says, gesturing toward the door. Could Treena be in there and not taking my calls? She wouldn't do that. Would she?

"Thanks, but I'd rather not interrupt them if that's the case," I say, even though I'm not convinced.

"You can hang in my room until they're . . . done," he says with a smirk, turning to walk, and then turns back and says, completely seriously, "That's not a pickup line. I'm being an utmost gentleman in offering my assistance, and not, you know, trying to get in your pants or anything, as I was told that was very much off-limits."

I remember the joke from last night and laugh, breaking my curiosity. "I see," I say. I stare at him waiting for me, and then get up and follow him into the building.

"Let me check her room first, you know, just in case," I say when we're in the elevator. That'll prove to him that she's not in there.

"Suit yourself," he says. "Maybe keep your eyes closed?"

I shake my head in response. I get off at her floor and run down the hall. Her door is closed, and I hear music coming from inside, and muffled voices. My heart sinks as I realize Bennett was right—she's in there. With Trey. And not answering my calls. When I turn around Bennett is behind me.

"I wanted to see if I was right." He grins. "I kind of feel bad that I am."

I smile and try to look okay, but really I'm hurt. This was supposed to be our time together. But instead of sulking, I shake my head and follow him up one more flight of stairs to his room.

We get to his door and it's decorated, like the others, but his has pictures of Buzz Lightyear on one side, and bikini-clad models on the other.

"My room," he says, getting his key out and fumbling with the lock, as if he's nervous for some reason. Inside, the room is much like the door—one side pretty neat with a picture of WALL-E, and on the other more girls in bikinis staring at me.

"My side," he says, gesturing to the fully clothed side. "My roommate's rarely here; he has a girlfriend in another dorm. He stops by to get clothes sometimes." He points to the piles of clothes strewn around the floor. "He's really considerate."

"I can tell," I say. I realize how funny it is that I'm here, in a guy's dorm room. Instinctively I want to tell Treena, but then realize I can't. And it hurts again, so I bite my lip as I walk around, reminding myself to act normal.

"So how'd today go?" he asks as he throws his bag onto his bed.

I sit on his desk chair and instead of moping, I open my mouth and find myself explaining everything that happened. I'd been so intent on telling Treena that it all kind of comes out. He listens, offering me a soda in the middle of the story, then sits on his bed.

"That's crazy," he says. "You actually met someone who knew your mom."

"I know, but she didn't remember her," I say.

"True, but she knew her at one time. And that's something."

"I guess you're right. But I'm still kind of disappointed."

"So what's next? Are you going to the high schools?"

"Yeah." I nod. "There's nothing else here. FSU is now a dead end, so I'm going to head to them tomorrow. I figure I'll start with the one she mentioned that's closest, Osceola, and go from there."

"You know, I volunteered at Osceola earlier this year for one of my classes. Helped them set up their new computer lab. I don't have any classes tomorrow, so I can take you, if you'd like," he offers, and though it's a nice offer, I'm not sure if it's what I want. What I'm doing is so personal, so just me. I don't want to say all of that, so instead I respond, "Maybe," and leave it at that.

He shrugs, leaning back on his bed.

"So . . ." I start, noticing his *WALL-E* background and matching toy. "You really are into Pixar."

"Ah, yeah. The pictures are inspiration and stuff, but this," he says, pointing to the figure, and then getting out a matching cup, "is my mom being overeager about my interests."

"At least she supports you," I say, thinking about how my mom got me my camera.

"She does, a little too much. I made her return the *Toy Story* sheets because having them wouldn't be embarrassing or anything."

"I loved *Toy Story*. But it kind of made me a hoarder. I never got rid of my toys because I didn't want to hurt their feelings."

"Yeah, that movie does make you feel crazy guilty,

doesn't it?" He looks down, then asks, "Want to watch it? I have to watch an animated feature for class, so you'd actually be helping me do my homework."

"That's your homework?" I ask.

"College is cool," he says easily. "So . . . ? Movie until you hear from Treena?"

I shrug. "Sounds good to me." I take a sip of my drink and put it down on his desk. He reaches over me and grabs his laptop from his desk, then rifles through a pile of DVDs on his nightstand.

"I'm not very organized," he says.

"Film guy down the hall would be very upset with you," I say.

"Ha," he says, putting in *Toy Story*. I realize that I can either stretch over and watch the movie from my chair, or join him on the bed, which is a little awkward. But he realizes the same and puts the computer back on his desk, so we can both see from where we're sitting, and I smile, hiding my face from him.

"Just FYI," he loudly whispers. "I'll try to be manly, but this movie totally makes me tear up."

I laugh, looking back at him, grinning.

"Me too," I whisper back.

Not long into the movie, voices outside bring us out of Buzz and Woody's world. A bang on the wall makes me jump.

"What's going on?" I ask.

"Not sure," Bennett says, reaching over to pause the movie. "But the guys down the hall are always doing something stupid. Last week they made lances out of paper towel rolls and ran at each other. I mean, they even had tinfoil knight helmets."

"Seriously?" I ask, raising my eyebrows.

"Seriously," he says, getting up. "Let's go look. Maybe they'll be luchadores this time."

I follow him to the door. Outside, a few people are standing around, cheering. In front of us, a girl is sitting on a skateboard. I look to the right and see a bunch of bottles set up like bowling pins, and I'm pretty sure she's going to skate over to knock them down.

"Seriously?" I ask Bennett again, because this is more like a movie than an actual Monday afternoon, right?

"Let's try," he says with a glint in his eyes.

"No way, I'll totally fall," I laugh, watching as the girl is pushed down the hall into the bottles. She knocks them down, then throws her hands in the air and cheers.

"You're sitting down, you can just put your feet down if you feel unsteady," he says. "Come on, take a leap." He grabs my arm and pulls me out of the room. I breathe in at the touch, and look up at him.

I've taken a jump so far; I've come here to find out more about my mother. This won't help, but it's not a bad thing, right? I'm taking leaps, so why not roll with it? Literally.

"Okay," I say, nodding my head and smiling. "Let's go."

"Yesssss," he cheers. "You first, I'll push." He walks over and high-fives a guy who's holding another skateboard. They put it on the floor and I sit on it, pulling my legs up so they're balanced on the front, and holding on to the sides so I don't fall in either direction, just like the girl before me did. It's not comfortable, and I'm pretty sure I'm going to topple over to one side, but I look back at Bennett and he's already crouched over, looking at me. I'm feeling unsteady, but it's not because of the skateboard.

"Okay, ready?" he asks behind me and I nod, unable to speak. His hands go to my waist, holding on tight, and he pulls me back slightly before pushing off.

The skateboard zooms forward and a laugh escapes me as I race toward the pins. I hear Bennett yelling, "Left, left," so I try to lean to the left, but get scared and straighten back up. And before I know it, I'm crashing into the bottles and throwing my feet down to stop. There's applause behind me, and I laugh, standing up to take a bow.

I run back down and hand Bennett the skateboard.

"Nicely done," he says, and I grin in response.

I catch sight of dark hair and look behind him to see Treena standing at the end of the hall with a frown on her face. My smile drops and I walk over toward her.

"Hey, I've been waiting for you," she says, a tone of annoyance and sadness coating her voice.

"No," I say, confused. "I've been up here waiting for you."

"If you've been waiting for me, why didn't you just come

to my room? I've been waiting for *you*," she says, frustration crossing her face.

"I thought you were busy," I exclaim. "Bennett says you usually hang out with Trey at this time, so—"

"Oh, Bennett," she says, shaking her head. "If you want to hang out with him, go ahead. I get it. I just thought you were coming up to see me and stuff."

"No," I say solidly. "I want to hang out with *you*. I came here to see *you*. I thought you were busy because you weren't answering your phone."

"You didn't call me," she says, shaking her head, and I eye her.

Where is this coming from? Why the sudden distrust in me? In us? "Yes, I did." I nod. "A lot."

She stares, purses her lips, then nods, and I follow her back to her room. I turn around and see Bennett watching. I shrug like I have no idea what's going on, and he waves good-bye. We head down the stairs and get back to her room, where she picks up her phone and sighs. "Oh."

"Yeah," I say, crossing my arms.

"I must have forgot to turn the ringer back on . . ." she says, putting the phone back down and looking at her desk. "I'm really sorry."

"Tree, I came here to hang out with you . . . I'm not going to leave you for a guy," I say purposefully, hoping she gets what I mean. She nods her head, then looks up.

"You just looked like you were having fun out there. And, like, last night you didn't even want to stay around during the party. I kept losing you . . . so I thought . . ."

"*I* kept losing *you!*" I say, stepping closer to her. "I just wanted to catch up with you, not go to a party. And when I finally found you, you were with Trey." I drift off, so she knows what I'm saying.

She opens her mouth, then closes it. "Ugh, sorry," she says, shaking her head. "Sorry. This whole thing is new. I mean, him, me, you being here. I promise I'll be better."

"Were you with him?" I ask, because I want to know if Bennett was right.

"Yeah," she says, cheeks reddening. "He came by and, um . . . I kind of lost track of time." She looks down and grabs her elbow self-consciously. "I *did* stay late after class, then came back to wait for you. I guess I missed your call at that point because, I swear, my phone was still on silent. Then he came over and I thought he'd leave quickly, and . . . ugh, I'm awful."

"It's okay," I say.

"No, seriously, I'm sorry. This is our time together. I shouldn't be so obsessed with him and all that."

"Tree, it's fine, seriously," I say, smiling at her, because it is. Okay, I was upset, but it's still Treena. "It's not a big deal. But now I totally require details about your rendezvous. I mean, not *detailed* details. You know."

She laughs and sits on her bed. I climb next to her. "First, tell me about today. What happened? Did you find out anything?"

"Kind of. I talked to the registrar and know she went

93

here. I saw her schedule and I met one of her teachers."

"YOU DIDN'T!"

"I did, but she didn't remember her. It was so long ago. So, I don't know."

"But did she tell you anything? About the class? Anything?"

"Not really, but she said my mother probably went to one of a few nearby high schools. So I think I'm going to go over to some of them tomorrow . . . if you're free to come . . ."

"Yes! Yes. I will be there," she says. "Organic chem isn't until later, so I can totally go in the morning. Did I tell you how much I'm hating that class?"

"That bad?" I ask, leaning back and thumbing through a book on her bedside table. It's a textbook for the same class she's talking about, and it looks terrible.

"The worst. I know some of the stuff from high school, but it's just . . . boring. And the teacher takes everything so seriously. And the people in the class are . . . I don't know, I just . . ." She trails off.

"At least you only have to take it this semester," I say. "Then you're done."

"I have a long line of similar classes if I want to get into medical school."

"*Do* you want to get into medical school?" I ask. She's always said that was her plan, but it never really seemed like her. More like something she felt she should do.

"I don't know," she says, biting her lip. "Between us, I'm

kind of second-guessing. I mean, I want to, and I know I'm okay at it, but it just doesn't make me happy, you know?"

"Tree, you're in college. You should take what makes you happy, not what you think you should take."

"Easy for you to say. Your parents are cool with you majoring in photography."

"Yeah . . . but Tree, your parents love you. They'll be happy with whatever you major in." I pause, then joke, "As long as it means you'll have a good career and a good husband."

She laughs and rolls her eyes. "I know, you're right. They were just so proud of me when I said I wanted to be a surgeon. . . ."

"What *do* you want to be?" I ask, not sure of the answer. I've never seen her want to do anything else. This is new, and kind of exciting to hear.

"Honestly? I'm really loving my English class. We're reading all of this beatnik literature and, to counter it, feminist literature, and it's all so good."

"Not surprising. You're always reading," I say, pointing to a small pile on her floor, near the bed.

"So, yeah, we'll see."

"I love it." I smile. "Though it might take away your study time with Trey."

"Ahhhh," she says, rolling her eyes. "We don't need studying as an excuse to get together anymore." She giggles.

"So I saw today!"

"I'm sorry!"

"I'm kidding, I'm kidding," I say.

She looks at me. "It's just, you know, I'm not used to this stuff. Guys didn't like me in high school. And he does, and it's just . . ."

"It's awesome, Tree."

"But he's so out of my league. I mean, why does he like *me*?"

"What do you mean?" I ask, and then I realize that her question makes sense. It explains her attachment to him, her nervousness around him, even her newer feel. She's acting different because she's trying to be different. We were never that in high school, and now she's here and wants to be someone new. "Don't think that way. You're so much better than him."

"Maude, I love you, but he's got girls hanging all over him. And, like, hot girls. The kind of girls who used to make fun of us."

"I don't think those feminist books you're reading will agree with your thinking right now."

"Yeah yeah yeah," she says, shaking her head.

"Well, I didn't see him making out with other girls last night," I mention.

"Oof," she moans, blushing. "Yeah. But that's all we did today, too, so don't get any ideas."

"Nope. None at all." I grin, and she pushes me. I tackle her back and we're laughing and just being silly.

We catch up more for the next few hours over chai just how her mom makes it (extra milky for her; no milk, extra sugar for my lactose-intolerant self), and as the time goes by, it feels oddly like we're not in a college dorm, but, instead, in her room back home and nothing is different, even though everything has changed.

TEN

For our big dinner with Trey and Bennett, we go for Mexican food. The restaurant looks like a normal, boring building on the outside, but inside it's bright and lively. A mariachi band is playing for a table in the corner, everyone is talking, and the menus are practically neon. I quickly take a photo of the multicolored chips and post it to my blog.

"This place is cool," I say, opening up my slightly sticky menu. There's a pronunciation guide, which I always find funny—who doesn't know how to say "taco"?

"Yeah! We come here a lot, so, I mean, we had to bring you," Treena says, cozying up next to Trey in the booth. I'm excited to have this night to figure him out, see more of him, since he still just looks like a jock to me. I'd love to know what he likes, and what he, himself, is like. I'm going to be nice.

Bennett and I sit across from them. I thought I'd feel underdressed when we left—in just jeans and a T-shirt— since Treena is in a cute little spring dress—but no one else here seems dressed up, either. Trey is wearing a football shirt, and Bennett has the same Tetris shirt he was wearing earlier, with a hoodie over it, and khaki shorts.

"So, Trey, what are you majoring in?" I ask.

"Don't know yet," he says with a shrug. "I'm undeclared at the moment. Thinking hospitality."

"Oh!" I say, completely unsure what that major entails. "That's cool. What's majoring in hospitality like?"

"Don't know. It's what most of the guys on the team major in. There's a wine tasting class, which is supposed to be epic. And, like, hotel management and stuff? I can see myself owning a resort." He grins.

"That sounds cool," I say, wondering what else I can add. I don't want to play twenty questions with him, but I want *something* to work with.

"I know a girl getting her master's in hospitality management, and she's already promised a job at the hotel downtown where, like, governors stay," Treena says, nodding enthusiastically. I smile and nod, too.

We sit in silence for a couple of minutes, pretending to read the menu. As if sensing the awkwardness, Bennett nudges me. "Okay, so if you weren't sure, this is how you say burrito," he says, leaning over to me and sounding out the word like *burr-eeee-tooooh*, while pointing to the pronunciation guide.

"I *was* wondering," I say, smiling at him. I look back, and Trey and Treena have fallen into their own conversation about something to do with swimming pools, so I dive into Bennett's distraction.

"Just wanted to make sure. Didn't know what you guys ate down there in *Orlando*."

"Ohh, I see, hating on O-town?" I ask, turning to him and putting my hands on my hips.

"Isn't everything made of pixie dust down there?" he asks, grinning, and I push him. After our skateboard bowling, things have been a lot friendlier between us, as if we've known each other for months, not hours.

"Aren't you the guy who loves *Toy Story*?"

"Touché," he says.

"Where are you from, anyway?" I ask.

"Miami. Trey and I went to school down there," he says.

"Oh, okay, since you're from Miami, you think you can teach me how to eat burritos?" I joke.

"*Sí.* I am half Colombian," he challenges.

"Uh-huh," I say, crossing my arms. "But what does that have to do with Mexican burritos?"

Treena suddenly laughs as Trey kisses her. I glance at Bennett, who rolls his eyes in response.

"Hey." He nudges me as the others ignore us. "Are things cool between you two? You kind of escaped earlier."

"Oh yeah. Yeah, things are fine. Just a misunderstanding."

"Okay." He shrugs.

"So anything you'd like to do while you're here, Maude?" Trey suddenly asks. I hadn't realized he'd stopped making out with Tree.

"Not really," I say. "I mean, aside from seeing Treena and the school and . . . stuff," I say, not wanting to get into the *other* reason for coming here.

"Well, if there is anything," Treena says, "let me know. I don't want you to regret not seeing, like, the capitol building or something."

"She should see the capitol!" Trey laughs, and it's the most animated I've seen him yet.

"Is it that great?" I ask, confused why he's so giddy about a building.

"Oh, it's *monstrously* great," Trey continues, still laughing, and Treena pushes him. My face starts to heat up as I realize I'm the only one not in on the joke.

"It's, um," Bennett starts while Trey continues to giggle across the table. "It's not what's inside that's great. It's just that it looks like—"

"A penis," Trey interrupts, guffawing. Treena slaps him, but laughs, too.

"Huh?" I ask, face still hot. This is not where I thought the conversation would go.

"Well, it's long and tall," Bennett says, scratching the back of his neck uncomfortably, "and behind it is the old capitol building, which has—"

"Two domes. So they're, like, the—"

"I got it," I say, cutting him off. "Great visual, but I think I'll pass," I add.

"You are *such* an idiot," Treena says to Trey, and then giggles, and I sigh.

Our waiter comes by and Trey's phone starts buzzing with texts, and I see Treena frown.

"What's up with your phone?" Treena asks.

"Dude, I have the best idea for tonight," he says, ignoring her question.

"What?" Bennett asks.

Trey looks at all of us, raises his hands, and then states: "Pineview."

"No way," Bennett says. Treena just looks away.

"Why not? It'll be *awesome*—I went there last week with some guys on the team."

"What's Pineview?" I venture to ask.

"It's this crazy haunted mental institution. It's abandoned and you can, like, break in and see all the old medical equipment. There's some creepy-ass shit on the walls and spray paint everywhere, and, like, dried blood on some of the floors. Some of the rooms are locked up, too, so you can't even go into those. A lot of people said they saw ghosts there, or, like, things moving."

"There's also asbestos, broken boards, nails, and cops guarding it. It's like the place villains take people hostage in movies," Bennett explains. "Seriously, Trey—don't."

"Dude, you haven't even been," Trey says. "Loosen up. You were so uptight in high school. We're in college now. Have some fun."

"I don't need to go to know it's dangerous," he says.

"Do people regularly break in?" I ask.

"Yeah, all the time. It's like a rite of passage. I had to do it for the soccer team—it was part of my initiation."

"What else did you have to do?" Treena asks, and I'm starting to suspect she doesn't know a lot about her "maybe" boyfriend.

"Nothing bad, baby," he says, kissing her on the top of her head. "But you guys should totally see this place. It's hella creepy."

"I mean, it could be fun . . ." Treena says tentatively.

"I don't know . . ." I say, siding toward Bennett's decision. The thought of breaking into an abandoned building scares me enough to give me the shivers. But also . . . it could be cool. I've never done something like this before, and I can only imagine the kind of photos I'd get. Not necessarily for my project, but just in general. If Treena's in, maybe I should be, too. . . .

"Come on, it'll be awesome," Trey says, and I can feel myself giving in, both not wanting to let him and Treena down, and also curious as to what might happen. What we might see.

My eyes meet Treena's and she looks pleading. I think back to our conversation earlier—how she doesn't feel good enough for him. Maybe this is what she needs, a chance to do something daring. Maybe this will make her feel better. And after having our fight this afternoon, I still feel kind of bad. And I'd rather do something *with* her than without her again.

Maybe this is more than just a crazy night out.

So I find myself nodding and hear Trey cheering while Bennett sighs on my other side. But like earlier with the skateboard, maybe it's time for me to push myself a little bit, too. And if I'm scared, I can always put my feet down.

ELEVEN

After dinner, we pile into Trey's car, Treena in the front with him and me and Bennett in the back. Bennett was mostly silent throughout the rest of dinner, and he isn't saying much now either. Trey turns a country song on rather loud, and he and Treena sing along. Another thing I didn't know about her—a newfound love of country music.

"Hey," I say to Bennett under the music.

"Hey," he says, playing with the hem of his shirt.

"You okay?" I ask.

"Yeah," he says, turning to me.

"Sorry we're going . . ."

"It's okay, I mean, it *does* sound cool and creepy, but I've done the whole breaking-in thing before."

"At Pineview? I thought you hadn't been. . . ."

"No." He shakes his head. "There's a place like this back at home. In high school I broke in with my friends because, you know, what else is there to do on a Friday night. First, I fell and got cut up bad on an exposed nail, so I was pretty sure I was going to die from that. Then, cops came and caught us, which almost cost me graduation. I mean, they let us go with a strong warning after bringing us down to the station, but still, my parents haven't really dropped it," he admits with a frustrated sigh. "So, I'm kind of not wanting that to happen again, I guess."

"So why'd you just give in?" I ask, moving closer so only he hears me.

He shrugs, glances at me, then at the seat in front of him, then pushes his curly mess of hair back. "It's Trey. He'll get his way eventually. He always does."

"How so?"

"I don't know, small things. I've known him for a while— since sixth grade."

"Ahh," I say, noting that I can always go to Bennett if I have questions about Trey. "So what was he like?"

"I don't know. Charming—everyone loved him. He'd magically convince teachers to not give us homework. Or convince people to *do* his homework for him."

"You're not making a good case for him right now," I say. "Best friend up there."

"He's not that bad. I mean, he's not a bad guy. He's just . . . Trey."

"Well, what happens when he doesn't get his way?"

"I don't know. He's never not gotten his way," he says with a raise of his eyebrows, and I shiver, wondering what it all means. For us. For Treena. I look away, but when I turn back, Bennett is looking at me. I want to ask more about Trey, but I also kind of don't want to know, don't want my opinion to be so changed without talking to Treena, so I change the subject.

"Do you have a scar?" I ask instead.

"Huh?"

"From the fall with the nail," I say.

"Oh, yeah, here," he says, rolling up his sleeve and pointing to his arm, between his elbow and wrist. The scar is long and pink, healed over a few times, and runs long and jagged.

"Ouch," I say.

He leans back, and when our eyes catch, he smiles, and with much bravado says, "It wasn't that bad."

"Of course it wasn't." I smile and nod.

"I've had worse, of course. There was the bus full of children I saved . . ."

"That was on fire?" I ask.

"And about to fall off a cliff."

"And there were babies on the bus, I assume."

"And bombs."

"Sounds scary," I laugh.

"Oh, you know, it was nothing," he says, waving me off.

"Then tonight should be nothing, too," I say, and he looks at me again and smiles.

After about twenty minutes, Trey stops his car, and

I feel my heart swell with fear. I look out the window and see the desolate four-story building, stony and dark against the night sky. Vines are growing up it, and some of the windows have been knocked out. There's a chain-link fence surrounding it, with a few streetlamps around casting an orange hue, and I swear it's a scene straight from a horror movie. I breathe in deeply and hold my breath. I do not want to go in.

"We're heeere," Trey says in a spooky voice, and I glare at him. I turn to my right and notice that there's a dimly lit police station across the street.

"Should we be worried about that?" I ask, pointing to the station.

"Nah, they set it up to scare people from breaking in. Most of the time the cops are out busting college parties and stuff."

"How do you know?" I ask.

"Told you, I've been here before," he says confidently, and I nod, not as reassured by his demeanor as Treena is. "But first," he says, pulling something out of his pocket. It's a silver flask, and I watch as he unscrews the top and takes a drink. My heart pounds as I wonder if he's going to pass it around, make us all take a sip. Another thing I haven't done before—drink.

He hands it to Treena and she doesn't look back before gulping some down. I guess this makes the second time she's taken a drink.

She turns around and gives the flask to Bennett, not meeting my eyes. And once again I'm in a position that I don't want to be in—not sure if I should go along, or just say no.

This is college, though. I guess next year I'll be faced with these decisions daily. And as I watch Bennett take a sip, I feel myself wanting to, too.

He hands the flask over to me, and I see an engraving on the side.

"Are these your initials?" I ask Trey.

"Yeah. My brother got married last summer. That was my best-man gift," he says, looking back. "Mom doesn't know, of course. She thought I got cuff links. Ha."

"Ha," I say, repeating him, before taking my own drink. I scrunch up my eyes as the liquid hits my throat and burns. I cough, then swallow, and have no idea how people drink this stuff normally. I hand the flask back to Trey, who takes another gulp before screwing the cap back on and putting it in his pocket. I can feel my face heating up.

"So, we ready? This is a rite of passage, guys. Prepare yourselves!" Trey whispers loudly, turning back around and shining a flashlight in my face. I block out the beam and look away. My heart is thumping louder than I thought possible. I am absolutely, 100 percent terrified, and the alcohol isn't helping. I look back and try to catch Treena's eyes, but she won't look back at me.

"Let's go!" he says, opening his door. Treena follows next,

and then me and Bennett. Standing outside is even worse. The silence is deafening. The building seems bigger, and I feel much, much smaller. Trey hands us each a flashlight he conveniently had—had he planned this all along?—and we follow him to the fence.

"You okay?" Bennett whispers to me, walking beside me as the other two are up front.

"Uhhh," I answer, unable to speak.

"Same," he says.

There's a large hole in the fence that Trey ducks through, and we follow. I contort myself, hoping the exposed metal doesn't scratch my skin. When I stand up, my body is shaking.

"This way," Trey whispers, and we follow him up the sidewalk leading to the building. We haven't turned our flashlights on yet, for fear of attracting attention, so it's still incredibly dark, despite the streetlamps' best attempts. My eyes are adjusting slightly as I focus on the door ahead of us. It's large and gray and does not look welcoming at all.

Trey gestures for us to avoid that door and go around the building. We step off the concrete path and into the grass, which hasn't been cut in months, it seems. It climbs up my pants and settles just between my ankles and knees. I keep my eyes trained to the ground, looking for movement. Every squish of the grass makes me think something is coming to attack.

We get to another door and Trey opens it. A screech

echoes out, and I jump back, fearing we've been heard. Heart thumping, I halt until the others move. I watch as they look around, take one last glance at the car, and then quickly go inside. Then I follow.

Aside from small beams of light filtering in, it's pitch black and smells like mildew. I wrinkle my nose and remember the asbestos Bennett mentioned. Trey turns on his flashlight.

HELP is written in red on the wall.

I gasp and jump backward, grabbing Treena's hand. Trey chuckles and shakes his head. "Sorry. Guys wrote that last time."

"Jesus," Bennett says, and I look back at him and can tell he's ruffled, too. Treena doesn't let go of my hand; instead she grabs it tighter, and I can feel her trembling. Despite this brave persona she's putting on, I know she's scared.

"Worse than the time we watched *Paranormal Activity*?" I ask her.

"A million times worse," she murmurs. "This wasn't a good idea, was it?"

"Nope. Why are we doing this again?"

She doesn't answer, and I turn on my flashlight and shine it on a desk with a bunch of books piled atop it. Behind it are file cabinets, some slightly ajar. I quickly move my light, afraid Trey will want to explore their contents. I'd rather not know what's in them. As I move away, I hear a jiggle and instinctively jump.

The other flashlights turn on, and I stand closer to Treena. I can tell she wants to run to Trey, but I hold on to her tighter. We follow Trey deeper into the building. The floor feels damp and soft, and squishy. The walls have peeling wallpaper and paint chips, along with words like FIND ME, I'M SORRY, and GO AWAY spray-painted on them. I'm sure all of those are fake, much like the HELP, but they still creep me out. Each time my beam lands on another message written in red, my heart jumps. I shake my head in frustration.

The smell gets worse the farther we walk in. It's like rotten eggs left outside in July's heat. And because of the moist floors, my body feels damp, too. I want to leave. Now.

"Right," Trey whispers, nodding his head to the right, so we follow him in that direction. He opens a door and exposes a room with two beds inside. There are chains on the beds, with shackles to hold the patients down, and instantly I want to cry. I don't want to see this. I don't want to be here. Treena's hand, still in mine, is shaking even more, and I know she's thinking the same thing. I flash my light at Bennett and it looks like all of the color has drained from his face.

"Cool, right?" Trey asks, walking up to the beds.

"Don't touch that!" Treena shrieks, running over to him.

"Why not?" he says, grabbing the arm rail.

"I want to leave," I whisper to Bennett.

"Me too," he says.

"Dude, Bennett, come over here. Dare you to lie on the bed?" Trey says.

"I think I'll pass," Bennett says.

"You did stupid shit like this when we broke into the building back at home."

"Yeah, and we were caught."

Trey rolls his eyes and shines his light on a few clipboards on the wall, an IV stand still standing by the bed. I can hear a faint dripping, and even though I know it's water, I can't stop myself from thinking it's blood.

"Let's go upstairs," Trey says, eyes shining in the night. With the light beam on his face, he looks like a demon, like he belongs here.

"I'm good," I say, backing out of the room.

"Yeah, I'm going to stay back, too," Treena says. "But you can go!"

"Bennett?" Trey asks, and Bennett doesn't even answer. "Dude, what's with you? It's like college made you lame. There's this creepy-ass doll up there. I'm gonna get a picture of it, then I'll be back down." He huffs off out of the room, back into the main waiting area, I assume, and then we hear him ascend a creaky flight of stairs. At his mention of a picture, I have an urge to take out my phone, but I don't want to remember tonight, and don't want to see what develops. I thought it would be cool originally, but not so much anymore. I keep getting a weird feeling that something might happen.

I walk out of the room and hear the others behind me. The stairs Trey must have taken are on the left—they're old and wooden and there are splinters all over them. They can't be safe.

We hear movement upstairs: doors groaning and loud footsteps.

"I hope he comes down soon," Treena whispers, and I put my arm around her shoulders.

There's a loud *bang* upstairs and we all jump. Then nothing.

"Trey?" Treena tentatively calls out.

A crash echoes through the hospital and we all jump again.

"What . . . was that," Treena asks, reaching down to hold my hand.

A screech comes from the right, like a wounded animal.

"I don't like this. . . ." I say.

A door slams shut.

"We should go. We should definitely go," I say, tugging on Treena's arm.

"No, not without Trey. We can't leave him behind," she says, then yells, "TREY!"

"I'm actually okay with that," Bennett says, grabbing my free arm and pulling me toward the door.

"NO!" a voice yells out, and Treena screams.

A growl sounds to our left and I jump nearly on top of Bennett.

"Trey!" Treena calls out. "TREY!"

I step backward and slip on water that wasn't there before. I quickly right myself and grab on to Bennett's arm.

"You guys . . ." I say, my heart racing in my chest.

"Yeah, no, we're leaving," Bennett says.

A bang erupts and then a book is tossed off the second floor.

"Oh my god," I say as Treena huddles into me, starting to cry. "We have to go, we have to go." I pull on her, toward the door, and she lets me, holding on tight. I'm trying to be brave, but I can't feel anything, I'm so on edge. The walls start making more sense. Maybe they aren't a joke; maybe there really are hauntings here.

"Just go through the front door," Bennett says behind us, guiding us out.

"OH SHIT! NO! RUN!" a voice calls, and I know it's Trey. My heart leaps into my mouth. I grab Treena's hand and then dash to the end of the room, dropping my flashlight in the hustle. I know the door is in front of me, but I can't see where.

"TREY! TREY!" Treena shouts, but I don't stop. I just pull her. There are feet coming down the stairs, more than two, and I don't have time to think of what that means.

Bennett runs ahead and shines the light on the door. He opens it up, and holds it open for Treena and me to run out. Then he shuts it behind him, and runs with us back out into the grass.

We keep running until we're out of the building, close to the car. I can't look back, I won't turn around. We'll hide out until Trey returns.

"Yooo-hooooo," we hear, and then a loud chuckle. Treena stops, which makes me crash into her, and Bennett into me.

"Trey?" she asks, whipping her head back. We turn to look, and he's standing by the door, doubled over laughing. There's another guy with him, one I vaguely remember seeing at the floor party last night, and two girls.

I wrinkle my face in confusion until I get it. They did it. They did everything.

"You asshole," Bennett yells out, and Treena goes running toward him. The leaving us behind, the laughing, it's all clicking into place. He tricked us. He did all of this to scare us. *It's a rite of passage*, he'd said.

And I hate him.

"Induction, bitches," one of the girls yells.

"Yeah, everyone's gotta go through this," Trey says. "Welcome to the club."

If this is a club, I don't know if I want to be a part of it. Is this what college is like—a series of trials that you have to brave out until you can't anymore?

My body, calming down from panic mode, feels like it's going to collapse. My knees go weak, and I sit down in the grass, not caring what's inside it anymore. I don't know if I want to cry, throw up, or punch Trey. My head falls into my hands as I gulp in breath after breath.

I can't believe he did this to us. What could possibly come over him, that he would think it was a good idea? I look up and catch Treena punch him angrily, and then fall into his arms, and he takes her and kisses her passionately in the shadow of a possibly haunted asylum. She forgives him so easily. Is that who she's turning into?

Bennett sits down next to me. "Are you okay?"

I look at him and he slowly puts his arm around my shoulders. I sink into his arms, feeling his body breathe in tune with mine.

"Did you know?" I whisper into him.

"If I did, do you think I would have gone along with it?" he answers.

I shake my head no, content that when the world is spinning and people are changing, he, at least, seems stable.

But why is Treena with Trey right now and not me? When did she stop being stable?

TWELVE

TUESDAY

That night I barely talk to Treena before we go to sleep. We say good night, and that's it. And as I lie in bed, all I keep thinking is that I want things to be the same. I want her to be the same, but she's not. She's someone who goes along with Trey's stupid ideas. She makes us do these crazy things that she herself would never do. Back at home, she was never the rule breaker; her parents would have punished her if she did anything remotely out of line. She, too, got the threat of being sent to India, but it was when her grade in math dropped to a B. She was always home five minutes prior to curfew, and that was when she *had* a curfew. Her parents didn't institute it until she started driving, which wasn't until last February, when she turned eighteen. I remember when she rolled her eyes at a kid in our grade who was busted for breaking into the school and climbing onto the roof after hours. *Why do something so stupid?* she whispered to me during class.

And maybe that made her—and me—lame or boring, but we had fun in our own ways. We didn't need wild parties or drinking for that. It makes me wonder what I'll be like next year, when I'm left to my own devices without guidance or rules. Will I do a complete 180 in college, too, taking up everything that scared me before because I *can* with no one telling me no? Will I try to be someone else because it's a chance to start over?

Maybe it's easy to change completely if you haven't changed at all. Treena was always the same. She never took risks. So now, she's risking everything. Maybe challenging myself every now and then will stop me from becoming someone I don't even recognize. It'll make the jump less tempting. Maybe I just need to allow myself to try.

Like what I'm doing here—trying to find information on my mother, trying to figure out who I am. Maybe that's my risk. Maybe that's my big jump, while Treena's was redesigning herself. Maybe in taking this risk, this chance, I'll know who I'm meant to become.

I wonder what my mother was like in college. Was she more of a Treena with me, or Treena with Trey? Did she change completely once she started? Did she become someone new?

Will I, after all this?

The next morning we talk casually, Treena and I—I tell her which high schools I'm planning to visit, and she nods along. But this morning she doesn't offer again to come, saying something about studying, and I don't ask. I need some time to clear my head. I leave the dorm room on my own. Something's changed; something's off.

I go downstairs to the snack shop to grab something to eat. I walk to the muffin aisle and hear a familiar voice.

"Hungry?"

I look up and see Bennett holding a granola bar.

"I was until I saw how sad the muffin selection is," I say, holding up a flat blueberry one.

"That's why I stick to this," he says, holding up the bar. "There's a cafeteria a building over, if you want normal food. Like . . . eggs and stuff."

"No, it's okay," I say, getting the sad muffin. "I want to get on the road."

"Oh yeah," he said. "I was wondering if you were still going."

"Why wouldn't I be?" I ask, and it comes out harsher than it should. But last night reminded me that I'm here with a purpose, not just to fit in. I don't need to fit in here. I have home to worry about.

"I dunno," he says, shrugging. "My offer still stands, if you'd like some company."

I look at him and see him as part of this new life Treena has, one that's far away from the one we had together. And, yeah, okay, he's cute and nice, but he's also a distraction for why *I'm* here. I don't want him taking this away from me. But still, he offered, so I ask, "Why are you so interested in my mother's story? I mean, not to be mean, but . . . I'm curious. I'm a stranger, really. Why would you want to help me?"

He musses up his hair, then says, "My mom's a social worker, so I've seen this before, you know? Not the whole searching-for-mother thing, but the adoption life. I guess . . . I've always seen the before, like, the getting adopted part, but never the after, like, what happens later."

"Oh," I say, surprised. "That's cool. I mean, that your mom's a social worker, and that you're interested."

"I'm also just a really nice guy," he says with a grin.

"Uh-huh." I smile back.

"Scout's honor. I got a badge in niceness."

"They don't give badges in niceness," I say.

"How do you know? Were you a Boy Scout?"

I look at him and shake my head. "You're stubborn, aren't you?"

"Annoyingly so," he agrees. "Come on, we can bike there. I'm sure you could borrow Treena's. I bike a lot around here." He sits down to tie his sneakers. "It's easier than driving. No traffic in the bike lanes."

"You sure a car isn't a better idea?"

"Nah, I like to live on the wild side," he says with a smile. "Well, the non–haunted house wild side. Speaking of, did you have nightmares last night?"

"Not really," I lie. I dreamt of dark rooms and shadows and dripping blood.

"I dreamt Trey was a murderer, living a double life in the asylum. I've kind of avoided him since."

"No," I say, laughing.

"True story," he says guiltily. "Come on, let's go ask Treena." He gets up and makes his way to the door.

"I—" I start, heart catching up with my mind. I don't really want to ask her for a favor right now, after everything.

"Yeah?" he asks, turning around to me. And it's the way he's looking at me—full of questions and excitement and a pinch of sugary granola bar—I don't want to say no.

"She should be in her room," I say, and he nods. We go back upstairs, and I knock and then enter.

"Hey, Treena?" I say once inside. She's at her desk, book open.

She turns around and looks surprised. "What's up? I thought you left?"

"About to," I say. "It turns out the school is nearby, so Bennett thought we'd bike there . . ." I start.

"Oh, you can borrow mine. It's downstairs. You know which one is mine, yeah?" she asks Bennett, and he nods.

"Yep. Purple one with the 'I Heart Trey' sticker on it."

"It does not have that!" she shrieks, seemingly back to normal.

"Kidding, kidding," he says.

She shakes her head and throws me the bike key. "I should be home around three today, so see you then!" she says to me, and I wave and say good-bye.

It's as if nothing happened. We've never fought before, really, so is this how we move forward? Pretend it never happened and go on with our day?

"Woo-hoo! Biking!" Bennett says as we get back into the hallway.

"What's with you and biking?" I ask, curious.

"I love it. There's something cathartic about being so exposed while traveling."

"Why not get a motorcycle?" I ask.

"I'd *love* to. But can't really afford one right now. So, bike it is."

"Bike it is," I repeat, kind of paying attention, and kind of figuring out how I'm doing this—going to a school that might have been hers. It might not have been, too, but I don't want to think that. I want to stay positive. I want to believe that each step I'm taking is getting me closer and closer to her past. Because if I find her school, I may be able to find out so much more about her. I'll be able to see a place that was a part of her.

Yes, it might be a dead end, but then I'll try the next school. And the next. I'm going to try as many as I can; it's my last hope right now.

I zone back in and he's still talking about biking. "It's the effort that I like. The putting one foot in front of the other and pushing on. It's awesome."

"I guess so," I concede. "I haven't biked in years."

"Why not?"

"No time, I guess? I liked it as a kid, but, I don't know, once I got busier I just forgot about it."

"You can always pick it back up again," he says, pushing the button for the elevator. It comes right away, and we get on. The flyer from the party is still up.

"I don't know . . . I still don't have much time."

"School?"

"Yeah," I say. "And photography projects, and thinking about college, and figuring out if I should get a job for the summer so I can afford those colleges . . ."

The bell dings, and the doors open on the ground floor. We take the hallway out to the exit. "Hey," he says, to a guy passing. When we get outside, the light hits us and it's kind of blinding. "So Osceola's not far; we'll be there in about thirty minutes. . . ."

"Thanks for coming with me," I say. "But . . . would you mind if I go inside the school alone?"

"I can work with that."

I follow him as he walks around the corner to the bikes.

"You don't mind? It's not that I don't trust you, it's that . . ."

"No, no, I get it." He shrugs. "But hey, there's this awesome place nearby for lunch, so I'm forcing you to go there after, cool?" He gives me a smile and continues to the bike rack where a bright purple bike (sans "I Heart Trey" sticker) is waiting for me.

"Deal," I say.

◇◇◇◇

Bike riding isn't bad. In fact, it's just as fun as I remember. Each press of the pedals equals another few feet behind me. My legs propel me on, and I feel the burn in every motion. It's so much better than walking or driving. Bennett was right.

I look over at Bennett and see him in a trance, concentrating purely on the road ahead of us. We're biking side by side along a small street where cars aren't passing us frequently. He's smiling as the wind hits his face, eyes focused and ready. He turns to look at me, I'm sure feeling my gaze, and I blush from him catching me staring.

"Fun, right?" he yells over the quiet wind between us.

"Yeah!" I yell back. He nods, then looks ahead of us.

We're not five minutes away from campus when I see a school across the street.

"Hey, that's not it, right?" I ask.

Bennett stops so I do, too. "No, that's a charter school. But, huh . . ."

"What?" I ask.

He scratches his head, then angles his bike to cross the street. "It has all grades, so technically she could have gone here."

"Wait, really?" I ask, nerves hitting me all at once. I

wasn't prepared to find this so quickly; I thought we still had time.

"I don't know, might as well ask?" he says. "Want to give it a go?"

"Sure," I find myself answering absentmindedly. "Why not?"

We bike across the street and pull up to a giant white-stone building that kind of looks like a prison—bars on all the windows, a closed, institutional feel. "What kind of school did you say this was again?" I ask nervously.

"A charter school. Fancy private school. Kind of . . . um . . . depressing-looking, though. Right?"

"Definitely," I agree. I keep nodding until I realize that it's my turn to go in. That I should start moving and walking and asking questions. But instead, I admit, "I'm nervous."

"You can do it, grasshopper," Bennett says.

I nod again, looking at the structure. "Here goes nothing," I say, heart pounding in my chest as I run up the stairs leading into the building. With no time to prepare, I might as well go.

Inside it looks similar to my high school and not nearly as imposing. Just an empty corridor and hallways full of classes and lockers. I head to the left, where there's an administration sign.

Inside the room, a student is sitting at the desk. I mean, I assume it's a student; he looks about as old as I am, with short blond hair and intense glasses.

"Hey," I say. "Do you work here?"

"Assistant," he answers, still typing. "What's up?"

He's like half professional, half not, and I don't know which angle to go with. I don't think sympathy will work, so instead I just say, "I was wondering if you could tell me if someone went to this school seventeen years ago."

"Why?" he asks.

"I'm trying to figure out where my mother went to high school. She's not alive, so I can't ask her."

At that he perks up and stares at me. "You don't go here?"

"No," I answer honestly, sticking to my gut reaction.

He rubs his chin, thinking, then raises his eyebrows in a way that makes him look evil. "I have access to the database of students," he says in a low whisper. "I've always wanted to use it."

"Now is a good time," I say, encouraging him.

He looks at me for a calculated second, then looks back down at the computer. His fingers fly across the keyboard, and he asks, "What is—um, was—her name?"

"Claire Fullman," I say, heart beating in excitement. This is it—he's actually doing this for me.

"Hmmm," he says, then, "Nope, doesn't look like she went here."

I let out a breath I didn't know I was holding. "Oh," I say, trying to hide my disappointment. "Okay. Thanks for looking, anyway." This is only the first school. We have a ton of other ones to try. I have to remind myself instead of surrendering to the thought of another letdown.

"No problem," he says, adding, "What are you doing tonight?"

"Huh?" I ask.

"I need someone to go with me to this *thing* tonight. This school function thing."

My mouth drops in surprise. "But you don't even know me."

"Yeah, I know. But you can't be worse than the girls here." He says it looking down, and it makes me think that he doesn't have it easy here. That he's more like me and Treena back home. That he might get picked on and pushed around, which is why he's here, hiding in the administration office.

I don't know what to say—it's not like I want to go out with him or anything, but I don't want to hurt his feelings. "College is better than high school. You have a chance to start over, and become a new version of yourself." I don't know if I believe it yet, but Treena's words seem to fit the situation perfectly.

"God, I hope you're right," he says, looking back up at me. "Thanks."

"No problem," I answer, turning to walk out.

"And hey, good luck," he calls, and by the time I turn back around, he's already typing again. He looks small in the office, alone among other computers, chairs arranged for those waiting, and a loud ticking clock on the wall. It seems empty, the space, but I guess to him, it's safe.

Outside, I shake my head as soon as I see Bennett.

"That sucks," he says. "But I guess not a huge disappointment, considering we weren't even planning on stopping here."

"Yeah." I nod. "You're right. Not a disappointment at all."

I jump on my bike and follow him off the campus and down the street.

Just past campus is the downtown area of Tallahassee where tall buildings dot the horizon. We turn and ride through another set of roads into a quiet neighborhood. It's strange how one city has so many different subsections— college town, business town, small town. There are cottages all around us, with wooden fences that are more logs of wood than actual barriers. Cars are parked right in the yards, and one house has a Confederate flag hanging outside.

Tallahassee is vast, and, though the chance is slim, I still wonder if my mother lived in any of these houses. If this was her life, among the ramshackle places. Or if she lived in the nicer houses out in the country area Treena told me about. Or in an apartment in the city. What was her home? How did she grow up?

"Over here," Bennett yells, and nods his head toward the left. I follow him and turn onto another small road with yellow CHILDREN CROSSING signs along it. I can see the school at the end—a big brick building with everything stuffed inside, so different from the open campus of my school, where a courtyard in the center connects many smaller buildings. With 1,500 students in my class alone, we would be suffocated by such a small structure.

"So, this is our next stop," he says, stopping his bike and lifting one foot off its pedal.

"This is it," I say, stopping my bike and breathing in. I turn around, taking in the entire view. The cars in the parking lot, the lampposts, the school itself. I touch the plant nearby, and rub my hand on the ledge. This feels right, for some reason. This feels more official than the first school. I have no idea why.

This school might have been my mother's school. I might be one step closer. I put my feet down and a shiver goes through me. Did she used to sit on those steps? Did she drive and park in that lot? Did she walk through those doors every day?

"How do you feel?"

I look at him, and then the steps ahead of me that lead into the school. "Weird," I admit, not knowing any other word that can describe the anxiety and excitement and also foreboding that fills my body. The thing is, only Treena can honestly understand how important this is to me, and it's odd not to have her here. "Okay, you really don't mind waiting?" I ask warily, but also still wanting the moment to myself. I forgot to ask last time; I was too wrapped up in the spontaneity.

"Nah, I've got homework to do," he says, gesturing to his backpack and pulling out a laptop.

"Thanks." I smile and turn. I walk in and smell cleaning bleach coming off the walls. There's a staircase in front of us, and the main office to the left. I walk that way, breathing in deep.

A high barrier is in front, painted the same off-blue as the walls. A woman with a mess of hair piled extremely high is sitting behind it, busily typing.

I walk up to her, hold my breath, and try.

"Hi, I was wondering if you could help me with something."

"You late?" she asks.

"Hmm?" I ask.

"Honey, are you coming in late? Bell rang an hour ago."

"Oh, no, I don't go here," I say quickly, remembering that I'm in a high school and am, still, technically, a high school student.

"Then why are you here?" she asks, finally moving her eyes from her computer to mine. This is not going to go well.

"Um," I say nervously, then continue. "I was wondering if you could give me some information. I'm trying to find out more about my mother, who died when I was born. I think she went to school here." I stop, and wait for some sort of reaction. A second goes by. Another second. I get nothing. No sympathy, not even a questioning glance.

I continue, extremely worried. "So . . . I was wondering if you could tell me if she went here? And if she did, maybe what her schedule was, so I can talk to one of her teachers? I know it sounds crazy, but I just want to learn more about her." I'm struggling, trying, and she's not giving me an inch.

"Honey, I can't just give you someone's schedule."

"She doesn't go here now. It would be from 1997," I clarify.

"Uh-huh. I can't give a random girl—who doesn't go here—personal information about one of our previous students."

"But . . . she's . . . she's gone," I admit. "She passed away."

"Uh-huh. And how do I know that? Do you have a death certificate?"

"Excuse me?" My mouth drops open in shock. I feel my face flushing, my heart thumping. A wave of emotion crosses over me as my ears start ringing. "No, because I never met her. Which is why I want to learn about her. Please . . ."

"I'm sorry you never met her, but this isn't my problem. I can't just give you information like that." She sighs. "Good luck."

I stare at her and feel my entire investigation floating away. I feel my mother walking away from me again, turning around and never coming back. A voice that's not mine says, "Thanks anyway," and then I make it back to the main area. The lights are bright, brighter than I remember. Blinding, almost.

I can't speak; I just stare at the bleach-white floor tiles, because I don't know what to do next. I can try another

132

school, but what if this was the one? And I wasn't given a chance? A student passes me. He's tall and looks like he's mostly asleep, and he's wearing a lanyard around his neck.

A lanyard that has his student ID on it.

And then I get an idea. I look back at the woman I was talking to and see that she's now engaged in another conversation. I rifle through my bag and pull out my independent study pass from school, which thankfully I didn't take out before coming here. It's not the same as the lanyard the guy was wearing, but it's similar enough. I silently thank Ms. Webber for letting me take an extra hour of lab time, for which I was given this pass.

I put the lanyard over my neck and quickly walk farther into the school just as the bell rings. Surrounded by students now, I keep my head down, as I usually do, and know no one will think anything is out of place. I'm just a student, after all.

Until I realize I have no idea where I'm going, or what I'm looking for. With the office not giving me any information, where can I go? Where would I find a record of old students?

Ahead I see a sign with an arrow pointing to the media center. I think of mine at my school, a place I haven't really been much, but I remember that it has old yearbooks. Since I'm on the yearbook staff, I had to grab one from a few years back. You never know. . . .

I open the door and it's small inside, with about six rows of books and a small computer lab; I'm assuming it's the one

Bennett mentioned helping set up. I wonder how he's doing outside. My heart swells, feeling guilty for leaving him out there, feeling hope that he's here with me, and feeling fear as I see a woman sitting behind the counter. She's probably in her late twenties, with cat-eye glasses perched atop her nose.

"Hi!" she says cheerily. "Need any help?"

"Um," I hear my voice say. "I'm doing a project, and was wondering . . . do you have any old yearbooks here?"

"Oh, they're over in the back, on the right, against the teal wall," she says.

"Okay, thanks." I nod and smile, turning toward the back and feeling relief. I still don't know if I'm at the right place, but I feel like I'm moving toward something. Just like riding a bike, I'm putting one foot ahead of the next and pushing forward.

There are those READ posters on the wall that every media center and library seem to have—these of The Muppets and some actors I don't recognize. They look older, with fading colors and outdated outfits. The posters might not have been changed since my mother went here, and the thought makes me smile.

I hit the wall and see a tall column of yearbooks dating back to 1973. I scan the titles until I find the one I'm looking for. And before I know it, my hand is touching 1997. When she would have been a senior.

I walk to a nearby table and sit, opening the book.

I know this could lead to nothing. I know I could just be fooling myself into believing that there will be answers in this book, but each page brings excitement. Until I turn the page and see it. A photo of my mother.

She's there. She's *real*.

I gasp and I swear my heart stops.

She looks similar to the one photo I have, but still different. Her hair is long, it goes out of the picture, and is dark brown like mine. She has the same bumpy, crooked nose like me, and piercing green eyes—which I don't have. She has a lazy smile on her face, like she's amused by these photos, and a tight seashell necklace around her neck.

"Wow," I whisper, afraid to disturb the photo, as if I'd wake it up. Afraid that if I move, the picture might disappear. Because here she is. I didn't find *her*, but I found another part of her, another view of her. I touch the page to make sure it's real, and continue staring at it for a few minutes.

She's pretty and young. My age, and that's crazy. She had a whole life, a whole eighteen years of life, that I don't know about. What's she hiding behind her eyes?

My fingers itch and I take out my camera. I want to steal the book, more than get a picture, but I know I can't do that. She left her mark here; I don't want to remove that.

I steady the camera in my shaking hands and focus on her smile, her eyes. The click sounds loud in the quiet library, so I quickly put the camera back in my bag. I don't want to turn the page, to lose the moment, but I know more clues might be hiding in the yearbook.

I breathe in, pushing myself forward, knowing that once

I turn the page, her image will be gone. But there might be more, so I pass the rest of the students and move on to the clubs. Cheerleaders and football players. Band, chorus, drama. It's interesting how the same clubs were around then. Do things really change? Or is high school just the same venue only with different outfits over the years? Comedy club, Key Club. Wait.

It's my mother, standing between three other girls and a guy. Their arms are around one another, and they're smiling at the camera. The five of them made up the Key Club—a volunteer club, apparently, from the description.

It's a full-body picture—she's standing up, and it's the first time I've seen her like that. Long hair with a headband holding it back, loose T-shirt, and long brown skirt hanging to the floor. It looks like she wanted to go to Woodstock or something, but it was the '90s, so maybe the style came back. She's looking away, not at the camera, as if something out of sight is more interesting.

She's wearing the same seashell necklace as in the yearbook photo, and the other girls are wearing similar ones, too. Maybe they were her friends. I grab my camera and take another picture. And then a picture of the caption, so I know the names.

I can't help but look at the guy whose arm is around her waist and wonder who he is, how she knew him. If she knew him well. If he, Chad Glickman, is . . .

It's only natural to wonder.

I wonder what she's thinking, what she was doing before

this photo was taken, or where they went afterward. Did she regularly hang out with these people? Did she have a lot of friends, or was she a loner? I wish I could ask her all of these questions myself, but the reminder that I can't trumps the excitement of my findings.

I look again at the caption, and decide to look the people up. Maybe they know something. Maybe the Key Club teacher, Mr. Wayne, knows something. Maybe he's still here.

I put the book away and grab the three years prior, hoping to see her through the years. And there she is. A junior. Then a sophomore. Then a freshman. Each year she looks a bit younger, a bit more innocent, and a bit less sure of who she is. No shell necklace yet. No hippie skirt. No clubs, either. I take a picture of each face and watch as she morphs more and more into . . . me. I gaze, taking it all in. It's weird, seeing myself reflected on these pages, but also right.

I put the books away and walk over to the librarian's desk. She looks up expectantly. "Find everything you need?"

"Um, yes," I say, then think quickly. "Actually, I have to take a picture of Mr. Wayne's classroom for . . . yearbook. Do you know where it is?" I ask, crossing my fingers that he still works here.

"Sure thing." She smiles. "He's down the hall, room 204 on the right. By the gym."

"Great," I say, all the air leaving my body in relief. "Thank you." I head out the door into a sea of students in the hall, and I figure it's a break between classes. I blend in, sticking to the crowd, and see the gym up ahead, so I look to the right for his room: 210, 208, 206 . . . 204. "Here," I whisper, stopping. I feel like I did just yesterday, standing outside of Professor Stark's office. Heart pounding. Breath deepening. I knock.

"Come in," a voice on the other side says.

I open the door and a man not much older than Professor Stark stands before a whiteboard, erasing something about the Civil War. He has a light beard, round glasses, and dark hair, and is wearing a button-down shirt with a sweater over it. It's like he Googled "What do teachers wear?" and chose the most stereotypical image.

"Hi," I say meekly, and he looks over at me.

"You don't look like one of my students. Can I help you with something?" he asks casually.

"Um, I have an odd question for you," I say, shifting my weight from foot to foot. "Were you, or are you, the Key Club sponsor?"

Mr. Wayne puts down the eraser and walks over to his desk. He sits on the edge and crosses his arms. "I was, a long time ago. We haven't had Key Club in . . . I don't know, ten years or so," he says, looking like he's mentally calculating the answer. "Did you want to start it up again?"

"Oh, no, I don't go here," I say, then realize what I admitted. His eyes grow large and he starts to stand up, so I continue quickly. "But I have a pass," I lie. "I just . . ." Okay, breathe. "My mother was in your Key Club, and I've been trying to get information on her. So I was hoping you might remember her."

"Who was your mother?" he asks, still looking skeptically at me.

"Claire Fullman. She would have been in it around 1997."

"Claire...Fullman..." he muses, scratching his beard. "I think I remember the name. Hold on." He gets off his desk, then rummages in one of the drawers. He pulls out a folder, and flips through a few pages. My heart is in my throat, hoping he'll pull out something, anything, that could help.

"This her?" he asks, showing me the same photo from the yearbook.

"Oh my gosh, yes! That's her!" I say excitedly, pointing to her. "Do you remember her?"

"Sort of," he says, sitting back on the edge of his desk. "I've had a lot of students over the years. I try to remember them all, but this was, what, seventeen years ago?"

"Yeah," I say, nodding, and still hoping.

He looks down at the photo, then back at me. "If you don't mind me asking, why are you looking for information on her?"

"She was, is, my mother." And I tell him my story, honestly and openly. He seems like someone who wouldn't mind hearing it.

"I'm sorry to hear what happened," he says, shaking his head. "So how'd you find me?"

"Yearbook," I answer. "I saw she was in the Key Club, saw your name, and then took a guess."

"I see," he says, looking back down at the photo, then up

at me. "She went by Clarabelle, I'm pretty sure."

"Clarabelle?" I ask.

"Yeah. I think it started because someone called her it as a nickname—reference to a cartoon cow way before your time. I don't remember, really, but that's what she went by. I guess what I remember most about her is that she knew who she was. Or, who Clarabelle was. She was confident."

I make a mental note to look up Clarabelle when I can, and think about exactly what he said. How she was confident. How she was Clarabelle.

"She was kind of hippie-ish, if you will. We studied the decade and she was all over it. I think I was her tenth-grade history teacher. I don't recall what year. But whenever it was, she really took to the decade for some reason, and went with it."

"I can tell by the outfits," I say.

"Right," he says. "She wanted to have class outside a lot and wore flowers in her hair. Girls copied her, which was great for Key Club. She got more people to join that way."

I take in everything he says greedily, overindulging on every sentence. I can't help but smile at the vision I'm having of this free-spirited person. She was real, with real thoughts and emotions and passions. She had friends.

"She did get into a lot of trouble, though," he laughs, and I jerk my head up. "She was a little *too* liberal, if you will. She skipped class a lot, and wasn't the best of influences on her friends. I remember some sort of trouble—"

"How do you know?" I ask defensively.

"I remember she was suspended a few times, which was the downfall of the club that year—it was hard to run a club without a leader."

"She was the leader?" I ask.

"The president, yeah."

"So . . ." I start, but don't know what to say. I didn't expect my mother to be perfect, but I guess I didn't think she'd get in trouble a lot.

"I am sorry to hear she's no longer around, though," Mr. Wayne says, lines forming on his forehead. "I never like hearing that one of my students is gone. It's never easy. Never."

"Do you think . . . her friends would remember her?"

"I would imagine so, yes," Mr. Wayne says, and I silently agree. This is just a teacher's side of the story—I'm sure there's more.

"Thank you so much," I say, and he nods.

"I'm sorry I couldn't be any more help, but hopefully that was a start. Good luck finding out more. Your mother, she deserves to be remembered."

"Yeah," I say. "I think so, too."

THIRTEEN

When I get out of the school, the sun beats down and I have to cover my eyes. It's like walking out from a movie theater; I've been in the dark for so long.

Bennett's sitting on a ledge and he jumps down when he sees me.

"How'd it go?"

"Okay," I say. I want to keep thinking about everything, going over it in my mind to process it all.

As if he understands, he asks, "Where to now?" Instead of answering, I unlock my bike and fill him in on some of what I found out, showing him the pictures. Some I want to keep to myself until I understand it all more.

"I'd like to look up those people I found," I say, and then feel my stomach rumble. "And I'm kind of hungry. . . ."

"Well, it's a good thing you promised to indulge in my obsession with food. We're going to this cool sandwich place a few blocks away, back toward campus. Care for sandwiches?"

"I do enjoy a good sandwich," I say, and then get on my bike. Before leaving, I turn around and take a picture of the school. There's my photo for the day. That's part of this story.

I follow Bennett down the street, past the quaint houses of my mother's past, and onto the main road. Ten minutes later, we find an empty booth in the back of Mimi's Sandwich Shop, a '50s-themed diner. We slide into a booth with red pleather seats, a white chrome-edged table, and a mini jukebox. I order a chocolate malt and the Turkey Twist, and Bennett orders the Cha-cha Chicken. I have no idea why the sandwiches are dance themed, and I'm not even sure if the dances are *from* the '50s, but it's cute.

Bennett pulls out his laptop while we wait for our food. "Let's look up the people from the photo," he says, loading Google. "Did you try looking up any relatives yet?"

"Yeah." I nod. "A few years ago. I just searched the last name a few times. There are a lot of Fullmans." I pause, then admit, "And they're not really nice. I actually tried calling them when I was younger."

"All of them?" he asks.

"All of them," I admit. "I was . . . really curious."

"I could imagine. I ask my mom about that a lot—if

people ever contact her about info on their parents."

"Do they?"

"Sometimes, yeah. She can't provide the information—sometimes it's a closed adoption, so the records are sealed. And sometimes it's open and she's able to give them names."

"We tried that, but after my birth mother died, no one from the family would talk to us. The adoption agency couldn't force them to, so that was that. I still don't know why . . . I guess my mother was more okay with keeping up contact with me, but my grandparents weren't. So, I don't know."

"Gotcha," he says uncomfortably. A waitress in a high ponytail and a poodle skirt delivers our food and we fill the awkwardness with eating and passing ketchup. The food is good, but I'm more interested in researching.

"Lisa Winger," I say, pointing to the name under the photo. A lot of search results pop up, all for ones from different areas, and mostly from those sketchy websites that ask for you to pay to get people's personal information. "Facebook? I know my parents are on it, so she could be," I suggest, and he nods. I pull the computer toward me and log in to my account. There are a few results again, so he narrows it down to just Floridians.

"Maybe that's her?" he asks, pointing to a woman who looks to be in her thirties and lives in Tallahassee.

"Check her high school," I say, to make sure.

"Yep, same one. Man, she should make her info private,"

he says, scratching his head.

"Or not. For us, it's good that she didn't," I say excitedly, pulling the laptop back toward me. "I guess I'll send her a message?" He nods and I breathe in, not nearly as nervous as I was earlier.

I read aloud as I type so Bennett is included.

Lisa, hi, my name is Maude and you don't know me, but you might have known my mother, Claire Fullman. She died when I was born, and I'm trying to get any information on her, since I've never met her. If you have a chance, I'd love to hear from you. Sorry if this is out of the blue. Thanks, Maude.

I turn to Bennett. "Good?"

"Great, send," he says. I click Send, and look up the next name.

"Jessica Cally." There's no Jessica Cally on Facebook, so we try Google. A few mentions of a person with either "Jessica" or "Cally" in their name, but not her. Nowhere. We try a Boolean search my mom taught me, but still nothing. "Huh."

"I didn't know it was possible to be invisible from the internet nowadays."

"Right?" I say. "How are *you* Google-able?"

"Ha," he says, messing up his hair, and then looking back at me. "In high school I made a computer-animated short that got some attention."

"Some?"

"It got me a place at summer camp."

"That's really cool," I answer.

"Yeah, it's kind of dorky. What about you?"

"Photography exhibit at a local gallery."

"Now *that's* cool. How many high school students get into a gallery?"

"More than you think," I say with a shrug. "But it was cool, seeing my photos hung up." More than cool. It was amazing. It was, I hoped, a vision of my future.

"Did you have a theme?"

"Childhood," I say, and the reality that my birth mother wasn't around to see it feels off all of a sudden. I shake it off. "Your film?"

"Superheroes." He smiles.

"What about them?"

"It was stupid," he says, trying to downplay it.

"Details . . ."

"Okay, okay, it was about an ordinary dog who became Superdog."

"That's really cute."

"The characters had these alliterative names like Brave Beagle, Champion Chihuahua, and Wonder . . . Weiner Dog."

"Weiner dog?"

"I couldn't think of a W, give me a break."

I smile at him, at his enthusiasm. He looks at me and

crinkles his eyes, as if trying to figure me out. As if he's trying to read me. I look down, not used to being looked at like that.

"Who's next?"

"Okay, um," I say, shaking off a feeling of . . . something. "Bee Trenton." When he goes to type her name in, his hand brushes mine, and I pull back quickly from him. It's not a bad touch; in fact I'd like my hand to stay there longer. And as my cheeks blush, I realize that wanting to stay there is the exact reason why I should move my hand away. I can't get distracted.

"On Facebook as well," he says, pointing to her. "I mean, I think that's her—she has that name listed, along with another last name—Shrayer. Guess she's married? She looks just like she did in the picture, right?"

"Yeah," I say, looking at an older version of the same girl we've just seen—long blond hair, big blue eyes, the tiniest nose. She just needs the shell necklace. I click the Message button and send the same note. "I guess we'll see what happens."

"Are you nervous?" he asks.

I shrug. "Not really," I admit, and realize it's true. I was terrified yesterday, but today it's become more normal, less surreal. "I mean, the worst that can happen is they won't get back to me. And the best . . ."

"Yeah . . ." he says. "How do you feel now? After learning all that stuff?"

I think about it for a second. "Honestly, I don't know," I say, shaking my head. "I mean, any information is new information, so everything is . . . shocking, I guess." I twist my napkin on my lap and try to put my thoughts into words. It's weird knowing I'm so different from her, which makes me wonder how I would have turned out were I raised by her.

I start, and then realize I don't want to discuss my insecurities with him. "Anyway, we have one more person to look up."

He looks at me for a second, then looks back at his computer. "Okay, last person, the guy. What was his name again?"

"Chad Glickman." I type it in. "And there he is," I say, as he's the only one to pop up. He's still in Tallahassee, too, and looks like he rarely updates his page. He's posed in front of a tractor, wearing a camouflage outfit. He's the exact opposite of the bleached-tips, all-American-looking guy from the photo. "Guess we'll try," I say, and send the same message again. Then I close the laptop without taking another look at his picture. I don't want the question of *who* he is brought up again.

I'm taking a sip of my chocolate malted when my phone buzzes with a text.

Meet me @ FAB @ 3. Bennett knows where.

"Huh," I say, putting my phone away.

"What's up?" he asks, finishing his sandwich with a triumphant bite.

"Treena wants me to meet her at FAB at three. Do you know what that is?"

"Ohhh," he says with a knowing smile. "I do."

"And it is . . ."

"I guess you'll see."

"This isn't some other sort of initiation, is it? I don't know if I can take—"

"No, no, you'll like this. Promise."

"Okay . . ." I say, then ask, "Hey, Trey is an okay guy, right?"

"Yeah," Bennett says, leaning back and meeting my eyes. "I've known him since middle school. He's an okay guy. He's not, like, my best friend or anything, but he's never done anything mean to me."

"Except getting you arrested for breaking into a building."

"Right, except that."

"But should I be worried?" I ask. "For Treena? She really likes him."

"You . . ." He looks up at the ceiling, then back at me. ". . . should be wary. I'm breaking about seven thousand guy codes in saying this, but as I said, we're not best friends. I don't think he's done anything to hurt her, but he gets a lot of, um, female attention. And he can be kind of douchey sometimes, like he was last night, but that's only when his soccer friends are around. Normally he's pretty cool."

"I see," I say, biting my nail. She's worried she's not good enough for him, when really it's the other way around completely. No wonder she's so paranoid about him leaving—he could, easily, with so much attention. The protective part of me snaps into action, and I start to distrust him even more. "If he has so many 'girls,'" I say, using air quotes, "why is he spending so much time with Treena? Not that I don't want him to, but, like, why not, I don't know, play the field or something. Isn't that what you guys do?"

"Us guys?" he asks, raising an eyebrow at me.

"Well, not *all* of you," I correct myself.

"Just the majority of us."

"Exactly," I say, smiling. "How many girlfriends do *you* have?"

"At least sixteen." He stretches his arms out and flexes. "There's a lot of Bennett to go around."

"You're ridiculous." I laugh and take a bite of my sandwich. "But, really, why's he with Treena?"

"Um. Have you seen your friend? She's kind of hot," he says, scratching the back of his neck, and jealousy hits me lightning fast. I always knew Tree was beautiful, but it's new to hear all the guys think she's hot. I mean, awesome and all, but still surprising.

"Ah," I say. "She is, isn't she."

"Very."

"Did you like her, too?" I can't help but ask.

"Nah," he says, turning a bit pink. "I mean, I never thought of her like that. I had a girlfriend when I came to college, and, um, we recently broke up, so yeah," he says, looking away.

"I'm sorry," I say.

"Distance is hard," he says with a shrug. "At least it was for her. Anyway, I'll keep an eye on Trey if you'd like."

"I would, thanks." I nod, wondering more about this ex-girlfriend, but not wanting to push. I'll find out later, maybe. "And what about you? You're cool, right?"

"I am the coolest," he says with a smile, stretching his arms to the sky.

"Eh, you're all right," I say.

"All right?" he answers, and pokes me in the side until I laugh. "I'm so much better than all right."

"You're better than all right!" I gasp, and he stops. I look up at him and he's grinning this wicked smile at me, so I nudge him back. I turn away, feeling flushed, and see an older woman smiling at us. Embarrassed, I clear my throat and sit up taller. "We should get going, right?"

"Yeah, right," he says, and I can almost detect a bit of sadness in his voice.

◇◇◇◇

We bike around campus a bit to kill time—Bennett shows me all of his favorite sights, including the ice-cream shop that I'll have to try later—until it's time to meet up with Treena.

"Hey!" she says a bit awkwardly when Bennett and I bike

up. She's sitting on a bench outside this round building, legs crossed, with a book on her lap.

"Hey," I say, getting off the bike. All of the information swirls in my mind—about her, about Trey. I don't want to say anything, not yet, so I'll keep it inside. Plus, I'm still a bit pissed about last night's events. "What's up?"

"Surprise. Lock up the bike," she responds. I glance back at Bennett and he shrugs.

"I'll leave you guys to your . . . surprise," Bennett says, spinning his pedals around while he stays in place.

"Okay, see you back at the dorm," Treena says, waving good-bye. I haven't broken eye contact with him yet, and feel conflicted about him leaving. Which is insane because I still barely know him. It's just—we've done a lot today.

"Hey, thanks for everything" is all I can say, though.

"No problem," he answers with half a smile, then looks down, turns his bike around, and pedals away.

"You okay?" Treena asks from my side. I jump, seeing her so close when, before, she was a few feet away.

"Yeah, fine," I say, then roll Treena's bike over to the rack.

"I wanted to . . . um . . . hey, I'm sorry about last night."

"It's okay." I shrug, locking the wheels up and playing it cool.

"No, it's not. We shouldn't have gone. It was stupid, and Trey was being such a jerk . . . I swear he's normally not like that."

"Uh-huh," I say, not really convinced, especially after talking to Bennett.

"No, I swear. I've never seen him act that way, like, so cruel. I talked to him about it this morning, and he's sorry."

"Well, maybe he'll tell me that later," I say, and it comes out mean, and I honestly don't care. I know it's Trey I'm angry at, and not Treena entirely—stuff like this happens; people can be jerks. But, I don't know. The fact that she's not upset with him bothers me.

"Maude . . . I don't want you to be mad at me . . . I don't like this . . ." she starts.

"I'm not mad at you," I say. "I can never be mad at you, Tree. I'm just, I don't know, worried."

"Don't be. I'm fine. And it was just a practical joke. I mean, stuff like that happens all the time here—we get bored and stuff. If he does something *really* bad, you know I won't stand for it."

I nod, somewhat convinced. She's small and shy, but she's also strong. She stood up when we championed for the school to get vegetarian lunch options. Not the same thing, but she raised her voice. She can raise her voice again. "I know," I say, seeing cracks of the old Treena slip out in her pleading eyes, her twisting hands.

"Okay . . . well, anyway, I want to make it up to you. Come on," she says, nodding toward the building.

"What's there?"

"Come see," she says, with a lift of her eyes, and I push

forward, trusting her once again. It's only then that I see the giant garnet sign that says FINE ARTS BUILDING. Oh, FAB.

"Tree—" I start.

She just gives me a taunting smile and walks past the sign, around the front of the building.

Inside it's garnet as well, with a few doors leading in different directions.

"In an effort to convince you that FSU isn't all that bad, I thought we'd come here . . . so you can see the art and photography department."

Immediately I grin because, yes, *this* is exactly what I wanted. Time with my friend. Time to see the school. Together. I grab her arm excitedly.

"A girl on my hall is majoring in photography. She said we can look around if we'd like. There are no classes right now, so you can hang out," she says with a smile. "Plus there's a real darkroom, too."

I gasp. Though I have a DSLR, I've always been fascinated with actual manual photography. My school got rid of its darkroom years ago, but a summer camp I went to had one, and it's where I learned the process of mixing chemicals and watching a photo appear. It's magical in a way. The process of developing.

"This is amazing," I say in awe. "I'm so excited." I shake my head. "Thank you."

"Anything for you," she says, bumping me with her hip. "So, okay, I've been here only once, but over there's the theater," she says, pointing to double doors near a ticket booth, "and that way is toward classes," gesturing toward another door straight ahead, "and art is that way." We head through a door on our left, down a blank, windowless hallway, and then she opens another door and we step into the blackness of a darkroom. It's similar to the one I learned in, only larger, with much newer equipment. I walk along the room, waiting for my eyes to adjust, and taking in the bottles of chemicals, the photos hanging up to dry, the beds waiting to be filled, undeveloped paper, the piles of film. "This is amazing."

"I thought you'd like to walk around and then see the editing labs and gallery," she says, rocking back and forth on her feet. She never did photography in high school, but she got how important it was to me.

I go over everything, and envelop myself in the sights, the sounds, and the smell of the chemicals. Metallic, like how nickels taste. I look up and see the photos being developed under the red light, see pieces of Tallahassee coming to life. And this would be a perfect photo for today, but I can't do that. I can't disturb a darkroom. Instead, I run my fingers along the tables and continue to take in the developing pictures.

"Cool, right?" Treena whispers.

"So cool. I want to do this again," I say, pointing to everything.

"You can." She grins, and I believe her; I really do. "I

think the editing room is next door," she says, and I follow her out. She shows me the computer lab with computers much newer than the ones I'm used to. There are a few students working who don't look up, and I wonder if I can be one of them. If I can do this every day next year. The thought fills me with hope.

"I'd say you can use the computers, but I don't have access . . ." she whispers.

"It's okay." I shake my head. "No worries."

"But there is an exhibit going on." She gestures toward another door in this maze of a building, and I follow her through.

There's a giant sign that says FALL SHOWCASE, and I excitedly walk around, losing myself to the art. Each piece is done by a different artist, and you can tell by how the photos are taken. Some macro, some landscapes. Some portraits, some extremely abstract. There's no theme. There's no rhyme or reason, but somehow all of the photos connect. As if the exhibit is showing small pieces of a whole. I slowly go from piece to piece, in awe of the talent surrounding me.

There's one picture of a girl sitting alone by the fountain, her hair blocking her face, and though I can't see her expression, she seems lonely. Like she wishes someone was there with her. She wishes for things to change. I think of Treena, and what she said about not having many friends when she came up here, not fitting in. And I get that feeling of wanting *someone*. It's how I was at home after she left. It's how I found Celine, and though she's nice and great, she's not Treena. She never can be.

I go back to my friend and give her a hug, silently thanking her for taking me here. She sighs and links arms with mine as I surround myself with the silence of the room, the beauty of the work, the hope for the future, and the pressure of today, and just . . . lose myself.

FOURTEEN

After visiting the FAB, we walk through campus, back toward Treena's dorm room.

"Oh! Let me show you some cool spots," she says as we make our way down the sidewalk. The campus is so green, with trees everywhere shadowing the redbrick buildings. It feels like college, like this is what it's supposed to look like. We pass a half-circle-shaped building with a statue outside.

"There are a lot of statues, aren't there?" I ask.

"Tons. That's, um," she says, looking at the plaque, "Claude, it seems. The building's named after him."

"He looks very stone-faced," I say, and she laughs. "Buddy Shot?" She nods and we run over and pose behind him, our faces on either side of his. I reach my camera out and we take a picture with Claude the Statue.

"Buddy Shots are better than selfies," Treena says factually.

"Definitely. I think we need more of them," I say, and she agrees. We get back onto the sidewalk and I ask, "So which buildings are yours?"

"I'm all around right now, since I'm still doing general classes, but mostly down on the opposite end. That's where the science classes are." She points to her left. "Over there, where you went yesterday, that's where the English classes are. That's where I think I'm heading."

"That building seemed really nice," I say. "Comforting, I guess."

"Yeah, I like it." We take a left and head off the main strip. More statues are around us, but not of people. As if reading my mind, she says, "Art installations," and points to a metal one that looks kind of like a giant asterisk. "That one's supposed to be a sumo wrestler or something."

"*Ohhhh,*" I say. "I guess I see it. Hey, remember that abstract art show I made you go to with me?"

"You were *so* excited about it! And, oh man, that was the worst. I mean, how is an empty bucket on the floor art?"

"Yeah, I didn't get it, either," I say. We get back to her building and it's nice out, so we sit outside like we did my first day here. I get out my camera and show her some of the photos I took throughout the day.

"That's really good," Treena says, looking at the picture of the fountain behind her building. I overexposed it a little, to make it darker, more haunting. I like it, too. Then I show her the yearbook pages I photographed. "Who's that?" she asks, and I tell her about the pictures I found of my mother.

"That's insane," Tree says, shaking her head. "God, you would have killed for this when you were first looking everything up a few years ago."

"I know, right? I mean, I still can't believe I saw it . . . I felt like I had to get a picture of the picture," I say, trying to explain myself, and she agrees, looking at the others I took of my mother, and then the one I took of Bennett. It's him riding away from the high school, fully content in his bike ride. His hair is blowing in the wind, and he's looking ahead, unaware of me.

Treena gives me a questioning glance, and I am suddenly embarrassed that I took it. "Uh-huh," she says, grinning. "So what do you want to do tonight?"

"I don't know," I say, thinking *not go to an abandoned hospital.* "Hang out? What do you usually do at night? I want to do that. I want to get the full Treena-in-college experience."

"Ah, but see, that would be boring. It's me reading *On the Road* in my pajamas."

"That sounds like the Treena I knew. How many times have you read that book?"

"Right?! I think that's why I like my beatnik class so much. We talk about it a lot, but also all these other amazing authors who just want to *live* and experience *everything.* You know?" I nod my head, because that's kind of how I feel right now, searching for my mother. I'm experiencing it all. "There's a part of me that wants to Sal Paradise it out of here—just go do something crazy."

"You never do anything crazy," I say.

"I know, and I think that's why . . ." she says, and I look at her, taking in her stretch for freedom.

"LADIES," a guy's voice says, interrupting us, and I look up to see Trey. My heart sinks because I was enjoying this moment with Treena, with seeing the old Treena.

"Hey," she squeals, jumping up to give him a kiss.

"Hey, baby," he says, throwing his arm around her. "Maude," he says down to me as I stand up. "Party at Jason's apartment tonight. You're coming, right?"

"Oh," she says, looking from him, to me, back at him, and then back to me. She wants to go, I know she does, but do I? I really don't want to spend another night with Trey; I really don't want to find myself in another position where I'm angry at Treena. But the look on her face, full of interest and hope, kind of sways me.

"Maude, what do you think?" she asks me.

"I, um," I say, knowing she wants to go, and knowing she'll be disappointed if we don't. "Sure, sounds great." I don't want to let her down. We don't have to stay long or anything. . . .

"YES," Trey says, giving me a high five. "I knew you were the cool friend. Be there by, like, ten. We'll get that thing started."

"Okay," Treena says sweetly, and kisses him before he turns to leave. Then she turns back to me. "Are you sure it's okay?"

"Sure," I say. Our friendship means more to me than our plans. Plus, it might be fun. I should at least try. And maybe Bennett will be there. "Let's go," I finally say, watching the smile spread across her face.

◇◇◇◇

At ten, we're in Jason's apartment—me, Tree, Trey, Bennett, and about fifteen other people. It's a small two-bedroom apartment a block off campus and we're all crammed in the living room area. How we're all fitting is a mystery to me, especially considering there's a long table in the middle of the room taking up a ton of space.

"Ladies," Trey says, handing both Treena and me a drink. I think back to last night and how horrible it tasted, but then I think about what Treena said earlier about doing something crazy. I want to try. I want to experience this; maybe testing the waters now will make my leap to college all the easier. I take a sip, and though it still burns, it's not as bad. So I take a second sip, and then a third.

I lean against the back wall, and Bennett comes up next to me. "Hey," he whispers. "Your boyfriend is here." He nods toward the door and in walks Film Guy, wearing all black yet again. I snort with laughter, then turn my head toward Bennett.

"*Not* my boyfriend."

"What, you don't like *Scarface*? It's, like, the Best. Movie. Ever."

"Actually, I prefer *Toy Story*," I say, taking another sip and meeting his eyes. He smiles, then looks away.

"Hey, Curls!" a voice calls out, and Bennett waves. I look over and it's a cute girl with a short pink pixie cut. She flits over.

"Curls?" I ask him.

He points to his mop of hair and I nod in understanding. "I see."

"It's like a poodle up there," he says, then turns to Pixie Cut. "Hey, Liz."

"Hey! Didn't know you were coming tonight," she says in a higher voice, all cute and bubbles. A surge of jealousy hits me, but I remind myself that I'm here for only a few more days. He can talk to Pixie Cut. He can like Pixie Cut. He's not *mine* or anything; he's just a guy doing a nice thing who happens to be kind of cute.

"Yeah," he says, brushing his hair back. "Have you met Maude? She's in town for a little bit." I smile and say hi.

"Oh, hey!" She looks back and forth between the two of us. I move a step closer to him. "Where are you in town from?"

"Orlando," I say. "Just visiting until the weekend."

"Oh! I was just there for a show. Much better bands go there than Tallahassee." She says the city's name in a low, lame voice and I laugh. I take another sip and everything starts to feel brighter, louder.

"Maude, come here!" I look over, and see Treena waving at me, so I excuse myself and head over, feeling slightly heavy as I walk away.

"What's up?" I ask. She's sitting on the couch, snuggled next to Trey. He has his arm around her and they're both holding empty cups.

"I missed you," she says, pulling me down with her. I laugh, falling in place, and she puts her arms around my waist. Her vanilla scent is gone, replaced by the fruity scent of the drinks we're currently consuming.

"Someone's been drinking," I say, patting her hair.

"Trey's fault," she says. "He's too generous when he pours."

I glance over at him, and he shrugs happily. "Don't get my friend too drunk, okay?" I warn him.

"I don't promise anything," he says, wiggling his eyebrows, and I roll my eyes. "You want anything? Treena's best friend is a best friend of mine." The sentiment feels forced, especially after we haven't really been that *friendly*, but still, I shake my head no and thank him. He's trying, so I will, too.

"Be right back, babe," he says, kissing her head, then getting up. He goes over and talks to a few other guys who look strikingly like him. All sports shirts, khaki shorts, and flip-flops. As if it's a uniform.

"Having fun?" Treena asks.

"Yeah, you?"

"Of course! Buddy Shot?" she asks. I take out my phone, and we smile, cheek to cheek. I check out the picture, and it's cute. We look happy. As I flip through a few photos, she says, "I think we're going to play beer pong next. You have to play! I'm bad at it; you'll totally win."

"What's that?" I ask.

She points to the two desks in the middle of the room and I watch some people play as she explains. "Four people play, two on each side. You throw Ping-Pong balls into the cups. If one team gets it into the cup, the other team has to drink."

I hold up my cup, "I don't know if I can handle one drink," I laugh.

"Come on, you have to! It'll be super fun," she says. "Trey will be on my team, and you can get Bennett. Where is he, by the way?"

I look back and he's still against the wall talking to Pixie Cut. He's smiling and laughing and drinking and I feel my heart drop a little. I finish my drink, gulping it down, and throw the cup in the trash.

The door opens and three girls come in. I vaguely remember one of them from the haunted asylum last night. Treena sits up quickly and mumbles an "I'll be right back." But it's not because she's *happy* to see the girls, it seems.

Alone, I fiddle with my phone to look busy and not like a high school girl with no one to talk to. I flip through my photos again, and then realize that I should document this for my project. Maybe not put up photos of us drinking, but the apartment, the people, the feeling. I snap one of Treena leading Trey away, a worried look on her face. I turn back and take a picture of Bennett, all curly hair and lanky arms effortlessly leaning. I take a picture of the room, of the strangers milling about and becoming new versions of themselves with every sip. And I observe, because here I am at another college party. It feels like an important moment, but also . . . not.

I feel my phone buzz and see that it's Celine calling. I look over at Treena, who's talking to Trey, and Bennett, who's still in conversation, and get up and head outside so I can hear over the music.

"Hey!" I say, feeling this immense need to talk to her for some reason. I feel like she'd be proud of where I am, what I'm doing.

"There you are," she says eagerly. "I'm having a bet with Mitch right now."

"Mitch?" I ask.

"The guy from Starbucks? Yeah, he's here. Say hi, Mitch."

"Hi, Mitch," he says, and I roll my eyes.

"Anyway, of all people, I knew you'd remember this. What's the name of that guy in our class who *always* falls asleep and snores?"

"Jace?" I ask, wondering *why* she's calling me about this.

I walk away from the apartment door and lean against the railing. I'm on the second floor, so I look down at the parking lot, at Trey's car, which we all came in.

"JACE, YES! Oh my god, Mitch, the funniest thing happened . . ." she says, going back to talk to him.

"Celine? Celine?"

"YES! Sorry, I was—"

"You called me for a name?" I ask, disappointed that she didn't want to talk, didn't care to find out how my trip was going.

"I knew you'd know it," she says, and I sigh. But then realize I have the perfect thing to say that'll get her interested.

"Okay, well, I gotta run. I'm at a party. . . ."

"Wait, what?" she nearly yells, and I smile because, yes, this is me at a party. "You don't go to parties."

"I do now, I guess. I'm here with Treena and she has a boyfriend. . . ."

"What! See, I told you. Things are totally different in college."

"They are, kind of," I say, turning around, and though I can't see into the party since the blinds are shut, I can guess what's going on.

"Is it amazing? Are you having a blast? What's her dorm like? What's this party like?"

"Dorm is cool, I actually went to a party my first night here, too. And last night we broke into an abandoned hospital. . . ."

"WHAT!" she yells again. "No, sorry, Mitch, I'll be right back, I need to get more details about this." The phone rustles again and I smile. "You broke into a place? This is not the Maude I know."

When she says that, I think about Treena and how I thought that exact same thing. It's funny how a few days can change someone. Though I don't think I'm different, not really at least. "I'm having fun," I say simply, because I am.

"I can't wait to go. Maybe I should have come on this trip with you." She laughs.

I lean my back on the railing when the door opens. It's Bennett, looking in both directions. When he sees me, he smiles. "Maybe," I say. "But hey, I have to go. Talk later."

"Definitely," she says, then hangs up. I shake my head because there she is, back in Orlando, flirting with Starbucks Guy. She's doing the same thing she was doing last week. And here *I* am, at a college party, one drink in, and about to talk to a guy. How did I get so far? She was right—a few days *can* change so much. And at the moment, I really don't mind it.

I put my phone in my pocket and feel Treena's bike key. It makes me think of riding and moving and feeling alive. It makes me think of learning about my mother today. Mr. Wayne said my mother was sure of herself, was confident and moved to her own beat. Maybe I can be, too.

So I look at Bennett and say, "Hey."

"I'm going to assume that whenever I can't find you,

you're hiding out in or nearby a stairwell," he says, pointing to the stairs and shifting his weight from the front to the back of his feet repeatedly.

"Phone call from home," I say, still leaning back.

"Boyfriend?" he asks.

"Girlfriend," I say, and his eyebrows shoot up. I laugh, then add, "But not like that. She's a girl. Who's my friend."

"Oh, okay," he says, leaning on the railing next to me. "I mean, it would have been cool if you had a girlfriend and all...."

"But I don't. Or a boyfriend, for that matter," I add, turning my body so I'm looking at him. "Did I miss anything in there?"

"Nah, Trey wants to play beer pong, so I was tasked to come find you," he says, and I feel a bit disappointed, knowing that he had to come, not that he wanted to.

"I see," I say, leaning back on the railing, away from him.

"I mean, I was tasked to find a partner, and obviously it was going to be you."

"Really?" I ask, turning my head. Our arms are close, nearly touching against the cold bar. One move and they'd be together. In fact, all I want to do right now is close any gap between us. I know it's probably the excitement of the day, and the drinking, but I feel myself being pushed toward him.

"Of course," he says, shoving himself off the railing and facing me. He's close, and I look up to meet his eyes. He stays

169

there, staring at me softly, then looks down, breaking contact. The air leaves my chest and my face feels like it flushes. "Come on," he says with a grin, then grabs my hand and leads me back to the party. "We can be the Wonder Twins and totally take them."

When we get inside, it's louder and more active.

"Hmmm," I muse. Bennett drops my hand and looks at me. I nod in the direction of Treena, who's lip-locked with Trey in another session I don't care to be privy to.

"Yeah," he says. "Treena and Trey are totally flirty drunks."

"There are different types of drunks?" I ask, feeling off—or, more so, feeling more on than ever. My senses are activated. The room is bright and dazzling, and Bennett is bright and dazzling, too. I want to feel what we had outside again, if only for a moment. I want to be that close to him again.

"Oh yeah," he says, bringing me over to the desks, where he sets up the cups to look like bowling pins. I help him, moving them around just so. "There are flirty drunks, who lose all inhibition and just want to, well . . ." he says, nodding his head toward Trey and Treena, who seem to have woven themselves together atop the couch. "Angry drunks, who start fights. Sad drunks, who cry about everything. Happy drunks, who cheer for everything. And sleepy drunks, who just fall asleep," he concludes, nodding toward Film Guy, who's conked out on the couch, on the opposite side of Trey and Treena. I laugh at the sight.

"So what are you?" I ask, meeting him in front of the table.

"I am a supremely awesome drunk," he says, leaning back.

"I don't recall that on your list. . . ."

"Right, it's a special category for just a select few of us."

"So what would that make me?" I ask, eyeing him.

"Hmm, let's see," he says, circling me and rubbing his chin with his hand. "You're not sleepy, definitely not angry. I don't see you crying, and you're not forcing yourself on top of anyone. . . ."

"So happy drunk?" I ask, wondering if I am, in fact, drunk.

"I think the verdict is still out," he says, stopping his circling in front of me. I feel a bit dizzy, but his steadiness is keeping me grounded.

"Out on what? Us beating your ass?" Trey's voice booms, ending our moment. I look over and he and Treena are on the other side of the table, ready to play.

"We'll just see about that," Bennett says, and I take my spot beside him.

Beer pong, it turns out, is not as easy as it looks. Especially when drinking. Trey shoots his first ball and gets it into one of our cups easily.

"I've got it," Bennett says, drinking the beer inside. They're not very full, thankfully, just a few sips. I don't know how much I can take. He turns the cup over, empty, then gives me a ball. "Ladies first."

I throw the ball and miss. Treena does, too, hitting the party's host on the head. He doesn't even notice.

Bennett misses his, but Trey gets his in again, and I drink this time. Beer is just as bad as the drink last night, but I take it down and put on a game face. I notice Bennett watching me as I take the ball and sink my shot in. We cheer and he gives me a hug. Trey lifts the cup and effortlessly finishes it in one gulp.

We keep playing until Treena leans on Trey and announces, "Sleepy," in a childlike voice. She gets whiny when she's tired; she always has.

"I'll take you home," Trey says with a grin, then literally picks her up like a baby.

"Wait," I say, rational despite how I feel. "How *are* we getting home? We can't drive."

"I can drive," Trey says, then wobbles with Treena in his arms.

"Not so much," Bennett says. "Night bus."

"Like Harry Potter?" I ask, confused.

"I wish. No, it's an off-campus bus system thing. You can call if you need a ride and are within, I don't know, so many miles of the campus."

"Oh wow," I say. "That's cool." Then I realize something. "So . . . the campus expects you to get drunk?"

Bennett laughs. "Guess so. I mean, college and all."

"Still sleepy," Treena announces.

"I think she's hit sleep drunk," I whisper to Bennett before walking over toward her. "It's okay, we're going home," I say, petting her hair. She's still in Trey's arms, and she looks cute, sweet.

Bennett looks at us and says, "Yeah, it's time. Okay, I'll make the call."

◇◇◇◇

The bus picks us up and drops us off near the dorm. Treena sleeps the entire ride, leaning on Trey's lap. When we stop, we all amble out into the night and into the dorm's elevator.

"Hey, I'm gonna take Treena home. You cool?" Trey asks me, and my heart jumps.

"Wait, what?" I ask. "Treena?"

She smiles, and leans on Trey. "We just want to snuggle. Nothing more," she says. "Okay, maybe a little more." And then she hiccups, and I remind myself that she's drunk. So she probably shouldn't be making this decision.

"Tree, I really don't think—"

"It's cool. I'm not an asshole or anything," Trey says.

"Yeah, I know, but she's drunk," I say.

He looks at me dead serious and says, "I'm not going to do anything. I promise."

I stare at him for a beat, and then nod.

"Benneeeeett," Treena whines. "Can Maude stay with you for the night? She's a great sleepover friend. She picks fun movies, and will jump in your bed with you if you're scared."

"Oh god," I say, my face turning red.

"This night has just gotten weird," Bennett says, and I refuse to look at him.

The elevator opens onto Treena's floor. "I love you, I'll call you in the morning, thank you," Treena says, all as one statement, and before I realize it, she's out of the elevator and the doors close, and I remember I'm with Bennett. Alone in the elevator. And I'm about to spend the night in his room. And I'm upset and worried that Treena just left me. This night *has* gotten weird.

"I've got you, don't worry," Bennett says. I look back at him and he's looking at his hands. He's not an angry drunk, or a sad or sleepy one. He's flirty, yes, and happy, definitely. But he's also shy. He wouldn't carry me out of the room in some big display like Trey. He wouldn't make out with me in public view. He'd ask my permission. He'd make sure things were okay.

"Okay," I say, and he looks up with shining eyes, and smiles. "Treena's okay, you think?"

"Yeah, Trey isn't *that* guy. She'll be fine."

I nod, and when we get to his room, he says, "You can take my bed, I'll take my nonexistent roommate's. I don't think he's changed his sheets since we've been here; I refuse to put you through that pain and suffering." He laughs awkwardly, standing in front of his bed.

"Are you sure it's okay?" I ask.

"Of course. Where else are you going to go? I'm not sending you to the common room. And I'm not making you go into *that* room," he says, nodding toward Treena's room, one floor down. I smile, then sit on his bed, still in my clothes. I feel tired, noticing that it's 3:00 a.m., but my mind is awake, alive. I look up and catch his eye and realize I want him here next to me. He's taken me in. He's helped me out with my trip. He's *interested*.

"Well, I don't want you catching some disease in those unclean sheets," I say, watching him.

"I think I'll survive," he says, not getting my hint. Maybe he still does have a girlfriend, or maybe he's just not interested. But I'm here, in his room, way past midnight. He looks at me and I know thoughts are running through his mind—I just wish he'd tell me what they were. He rubs his hands together, then says, "Right, so, good night?"

I sigh inwardly, then smile at him. It's not the right time, maybe. "Night, Bennett. And thank you. For everything."

"Of course," he responds, then retreats over to the other bed. I lie down, facing away from him, and wrap myself in the blankets. The scent of him is overpowering, and I have to inhale deeply to stop my heart from pounding out. One breath. Two breaths. Three. I hear every movement he makes, and I'm sure he can hear me. So with every nerve on edge, I close my eyes and try to sleep, but I know, despite exhaustion, it'll be a while until I pass out.

FIFTEEN

WEDNESDAY

It's morning. I know that when I open my eyes, but that's the only thing I know. I have no idea where I am. The sheets are soft, but not the same as the ones in my room, or the ones in Treena's. I lift my head and look around. There's a laptop, a lamp, a desk, some DVDs, including *Toy Story*.

Bennett. I'm in Bennett's room.

The night's events immediately fill my consciousness. The party. The talks. The cups. The drinks. Treena leaving with Trey. I'm in Bennett's bed. I open my eyes wider and freeze.

I'm in Bennett's bed.

I hear movement from the other side of the room and

remember that he's still here, only not in the same bed. I roll on my back slowly, quietly.

"Does your head hurt?"

I look over and he's sitting up, legs off the side of his bed. His hair is everywhere, a mess of curls. He's wearing the same thing as last night, and he looks so cute there, first thing in the morning, despite hanging his head on his hands.

"I'm not sure yet," I say, then sit up. There's a sting in the back of my head, and I squint my eyes shut. "Ouch."

"Yep," he says. "Sorry."

"For what?" I ask, leaning forward and copying his position. I roll my legs off the bed so we'd be looking at each other, were we looking up.

"We shouldn't have played the game. Drank too much. Didn't drink water or eat anything before bed. Hangovers suck."

"So this is a hangover?" I muse, looking up at him. Another rite of passage? An induction Trey would be proud of?

"Yeah. First one?"

"Yep. Yaaaaay. Ouch."

He looks up and smiles at me. "I'd like to point out that, despite you being hung over and in my room, I've still not gotten in your pants. Promise still kept."

"Thank you for being a decent guy?" I laugh, then wince.

"Okay, here's the deal," he says. "I'm going to run

downstairs and get us something to eat and drink. Make yourself at home."

"I can come with . . ." I start.

"Nah, no use both of us suffering." He grins.

"Thanks," I say, and he waves, then leaves.

Once he's gone, I flop back down on the bed and smile to myself. I'm conflicted because, no, I shouldn't be here. But I am. In his room. He invited me here, and though nothing *happened* between us, I felt something.

And I like something.

I grab my phone off the desk to tell Treena, but as I pull up her number, I remember last night again. How she chose Trey over me. I wasn't hurt about it then, but now I feel torn. Sure, she was drunk, but . . . I'm visiting her. And she just left me behind. She *never* did this—or would have even thought of doing it—in high school. And why'd she get so drunk anyway? For Trey? The thought that she does all of this for him festers in my mind until I shake it out.

But still, I want to talk to her. I want to make sure she's okay. So I shoot her a quick text.

Awake @ Bennett's. Wha! Call me xo.

If I don't hear back from her in twenty minutes, I'm going to the room.

I shake my head and focus on where I am. Once again I feel Bennett all around me. His smell of grass and sunshine from yesterday's ride. I smile at the thought. I sit up and flip through my phone, deciding to check Facebook. And, maybe, while there, take a brief glimpse at his profile because . . . why not?

There's a cute picture of him in a classroom, looking off to the side, off the screen at something else. There's a hint of a smile in his face. There are a few comments on his page, friends from home it looks like, who are arranging something for his Thanksgiving break. I click over to his About section. He likes *Adventure Time* and *The Catcher in the Rye* and *Star Wars*. He likes video games, and dinosaurs, and animation. He plays Dungeons and Dragons.

I bite my lip and click Photos, in full investigation mode now. He's tagged in a few from graduation, a few from here. One girl is in a few photos with him on the beach. Maybe that's the ex he mentioned?

I look at the time and realize I've spent the last five minutes poring over his profile. I shake my head, slightly embarrassed by what I did, and go back to my homepage. It's then that I see I have an unread message. I open the screen. It's from Bee Trenton-Shrayer. My heart leaps as I open the message and read.

Maude, I can't say digging up the past and discussing Claire is a pleasant task for me. We did not get along well, and though I should be over it by now—it has been 17 years, after all—some scars never heal.

179

What I can say is this—we were friends, we were not friends, and she did things in between that contributed to our falling-out. I am sorry to hear about her, however, and wish you luck in finding the information you seek. I'm sorry that I cannot help you. —Bee.

Whoa. I sit up straighter and read it again. And again. Each time it seems meaner, and a wave of emotions comes over me. What could have happened that made her feel this hostile toward my mother so many years later?

I think about what Mr. Wayne said about my mother, remember that she was a ringleader, a popular person who might have been a bad influence. Maybe this Bee was jealous. Or maybe not.

My heart is pounding in my chest as I drum my fingers on the bed. The door opens, and I jump up, practically attacking Bennett.

"Whoa," he says, balancing two coffees in his hands.

"Sorry! Sorry, I have news," I say, backing away.

"Really? What news?" he asks, handing me a cup. "Sorry, no food—the line was crazy long. Like, *Lord of the Rings* extended version long. So, coffee now. We'll go out for breakfast."

"Oh, okay," I say, looking down at the drink and smiling at the reference. He wants to go to breakfast with me.

"So what's up?" he asks. He sits on the bed behind the

desk and takes a sip of coffee.

"I got a response from Bee."

"What's it say?" he asks eagerly, leaning forward.

"Nothing good." Before I know it, I'm showing him my phone and letting him read the terrible message.

I watch him take in the words, and notice how his eyebrows immediately go up.

"Wow. She hates your mother."

"So it seems," I say, putting my phone down.

"Like, seventeen years later still hates her," he says, leaning back on his arms. "That's some grudge she has."

"I know. I want to know what happened. It's annoying that she won't tell me *anything*."

"Yeah. You'd think she'd have some sympathy."

"Apparently not. I want to respond, but she doesn't seem keen on hearing from me again."

"I think you should respond. The worst she could do is not answer. And the best is you can learn some more, even if it is all bad news." He adds, "You don't believe her, do you?"

"That my mother ruined friendships and made someone hate her for my entire lifespan?" I ask.

"Yeah. Do you think your mom . . . mom? Mother?"

"Mother. Birth mother," I explain. "My mom is the person who raised me. I like to differentiate between the two."

"Noted," he says. "Anyway, do you think your mother was the kind of person who left people with scars, like Bee insinuated?"

"No, not really. I mean, I don't know. I guess she could have been. . . ."

"But you're not like that," he points out.

"Thanks." I smile. "But I wasn't raised by her, remember?"

"True," he says. "And I'm sure that affects things."

"You think?" I ask. "You don't think certain traits run in the blood? Like, will a bully have a baby bully?" It's exactly what I've been wondering, especially since starting this quest. And I know Bennett won't have the answers, but his mom might have seen progress, his mom might have witnessed changes. And it feels good to kind of discuss this out loud. Am I who I am because of my mom? Would I be different if I was raised by my mother? It makes me wonder who I'm *supposed* to be, and if I went astray somewhere along the way.

"Well," he starts, "what if the baby bully is brought up in a loving, bully-free home?"

"Like me?" I ask.

"Like you." He nods. "I think we're getting into a nature versus nurture philosophical conversation."

"So you think it's nurture, then. That no matter what genes I have, I can change. Everything can affect who I am, including my mom and, I guess, my own decisions?"

"I guess," he answers, massaging the back of his neck. "I haven't thought much about it. But I'd like to think that we could change. Like prodigies—are they good at, like, piano because their parents are professional musicians and it's in their blood? Or are they good because they practiced a lot? Or, look at me. I love animation, but my parents aren't artistic at all. Not that I'm great, but you know."

It's true; I don't know what my mother liked, but my parents are bringing me up to like everything, to try everything and see what works out. Which is how I found photography. I wonder what my mother liked.

I look at him, and he leans forward, touching my arm. "I think it's up to you, to be who you want."

"Thanks," I say, because it's the most honest thing I've heard in a while. I look down, hiding my blush, and when I look up again, he's staring at me.

"So what should we do now?" I ask, going back to the task at hand. Realizing it's easier talking about that than my personality.

"Respond to her. And then, I don't know, wait?"

I nod and look back at the message. I shake my head, steady my shoulders, and right myself for the problem at hand.

Bee, thanks for your message, and I'm sorry for the pain it seems to have brought up. I never knew my mother, like I said, so I don't know what happened between the two of you. I would love to, though. Any information would be extremely helpful. But I understand if you'd rather not talk. Thanks, Maude.

I reread it a few times, and then look back at Bennett. He leans forward to read it, then nods his head. With a deep breath, I press Send. I sit back and impatiently wait for a response, refreshing the page repeatedly.

"She'll get back to you," he says reassuringly. "She can't be heartless."

"I'm not so sure. . . ." I say, raising my eyebrows.

"Hey, this may be obvious, but is your father's name on your birth certificate?"

"No." I shake my head. "I've asked my mom before, and she didn't know anything either."

"What do you think about that?" he asks gently, and I wonder . . . what *do* I think about that? I've always speculated on why he wasn't listed. Did he just split when he found out about me? Or did she honestly not know who my father was? Both options are bad in their own ways, but I still can't help but wonder what he would have thought about me.

I look over at Bennett and then think of another situation—what if I wasn't just an accident? What if I was a product of something worse? I shake my head, not wanting to think about that. Not wanting to feel my own skin.

"I don't know," I finally answer. "I guess she had her reasons. I mean, I want to know, but . . ."

"But maybe you don't?"

"Yeah, maybe I don't," I answer, somewhat uncomfortably. I look down and realize I'm still in yesterday's clothes. This is a good excuse to split before I start confessing and unearthing deep dark secrets that I haven't even had time to realize. Also, I haven't heard back from Tree and, despite everything, I worry. "Hey, I think I'm going to get ready for the day."

"Yeah, I should, too. I smell, don't I? Be honest."

"You don't smell," I say.

"I smell. You're just nice. Anyway. What are we doing today?"

My heart lifts at this question—he's inviting himself along again. I like that he wants to spend time with me, despite my oddly philosophical questions and, more than likely, morning breath.

"I don't know—I guess I'm just waiting to hear from everyone. Maybe I'll go to the school area again? I guess my mother lived over there, so maybe we could check the area out? See where she grew up?"

"Sounds good," he says. "I have classes from one to six, so I'm all yours this morning." He smiles, and I smile back. "So, yeah, get ready. Then, breakfast."

"Deal," I say, getting up. It's odd, being this comfortable around him, when I'm not like that with any guys at my school, guys I've known for years. What is it about Bennett? Maybe today, as we continue my quest, I'll find out.

SIXTEEN

Treena's door is unlocked, but she's gone. There's a note on her desk.

Early class. Chai and gossip later?
Love, T

I put it down and sigh. Short and to the point, with no mention of last night. Either she forgot what happened, or doesn't want to address it. Probably the latter. She's never been one for confrontation.

After showering and getting ready, I call my mom to check in, not going into many details yet about what I've been up to, then meet Bennett outside his room.

"How do you feel about bagels?" he asks, locking his door. The smell of soap rushes out, and his hair is still wet, hanging limply on his face. He's back in his uniform of cargo shorts, red T-shirt, and hoodie.

"I'm in full support of bagels," I say, ready to start my day.

"Great, I know a place," he says, raising his eyebrows. I smile and follow him down the hall.

◇◇◇◇

"You are oddly excited about this place," I say when we walk in. It's not much, really, just . . . a bagel shop. Not a fancy one, either. There's nothing on the walls; they're just painted an off-white that looks like it hasn't been repainted in years. Decades. There are a few small two-person tables, and a food counter, and that's it.

"It's really good!" he says excitedly. "It's been here for, like, a million years apparently. I don't know, I just like it," he ends with a shrug. I nod and follow him to the counter.

I still have Treena's bike key, so we rode bikes here, because why not? The weather was nice, and I kind of wanted to feel the movement under my feet again, especially now, when we're at a standstill on my search. I need to know that I'm going somewhere.

"I usually get the everything bagel, but it's a bit . . . garlicky, so I'll pass today," he says, turning around to me.

"Please, do not let me tear you away from the garlic," I answer, looking at the baskets of bagels. I will agree with him—they do look good.

"Nah," he says, then turns back to the counter. "I'll have one sesame seed bagel with cream cheese. And an orange juice."

"And you?" the guy behind the counter asks, not acting entirely polite. He has a thick black mustache that must have a story of its own.

"Um, cinnamon bagel with cream cheese, and just a cup of water," I answer.

"I've got it," Bennett says, taking his wallet out of his pocket.

"What? No, it's okay. I can pay."

"Maude, it's, like, a dollar. Plus, you're taking me on an awesome adventure, so I owe you," he says, handing over a few bills to the mustached guy.

"It's you who I owe. You're the one showing me around."

"Let's just say we're even," he says, putting his change into the tip jar and picking up our bagels.

We walk to an open table and sit down. There are a few other people here, but not many. I guess it's not packed at 10:00 a.m. on a weekday.

"It's usually more crowded on the weekends," Bennett says, as if reading my mind.

"I'd imagine," I say, and take a bite of the bagel. It's just the right mixture of crisp and bready, with the perfect amount of cream cheese. "This *is* good!"

"See? Told you. Best bagels." He smiles, taking a bite of

his. "Especially for hangovers. How're you feeling?"

"Better." I shrug. "It really wasn't that bad."

"You really weren't that drunk," he points out.

"Uh-huh," I say, not really able to agree or disagree. "How'd you find this place, anyway?"

"Know how I used to help out with the computers at the school? I was in this area, so I just dropped in. I like trying the local places."

"Has it really been here for a long time? I wonder if my mother ever came here."

"Who knows? It's been here for almost fifty years, though," he says, pointing to a small plaque that says it was opened on April 14, 1968.

"Very cool."

We eat our bagels and quietly laugh when someone asks for a venti coffee, as if Starbucks lingo is the norm.

"So what do you want to see on this side of town?" he asks, wiping his mouth with a napkin.

"I don't know. I guess we can bike around until we find something that might be cool?"

"Yeah. Okay. Later, we can go around campus again, too, if you'd like."

"Oh, that'd be awesome. My mom asked me if I've seen much of it yet, and I, um, haven't," I admit.

"You saw the FAB," he offers.

"I told her that!"

We finish up our bagels and are walking outside toward

the bike rack when my phone buzzes.

"A new message?" Bennett asks, getting on his bike and seeing my phone in my hand.

"Yes, from Bee. Oh god." I open it and Bennett jumps behind me to read along.

Maude, I really would rather not talk about Claire. It's been too long, and in this case, absence does not make the heart grow fonder. Just know that our problems, like many others, stemmed from a boy named Chad. They started and ended there.

"Oh," I say. I put my phone in my bag and sit back on the bike's seat.

"So, Chad—" Bennett starts. "The guy in the picture . . ."

"I'm guessing he dumped Bee for Claire? Or cheated on her with Claire," I say, and Bennett flinches. "Still, why hold a grudge so many years later?"

"Maybe there's more to it?"

"Well, it doesn't look like she's going to tell."

"Maybe we can track her down?" Bennett says. He's fiddling with the handlebars on his bike. His fingers are long, and they snap the gears back and forth distractedly.

"Maybe," I say.

"No, come on," he says. "Pull up her message again."

"Okay," I say, getting my phone out. "Here."

"Let's see how public her profile is," he says, taking my

phone. He clicks her profile and scans down. "Look, it says she works at the capitol, in the museum area."

"We can't just go and track her down at work," I say.

"Who says we can't? Like everything else with your quest, the worst that can happen is she won't talk to us. And the best . . ."

"Yeah, I know, but it's very clear that she hates my mother. How thrilled would she be at me turning up at her job? *At the capitol?*"

"Are you more worried about seeing Bee or the phallic monstrosity that is the capitol?" he asks, grinning.

"Shut up," I say, but still smile. I reason with myself that this is a terrible idea, that we'll probably have the cops called on us, but, really, they can't do anything that bad. We're not going to be arrested or thrown in jail. If anything, they'll just escort us out, and Bee will have another reason to hate my family. But maybe she won't freak out; maybe she'll talk to me. I do *want* to see her, now that I know the connection. "Okay." I nod. "Yeah, okay, let's go."

"Bennett Holmes and Maude Watson are on the case!" he says, hopping onto his bike.

"Hey, why do I have to be the sidekick?" I complain.

"Because it was my absolutely brilliant idea," he says, pushing off the ground triumphantly and heading toward the capitol.

The neighborhood is empty, so I move my bike next to his in the middle of the street. We're off the main roads and ride for about twenty minutes through the streets. Houses are stacked close to one another on both sides like dominoes. There are tires scattered about on front yards, and multiple cars in the driveways, each crappier-looking than the last. Some people are sitting outside, just resting and following us with suspicious eyes.

I wonder if my mother lived here, among the crowded front yards and discarded bicycles. I wonder if this is why she was so free-spirited, so rebellious—because she always dreamt of leaving it. Flying away from cars backfiring and the glares of the neighbors. From the broken fences and clusters of crows. It all feels like a home, but not one I'm used to.

"There's a park over there," Bennett says, nodding toward the right. "Take a break?"

I'm eager to get to the capitol before my nerves catch up with me, but I'm also tired from pedaling, so I nod and follow him down a side street, past more run-down houses, and at the end find a small swing set and slide. When I check my phone again, I see that we've been biking for over half an hour.

I walk over to the swing and he follows, sitting on the one next to me. I hold my phone and take some pictures of the slide, the houses. Of the neighborhood that feels more forced than friendly. I quickly post one to my blog without a caption.

"It's kind of insane," I say, moving the swing with my feet. "Being here."

"Yeah. I'd imagine. I mean, she could have sat in that swing, right?"

"Right," I say, thinking about the possibility. "Do you think she liked it here?"

"Don't know. I guess if this is where you grow up, it's all you know, so you just deal with it, right? It becomes home."

"Yeah."

He adds, "I mean, it could have been nicer back then?"

"Maybe." I pause. "What's Miami like?"

He starts pumping his swing, pushing and emphasizing his words. "Miami is crazy loud. I think that's the best way to describe it. Just, so loud and bright. I mean, depending on where you are, you could walk down an entire row of neon buildings."

"That is bright."

"Yeah. And it's huge. I live in the outskirts, like, away from the craziness and beaches, but still."

"Same here."

"You live in the outskirts of Miami, too?" He eyes me jokingly.

"No, no, the outskirts of Orlando. There's Disney and the parks, but they're, like, forty-five minutes away. I live away from that and the beaches and stuff."

"Suburbia at its best."

"Exactly."

"You graduate this year, right? Are you going to stay in Orlando for college?"

I shake my head. "No, I'd rather go somewhere else. I mean, I like Orlando and all, but I want a new experience. So, I'm looking here, among other places," I say, pushing a little harder on the swing, and letting my feet leave the ground. "What brought you here?"

"Animation scholarship. Also, it wasn't too far away, but wasn't too close. Like, I could go home if I needed something, but didn't have to if I didn't want to."

"And your girlfriend was there, right?"

He doesn't answer, just stares out ahead of us.

"Sorry, I shouldn't have . . ."

He skids his feet and stops his swing, turning to me with a weary look. "No, it's okay," he says. "But yeah, that was a consideration when I came here. She stayed in Miami, so it wasn't extremely hard for us to visit each other."

"And it still didn't work out?"

"She cheated on me within the first two weeks, so, no, not really," he says, with a slight laugh.

"Seriously?" I ask, surprised.

"Seriously." His hands grab the metal chains and hold on tight. "So . . . that was that."

My heart falters for him, and I want to reach out, comfort him, after all the times he's helped me, but I'm still unsure if I can or should, or if he even wants me to. So I simply say, "I'm sorry."

He shrugs, and then continues. "It sucked, but better I learned who she was sooner than later, right?" He looks at me with questions in his eyes. "I guess I kind of hoped that when I'd see her back at home for Thanksgiving we'd magically make everything right again," he says with a flourish of his hand. "But . . . it turns out she's on guy number four or something, so, yeah, that's not happening." I watch the emotions wash across his face, from disappointment to embarrassment to acceptance.

"Wow. She moves fast," I mumble. I can't imagine how he feels—I've never dated before. And I guess not dating has saved me from the pain of being cheated on, but unrequited crushes have their own pains, too.

"You're telling me." He laughs halfheartedly. "Clearly I wasn't enough for her."

"Hey, I'm sure that's not it," I say. "Some people go wild in college, from what I hear. I mean, Treena has a guy. And that's . . . different."

"She didn't in high school?" he asks curiously.

"Nope." I shake my head.

"And you . . . ?" His voice is tentative now.

"Nope. We're kind of loners," I joke, letting out my nerves. "I mean, it's not that I don't *want* to date or anything, I just haven't, I guess. I hang out with the art crowd, and everyone is either weird, introverted, or both—like me, I guess—or outgoing like my friend Celine. And aside from me, Treena was mostly with her family friends, and her parents were pretty strict about no dating. So we had each other, and that seemed like enough sometimes. But, you know, not always."

"I get that. I mean, I've only had one girlfriend. And she was already a friend, so it was easier, I guess. I don't know."

"We can be loners together," I joke.

"And bask in each other's awesomeness," he says, and I can tell he's feeling less down, less reflective on what happened.

"You're different."

"And how's that?"

"Well, for one thing, you're a total dork," I say, trying to cheer him up.

"If you're trying to cheer me up, it's not working," he says, pushing my swing to the side.

"And another"—I laugh, trying to regain the swing's balance—"you don't make me nervous." I wasn't intending to go that far, but the words just naturally come out.

"Good." He smiles, and I look down.

I move my swing closer to his so we're facing each other, knees touching, and all wrapped up in the chains. He reaches over and grabs my swing, bringing me closer and wrapping me in a hug. I let go and hug back, for the first time allowing myself to see Bennett, really see him, without any sort of apprehension or barrier in the way. Without wondering if I was wrong to be here with him. I hold on tight, closing my eyes and memorizing the feel and shape of his body.

We let go and swing away, untwisting as we go, and I feel

both faint and shy from our embrace. This is all new, opening up to a guy. I don't know how to feel. I don't know how to do it.

"You're a good guy, you know," I say, kicking his swing so it spins again.

"Oh god, that's the worst thing to hear," he laughs. "Actually, I'm a pathetic guy. I keep hearing my story in my head and it sounds like such a sob story."

"Hey, don't make fun of my friend's pathetic sob story."

"Oh, so we're friends now?"

"Bennett. We shared a bedroom. I think we passed friends a long time go," I say, and he smiles, and I can't help but blush at the thought that I made his face change like that.

SEVENTEEN

We walk from the swing set back to the bikes, where they're locked up by a bus stop. There's a public board posted by a bench, full of Help Wanted, For Sale, and For One Night Only flyers. I browse them quickly, and just as I turn away, a bright orange poster catches my eye. It's right there, under a gig poster for a band called the New 52s—an art exhibit opening at Full Moon Café. The artist is named Jessica Cally.

Jessica Cally. I jerk toward Bennett and point it out to him.

"Isn't that . . ." he says, touching the sign.

"Yes!" I gasp. "Jessica Cally was in the picture with my mother."

"Do you think it's the same person?"

I'm nearly jumping in excitement. "I don't know! Maybe?"

He grabs my shoulders and says, "We should go."

"The opening was yesterday, though," I say, noticing the date, and letting that information hit.

"I'm sure the show is still going on. We can call and ask when the artist will be there again."

"True," I say, not sure if it'll work, but eager enough to find out. "When I had my exhibit I was only there for the opening night, but mine was just a high school thing, and this is something bigger, right?"

"Right," he says, removing his hands, and I toss the thoughts in my head. It can't hurt to look, right? I'm determined to try. If there's a chance I can see her, I'll take it, as small as it is.

I call the place and learn that, yes, Jessica Cally's exhibit is still up, and yes, she'll be there today around noon. My heart leaps with excitement, so I tell Bennett as soon as I hang up.

"She'll be there after twelve. We're gonna meet her!" I say giddily.

"We? I'm included this time?" he asks, but he doesn't look upset or insulted that I didn't let him stay last time.

"If you want," I say, but I'm still not sure. It's important for me to go, I just don't know *how* I want to go.

"Tell you what. I have class at one. Campus is on the way to Full Moon, so let me show you around for a bit until noon. Then you can decide. If you want company, I'll come along. If not, I'll just head off to class. Deal?"

"Aye aye, Holmes," I say, and he smiles.

◇◇◇◇

The campus is beautiful—all of the buildings are similar to the ones I saw just yesterday with Treena. Trees dot the sidewalks, and there are even a few small hills, which are nonexistent in Orlando. It *feels* like a college campus, which seems so foreign to me. And it's once again surreal thinking that seventeen years ago, my mother went here, too. She might have biked these streets, walked the paths.

"Okay, so here's one of my favorite buildings," Bennett says, pulling up in front of another brick building, this one with a beautiful stained-glass entrance. Under panes of blue and yellow and green glass are the words "The half of knowledge is to know where to find knowledge."

"That's kind of fitting, isn't it?" I ask.

"Especially for you."

"So, does the act of finding where to find knowledge make us smarter?" I ask. "We don't know where to look for knowledge, but we're trying, and we're finding those places. Slowly."

"I'd like to think so," he agrees. I take out my camera and take a picture of the phrase, zooming in so it's the only thing in frame. I can feel Bennett watching me, even though I'm absorbed in the picture. Then I take a photo of some of the people walking, the students I might one day be.

"Come on, there's more to see." Before he turns, I aim

my camera on Bennett and take a photo. He kicks off his bike and we pass the English building I visited that first day, and then we're going around a larger, more statuesque building with a fountain out front. He stops again, and I pause behind him.

"Okay, so this is the main auditorium on campus. A lot of big people come and speak here, like Elie Wiesel and B. B. King and Anthony Bourdain. But more importantly," he says, turning toward the fountain, "this is the fountain."

"How is the fountain more important than Elie Wiesel?"

Bennett smiles. "The fountain is important because it's tradition for people to be thrown in here on their birthdays."

"Seriously?" I ask.

"Seriously! It's not just birthdays—celebrations and stuff. It's a bizarre thing, but I thought you should see it."

"Have you been thrown in?" I ask, picturing him popping up from the water, soaking wet.

"Yeah, my second week here. I was one of the first. The water was . . . cold."

"I bet," I agree.

"Okay, next stop!" he says, pressing down and pedaling on. We ride behind the auditorium, and Bennett points out both the music and psychology buildings as we pass by. "The music dorm is supposedly haunted," he says, still biking, and pointing to a dorm across the street.

"I think I've had enough of haunted buildings for one

trip," I say, keeping up behind him, though it's harder now. We can't bike side by side as we were earlier. Instead we're single file on a sidewalk, avoiding other bikers and walkers.

"You're planning on majoring in photography, right?" he asks as we stop outside the lab I went to just yesterday.

"I don't know," I say. "I mean, I want to, totally, but . . ."

"But your parents think it's not a good idea to major in it," he finishes.

"Not that, exactly. I just—they know it's something I'm super passionate about, and know I want to and are supportive of it, but I think they also assumed I'd major in something more . . ."

"Lucrative?"

"Professional," I say. "I mean, they're both professional. I don't know, I haven't really talked to them about it much."

"Really?" he asks, surprised.

"Yeah."

"You seem pretty open with them. I mean, they're cool with you searching out your mother and all . . ." he says, scratching his head.

"Kind of. I mean, they weren't like throwing me out the door to do it. They were wary, my mom especially. She's open about everything, but she's still . . . worried. They *are* supportive, and I know they wouldn't mind if I majored in it. . . . I guess I just want to make them proud and all that."

"So let me ask you—what do you like about photography?"

I think about it for a second, then say, "I just do. I always have. It's part of me." I pause, then add, "It's the process. The focusing in on something so you can show the perfect image."

"You like the end result."

"No. I mean, yeah, but I like the process of getting there." And I realize what I'm saying as I'm saying it. I like the process. I'm *enjoying* this process, this uncovering of information about my mother. The daily documentation on my blog. The discovering and analyzing of things as I go, even if I don't understand them at the time. This slow developing to create some sort of story. I'm enjoying figuring everything out . . . including myself.

He nods and says, "My parents were cool with computer animation because I liked it. I'm sure yours are like that, too. They want you to be happy, not do what they want."

"And how do you know that?"

"I don't know," he says, stepping back onto his bike. "Just a hunch."

I look at him, then ask, "What do you think my mother would want?"

"You'd know better than me," he says, and the truth is, I don't. Not really. But I know she was a free spirit—I know she did what she wanted. Maybe she would have pushed me toward photography, toward what I really wanted, even if it was a bad decision. Maybe, sometimes, bad decisions are actually okay.

"I feel like, I don't know, I'd want to make her proud, too. Even though I don't know her."

"Not weird at all. I mean, you don't know much about your mother, but you do know she wasn't, like, a crazy person, right? Like, my mom's been through some serious cases with kids—fostering them out and all after terrible home lives. Yours wasn't like that, so it's normal to want to know what it would have been like. At least I think so."

I nod my head. It *wasn't* like that, was it? I still don't know much about her, but my parents said she wasn't horrible when they met her. She wasn't crazy or mean or an alcoholic or anything like that. She was just a girl, not much older than me, who was scared. I want to know what happened. I want to know her, still.

"You know, she did start college, so she had to have wanted to do something . . . she took English, that I know. I didn't learn what her other classes were. . . ."

"Maybe we'll find out later today what she wanted to do," he answers simply.

I jump on my bike and follow him, thinking of what he said. Which path am I supposed to take—the one my mom thinks is smart or the one my mother might have been more keen to take? Or maybe a bit of both? More importantly, which is more *me*?

Full Moon Café is only a five-minute bike ride from campus. We get there in four because I'm anxious. When we get inside, I'm surprised by how lively, how eclectic it is. There are mismatched, worn-looking couches and tables, crowded with newspapers and used books, making it resemble a messy person's living room more than a coffee shop or an art studio. Each wall is a different color—burnt red, teal, purple, and yellow—and they're all covered in framed artwork. Artwork that I assume is Jessica Cally's.

"Do you remember what her photo looked like?" Bennett asks as he follows me inside. I let him come with me this time. Knowing she'll definitely have something to say, and worried she'll react similarly to Bee, I want someone with me. We walk toward the walls to see the exhibit; I want to see her artwork before I see her. She makes collages, it seems—mixtures of paints and newspaper and pen drawings. They're interesting, though I have no idea what they mean. I like the splashes of color on threaded newsprint. I like the swirls drawn over them.

"Kind of. Red hair, that's all I remember. She's in her midthirties now, I guess. I can pull up the photo—"

"Her?" Bennett asks, cutting me off and nodding toward a woman with wavy red hair in the corner, standing before an easel. My heart flips because yes, that's her. That *has* to be her. I might not remember the photo, but I remember the curls.

This woman knew my mother.

"Definitely," I whisper. "What should we do? Should we go ask if it's her?"

"Sure," he says. "You go, this is your thing. I've got class anyway."

"Really?" I ask, actually sort of sad to be losing him.

"Really." He smiles. "You'll be fine, and we'll meet up later, cool?"

"Okay." I nod eagerly, because while I definitely want to see him later, I also want to go in the direction of the woman with the wild red hair. I put one foot in front of the other and walk in her direction. I can do this, I remind myself. She's just a person, after all.

"Excuse me?" I ask the woman, and she turns around to face me. She's in a long, flowing light purple skirt, with a dark purple shawl wrapped around her waist. Her hair is falling around her shoulders, spilling down over her loose blue tank top to her elbows.

"Hi." She smiles. "Can I help you?"

"Are you Jessica Cally?" I ask.

"I am!" she says, giddy. "Are you here for the exhibit? I can show you around if you'd like. Not like this place is big!" She laughs loud and deep and it makes me smile.

"I actually . . . I have a question for you," I say, breathing slowly. My heart thrums with anticipation. "Back in high school, did you know someone named Claire Fullman?"

Her face goes from pleased to surprised in no more than half a second. Her eyes get wide and her mouth drops open. "I did," she says slowly in a slight southern accent. "And who might you be?"

"I'm Maude," I say slowly back. "Claire was my mother."

"You're . . ." she starts. "You're Maude . . ." And then her eyes get even wider and it clicks. I click for her. "Oh my *god*," she says loudly, bringing her hand to her heart. "Oh my god! I never thought—I mean, I never imagined—how did you find me?" And just like that, it all breaks and tears come to my eyes and I smile a crazy smile because *I found someone*. Someone who knew my mother, who seems to have liked her. My mother is not a villain in Jessica's story.

"Do you have time? To talk, that is?"

"For Claire's daughter, I've got all the time in the world," she says, shaking her head. "I can't believe this. I cannot believe this. My heart is *pounding*!" she says, and I know the feeling. She points to a fuzzy red couch to her right. I sit down and she takes a chair with sky-blue cushions across from me.

"I don't know why I didn't recognize you! You are the spitting image of your mom. Identical. I should have known as soon as you walked in. But I never thought . . . It's been how many years? How could I have expected . . ." She trails off, then shakes her head. "Too long. That girl. Every day I miss that girl," she says, sadness blanketing her voice.

"What was she like? I don't know," I admit.

"She was everything. I'll tell you that," she says wistfully. "But tell me about yourself. How'd you find me? Do you live in Tallahassee?"

"No, I live in Orlando," I say, then fill her in on the important things. My adoption and my photography project. My trip to FSU and then Osceola High and talking to Mr. Wayne. I tell her about the yearbook and the internet search and the flyer at the park. And she sits and listens attentively, shaking her head every now and then. I keep rambling because I'm afraid that if I don't, this will all just disappear.

"You talked with Mr. Wayne? Wow, you are *determined*. Just like your mother."

"Really?" I ask eagerly.

"Oh yes." She shakes her head, lost in thought. "Clarabelle always got what she wanted, be it grades or guys or . . ." She cocks her head, then carefully says, "Other things."

Other things. That can refer to a lot.

"Anyway," Jessica continues before I can ask her to elaborate. "She was a force."

"You called her Clarabelle," I point out.

"Oh yeah," she says, waving her hand. "Some guys started calling her that as a joke in middle school, but Claire wouldn't put up with that, so she *owned* that nickname. She made sure everyone called her that. She got the last laugh there."

"That's awesome," I say, noting that her story matches up with Mr. Wayne's. I wish I had the same confidence as my mother, the ability to own up to insults. Celine is like that, and maybe that's why I like her. Maybe it's a part of me wishing I was more like that, and less shy and nervous. Maybe it's why I'm kind of jealous of Treena—not just because she's hanging out with Trey, but because she's with him. She's figuring herself out and dropping her cocoon. I haven't yet, and I don't know how to. But here, doing all of this, is helping me. Maybe learning more about my mother will, too.

"What else can you tell me about her?" I ask.

"What else do you want to know?" She leans back, looking so at home in the café.

"Everything. Anything," I say. "I don't know much at all. . . ."

"I could go on for hours. Claire was my best friend, you know."

"Really?" I ask excitedly. And I immediately think of Treena. She was her Treena.

"Oh yeah, we did everything together. Man, I loved that girl so much. . . . It was really hard for me after, you know," she says. "Really hard."

"I'm sorry," I say instinctively.

She wipes her eyes and shakes her head. "Not a day goes by that I don't think about her."

I let her reflect, not wanting to ruin her moment, and then carefully ask, "How'd you meet?"

"Detention, actually. Funny, right?"

"Oh! Why were you there?"

"Oh, I don't remember." She waves her hand, mood visibly changing for the better. "Probably skipping class, nothing huge. We got away with a lot more than we should have, I'll say. Your mom, she had a way with words."

"How so?" I ask.

"Well, for one thing, that Mr. Wayne you met? She convinced him to start the Key Club for us. Neither of us were the best of students, you know, and we needed some extra credit to graduate, so we got him to put that together for us."

I think about what she's saying, try to process it, and it seems so foreign. I never would have done something like that, and it's weird thinking my birth mother did. I didn't expect her to be like my mom, but I also didn't expect her to be the opposite.

"He tried so hard," she sighs, "and, oh, he was cute. Is he still cute? Your mom had a big crush on him for a while."

"He was okay," I say, blushing, because he's more than twice my age.

"God, I miss her," Jessica says. "We started hanging out after school, on the weekends," she continues, resting her arms on her knees and kind of in a trance. "We'd say to study, but we usually just snuck out. Her mom was *never* home, so we'd bring friends over, or just stay out late. Oh, that girl got me into so much trouble with my mom."

"Wait," I say. "You say mom; did she not have a dad around? I was never sure. . . ."

"Oh," she says. "How much do you know?"

"Not much at all. Nothing, really," I admit. "Which is why I'm here. I don't know if I have grandparents, honestly. . . ."

"Oh, honey," she says sadly. "I feel so guilty, knowing so much of her, and you knowing so little. . . . Okay, so she never knew her dad, from what I knew. So, I don't know any more about that, I'm afraid."

Disappointed, I murmur, "Oh." It's not that I expected to figure out who my grandparents were or anything, but I guess I kind of hoped I might. Maybe that's a main reason why she wanted to give me away—because she didn't want me to end up in a broken home like hers. The thought makes me sad—she gave me to perfect parents because she herself didn't have them.

"But she lived with her mom. I don't know what happened to her, honestly, but boy, we gave her a run when we were younger," she laughs. "She was a great woman, and great second mom to me."

She says it offhand, like it means nothing, but it's shocking how much that hurts me. This woman who's my grandmother was practically a parent to Jessica, but wouldn't even talk to me when I tried calling her a few years back, during my stint in calling everyone with the last name of Fullman. I know it was her on the phone; I know she answered and hung up on me. I just don't know why.

"So, yeah, she was out a lot and, you know, Claire loved the freedom. She had these amazing parties at her house, oh my gosh, they were the best. I mean, she did most of her art at her parties. She'd make people come over and then draw them."

"Wait, really?" I exclaim. I take a breath and everything. "She was an artist?"

"Oh yeah, paintings, mostly. She made these abstract drawings of people and animals. Like, a human body with a boar head, or vice versa. *So* insane, but so . . . inspired. I always loved her stuff."

"That's amazing," I say, thinking about my photography, and how we have that in common. How we could have shared that passion. How maybe I got it from her. I can't help but grin.

"We took painting together in twelfth grade. Teacher *hated* us because we never followed the rules. But, I mean, who wants to paint an orange when you can paint the sky? Or something wild like a two-headed dog? That was your mom—she loved painting the bizarre. So she'd turn our friends into beasts and dragons and it always amused us."

"That's so cool," I murmur, picturing her controlling a party. Having everyone sit down so she could concentrate, and then, within seconds, creating an amazing work of art. Maybe that's why she wasn't a great student—her mind was always on something else. Maybe it just needed to be let free. My fingers twitch and I know I want to take a photo of this moment, but I can't. Not yet.

"Oh, it really was." She smiles. "Everyone came. Let me ask, are you an artist, too?" She leans back, playing with her scarf.

"Kind of, I mean, I want to be. I'm a photographer," I explain.

"A visual medium. I'm into that, too. I use photos as an inspiration for my pieces." She pauses, then smiles. "I bet you're just like her. Let me guess, mind always wandering? Fingers itching to create?" she asks, leaning forward and staring at me, as if she's trying to really see me.

"Yes." I nod, because that's exactly like me. Maybe I'm more like her than I thought.

"And how often are *you* in detention?" she asks with a slight laugh.

"Ha," I say. "Um . . . that part I'm not like at all."

"Uh-huh, sure," she says with a smile. "I could never have imagined Claire's daughter ending up boring."

She says it offhandedly, but I feel her words deep down. I think of my life in Orlando. Celine has an exciting life there, flirting with guys at Starbucks and having inside jokes with them. I'm behind my camera. I go to school and come home.

Am I boring?

Would my mother have considered me boring, or a disappointment? And if I was still with her, would I have turned out more like her?

"Tell me a fun, unboring story about my mother," I say, because I have to know what I'm missing out on.

"There are so many. Hmm. Well, there was this one time," Jessica continues, overriding my thoughts, "that Claire and I got drunk, then went streaking across her neighborhood. Oh my god, you should have seen the boys' reactions! I mean, they were all there, of course, all her boys. My lord, that girl attracted the guys."

"Really," I more say than ask.

"Oh, the guys loved her. She was so . . . passionate and engaging. I had a boyfriend at the time—god, I haven't thought about him in years—but your mom? She had a few. They were always coming over after school. . . ." She stops, then looks at my face, really looks at it. "But I guess I shouldn't be telling you any of that stuff."

"No, please, I want to hear everything," I say quickly. I want her to keep talking, even though I don't know what to say, how to take it. It's a strange feeling, knowing more about her. I saw her as this dominant force, this aura who lured people in with her dramatic speeches and personality, and that wasn't her, not really. She did do those things, she was strong and proud, it seems, but she was also young and reckless. She made mistakes and went crazy. I can't be upset about what she did back then, but it still feels off connecting the pieces and drawing out a new image of her. She was this wild and daring person who I can't even imagine.

"I mean, you can probably guess some of the stuff that went on—you were a product and all," Jessica says, motioning to me and emitting a high-pitched, single-syllable laugh.

"Can I ask . . . how'd she react? When she found out about me?"

"She was pretty devastated."

My face falls when I hear her words, and my heart thumps.

"Oh, honey, no offense!" she says quickly, noticing my

reaction. "I mean, she just wasn't ready to have a kid, you know? She was eighteen. Who's ready to be a mother then?"

I nod because I guess it's true. If I found out I was pregnant, I'd be devastated, too. But it doesn't hurt any less.

Jessica continues, "She thought about . . . *you know* . . ." Oh, I know. If she had gone through with *you know*, I wouldn't be here. I feel my heart race with the realization. "But she didn't think she could go through with it. So she contacted the adoption agency and heard she'd make some money . . . and you probably know the rest from there."

"Yeah . . ." I nod. "Wait. Do you know who my father was, then?" I ask this quickly, before I even realize what I said.

"She never told me, not that I didn't ask a bunch. She was dating a few guys at the time, so . . ." Not only does she not know who my father is, there could be multiple suspects. Which makes me feel . . . uncomfortable. She registers my face, and adds, "She liked one of them, this guy Chad, better than the others, and was with him longer. So you never know."

Chad was in the photo; Bee mentioned a Chad. We were right in suspecting they were dating. At least that's something.

"Do you know where Chad is now?" I ask, and she eyes me.

"Here in Tallahassee. I haven't kept up with him, but I think he's a car mechanic. But don't go thinking he's your father or anything," she warns quickly. "He was always kind of a strange guy. Very clingy to her. Followed her around like a puppy dog."

"Do you know a girl named Bee Trenton?" I ask, moving forward.

"Bee! How do you know Bee? Ahh, I guess she was in that photo, too. Oh, Bee . . ."

"What about her?" I ask.

"She was a friend of ours for a while, but then things got messy, you know how they do. She and your mom got into a huge fight and that was it."

"Do you know what they fought about?" I ask. "And why?"

"Oh, honey, I don't remember. It was a long time ago. She was more friends with Claire than me. They knew each other before I came into the picture."

"It's okay," I say, disappointed. "I'm sure it was about a guy or something."

"You know, yes, that might have been it. Bee was with Chad before Claire was. God, I forgot all about that. Anyway, I don't have all the details. Your mom . . . she was always a bit secretive about things, so you never know."

"Like what?" I ask, wondering what a girl who was okay with streaking was truly private about.

"Oh, she had guys, but she never kissed and told. She didn't talk about her mom much. The only time she really opened up was when she was drinking or high, you know?"

"Of course," I say, my heart faltering again from this roller coaster of a conversation. Because, again, I'm finding out more information that pushes her farther and farther away from me. I don't know what to make of it all, and Jessica says it all so casually, as if it means nothing. The image I had of my mother keeps changing, morphing into something new, and I don't know what, or who, to picture anymore. I knew she was different, but if I'm part of her, how am I not more like her? What does her lifestyle say about me? About what I will become when I'm away at college? Will I become someone I won't even recognize? Treena pops into my head, and I think about how much she's changed since going away. She wanted to create this new version of herself, and she did.

The thoughts are tangling through my mind, and I can't grasp any of them. I don't want to. I want to go back to this clean, pure image I had of my mother, when everything was still unknown and innocent. I want *that* to be her. I want to still have hope that I'm like her, that there is part of her in me. That I'm not alone.

She wasn't bad, but she wasn't what I wanted. I wanted perfect, and it's only now that I realize I never could have had that. It's irrational to think so.

"But enough about her! I want to know more about you!" Jessica says, snapping me out of my thoughts, and I look up, unsure of where I am, who I am. I don't want to be here anymore; I can't.

"I, um, I live in Orlando. And I'm here, at FSU, staying with my friend," I say slowly, carefully.

"How fun! What're your plans for tonight?" she asks, and it clicks in a way. She is two people—she's the Jessica from high school and the Jessica now. She's the Jessica who was best friends with my mother, and the Jessica who lost her so many years ago. And I wonder what would have happened if she hadn't died. Would they be here together, launching exhibits and talking about old times?

The realization saddens me, so I look at her, nod, and smile.

"Not sure, I guess we'll see. I, um, I just realized what time it is, and I have to . . . go meet my friend. But, hey, thank you so much for talking to me, really. It was . . . something, really. It was . . . great," I say, because I don't know what else to say.

"Oh, I'm so sad you're leaving! But I understand." She looks sad, but also maybe relieved? Maybe this was weird for her, too. "Please let me know if you have any more questions, I'd love to talk. It was *so nice* going back in time. I don't do it nearly enough!" Jessica says, handing me a business card that's also collaged, just like her art.

"Yeah, yeah," I say, standing up. "Thank you, really."

"Keep in touch!" Jessica says, bringing me in for a hug. She smells like cigarette smoke and when she pulls away I see a wonderful, crazy artist, but I also see her wrinkles and scars. I see that this is her, daily, painting in a café. This is the life my mother could have had, would have had. This could have been her. And, maybe, me.

"Oh! One last thing. While you're here, you need to visit Lichgate. Your mom absolutely adored that place. It's not far from here. Be sure to see it."

I nod and turn around, filing the information away for later. I take a picture before I leave, of Jessica going back to her canvas. She broke the image I had of my mother, shattered it into a million pieces and reformed it into something new and not yet understood. I need time to get to know this mother, this version of her.

EIGHTEEN

I walk outside and am surprised to see Bennett on the sidewalk, scrolling through his phone. I slump down next to him and simply say, "Hi," because I don't think I can process more words.

"Hey," he says, putting his phone down. "Class was canceled."

"Was it really?" I ask.

His cheeks turn a tint of red and he shakes his head. "Okay, no, I just didn't want to leave you with Crazy Redhead in there."

I nod, too exhausted to say anything.

"What happened?"

My throat fills with angst and my eyes overflow with tears. I try to hold it in, but I can't.

"Oh, crap, okay," he says as I silently weep in front of him, tears spilling from my eyes into my hands cradling my face. I cry for what I didn't know, and what I thought I did. I cry for the mother I never knew and am so different from. I cry because it all makes sense, even though I don't want it to. I cry because this complete trip was an utter failure. I shouldn't have found all of this out. I shouldn't have known. It would have been better for me to keep my pristine picture of my mother—for her to be the scared girl who bravely gave me up. Not a partier who made a, to her, devastating mistake.

I feel Bennett's arm go around my shoulder to keep me together, but it makes me cry more. He turns me to him, and I rest my forehead on his shoulder, aware of the tears seeping through his shirt. But I can't turn them off. They've been held in for so long. Both his arms are around me now, rubbing my back, and I try to concentrate on that movement, on their rhythm, and not the fact that my mother maybe never cared about me. She was too young to; she didn't want me in the first place, of course. I should have known that, realized it, but it never really hit. The thing is, there's no hope of making her proud, because I was never a part of her life.

The nicest and bravest thing she ever did was give me up. She gave me the life she herself didn't have. And the thought of her life, and what wasn't lived, fills me with tears again.

Once I have calmed down a little, I tell Bennett some of the stuff I learned, and he nods and shakes his head along the way. When I'm done, he says, "I get why you're upset, but it's okay." I look at him sadly and shake my head.

"But what—?" I start.

"Let me ask you something. What's your mom like at home?"

"My mom?" I ask, confused. "She's . . . a mom. She's nice and protective and smart. She's a teacher, so I have pretty good grammar because of her. And she's always moaning about her students, but I know she actually likes them."

"Right. So that's who you're around all the time. You're surrounded by that, by her, not by your mother. What were you doing before this trip?"

"Going to school and working on my photography."

"You weren't going to wild keggers or anything?"

"No!"

"Right, so you're not like your mother at all. If you never found out about it, things wouldn't change, right? And now that you did . . . they still shouldn't change."

"That's easy for you to say. You know your parents."

"And you know yours."

"It's different," I say.

He looks down, then says, "So there was this kid who used to come by our house every now and then—one of the kids my mom was trying to get adopted. He was, like, four, and kind of messed up, so my mom wanted him to see a solid, 'normal' family, I guess. I never liked him because he pushed my younger sister. But anyway, he got adopted and we ended up going to the same high school. And he's kind of cool now. So, I don't know; how I see it, he's not like the mother who left him when he was a baby. He's like the mom who has him now. Nature versus nurture, you know."

I nod; I see what he's saying, but though his words are nice, they're not making my struggle easier. I'm still confused. I'm still . . . lost.

"I get it, I do, but I don't know."

"So, wait, you're worried about next year? College?"

I wipe my face again. "I could change. I could want to change without realizing it. I mean, before this week, I never drank. And a few days in I woke up in a guy's bed with a hangover," I say. "I can change, and I might, and that terrifies me, because I don't hate who I am now. I mean, look at Treena. She's completely different. It's not entirely bad, it's just . . . new. How do we change so easily? And what do we do with the old versions of ourselves?"

"Okay, I didn't know Treena before, so I can't comment on that. And sure, your mother's DNA is in you, but you weren't raised by her. You were raised by your parents, who taught you to *not* be like her."

"Their three rules before I left were no drinking, no boys, and no partying. I broke all three of their rules by the second day I was here."

"Oh come on. You could have done much worse. You hid during the first party, you didn't go wild last night, and look at me, I'm harmless. That's actually my middle name.

Bennett Harmless Walker."

"Uh-huh," I say, realizing he's trying to cheer me up.

"Plus, it's college! You're supposed to loosen up and explore things. It's part of the whole experience. You're only here with me because Treena's been preoccupied," he says. I shake my head no. "Well, it's not because I'm good company. I mean, I take you to bagel places—talk about fancy."

I smile a little and agree because he's trying. "You're right. You do make poor decisions."

"The worst. Like, not seeing the new *Star Wars* on opening night poor decision."

"Oh, that is bad," I chuckle.

"Why are you with me again? It's the bike, isn't it? Chicks dig the bike."

"Has to be." I smile, and then look down.

"You're okay. This means nothing in the long run."

Maybe he's right. But still, I can't deny the fact that all of that happened, that it's linked to me now, whether I like it or not. "Come on, let's go back to the dorm," he says.

"I should talk to Treena," I sigh, wondering what I'll say. I'm still kind of upset she had me go to Bennett's room last night. Not that that was bad, it's just . . . she's my friend. And I'm here to see *her*.

"What are you going to say?" he asks, helping me up and walking me back around the building. He drops my hand and I do everything in my power to not grab his back.

"I have no idea," I admit. "But I want to tell her about today. I want to hear what she says."

When we get back to the dorm, Treena's door is shut and we already know why, and it makes me want to cry. I follow Bennett up to his room.

"Well, that's . . . frustrating," I sigh, sitting on his chair. "I guess I could knock, but . . ." I shake my head. "I feel like I'm in your room more than hers."

"Well, my room has one hundred percent less making out, so, you know, benefit."

I smile at him and blush, thinking of the not-making-out going on in here.

"Oh, crap," he says, looking at his clock. "I actually have to run to this class. I completely forgot." He gets up and grabs some books on his desk. "I'm sorry. You can stay here, if you'd like."

"No, no, it's okay, I can hang out outside."

"Seriously, it's okay."

"I want to go take some photos, I think."

"Okay, well, give me your phone." I reach into my bag and hand it over. He dials a number and then his phone rings. "Okay, I've got your number, you've got mine. If you need anything, just call. I'll be done in a few hours, and then hopefully they'll be, um, free," he says, nodding in the direction of Treena's door.

We leave his room, then head downstairs. I stretch out on the green lawn just outside their building and look around at the people going to and from class. They all look like they have a purpose, a reason for walking. Even the girls giggling over something on a phone they're passing back and forth between each other seem to be on their way somewhere. There are other people sitting around, like me, and they make me feel less lazy. Some are doing schoolwork, with laptops and books open. Some are just lying down and enjoying the sun.

I take my camera out and snap a few pictures to capture the moment—the isolation of being surrounded by people but not being part of any of them. The tranquility of being alone on an expansive grassy knoll. And the feeling of contentment from just sitting still after a day of movement.

I needed this.

I lie on my back and let the grass tickle my skin and dig into my exposed arms. The sun is bright overhead, the clouds not blocking its beams. I close my eyes and think about all I've done so far.

I've always had this image of my mother in my head. The one from the photo hidden in my dresser, but also one I concocted late at night when I was trying to figure out who I was. Why I was me. She was a vague image, and, in my mind, she guided me out of my weariness and into more stability. All of my questions were answered by this idea of her, and part of me always felt I'd find something about her that would prove my vision to be real.

But I found something now, and that idea I concocted isn't who she was. The perfect mom/friend. It never could have been, really, because I just made it up. Now she's a real person with hair and eyes and arms and a personality. Now she's some*one* and not some*thing*.

And in a way, I'm still a part of her. And she's still a part of me. And I'm not sure how I'm supposed to feel now.

I squint my eyes and groan in frustration. I'm not going to figure out anything here, lying alone on the grass.

I sit up and grab my phone again, then realize that I haven't checked my email in a while. I haven't wanted to, not after the café with Jessica, but there are still answers out there, and it's my job to finish this. I can't back out now.

But there's nothing new, so I absentmindedly flip through the photos I've taken so far. Lots around campus; of the people we've encountered, both good and bad; of Bennett and Treena and Trey. Pictures from the party last night, from all of our destinations today. And as I flip, I'm starting to see a story unfold, my story. There isn't an ending yet, but there's a start and a middle. There are questions in these photos that have yet to be answered.

I post another photo to my blog, one of Bennett riding his bike on campus. It's just his back, but I like it. I then check my comments and see that there's one on the "Unconquered" photo.

It's easy to give up, and hard to stay unconquered.
Greatness didn't come from giving up.

It's from my teacher, Ms. Webber. I knew she'd be looking, but I didn't think she'd comment. I look at the photo, and then the ones I posted before. And though they're only a fraction of the ones I've taken, the same story is unfolding in them. But I'm not showing defeat in them. Maybe she's just guessing? Maybe she has a feeling. . . .

I guess, in a way, it's like me getting an impression of my mother. I don't know all of the details, I don't know what she was really like—just some stories from people who knew her—but I'm already assuming I know who she was.

Maybe I need to keep an open mind.

And maybe I need to find more people, maybe someone related.

Like her mother. My grandmother. I've tried reaching out to her in the past, with no success. I wasn't sure if I could handle another rejection, but I think it's time.

I need to find her, too.

◇◇◇◇

A few hours later I find myself pacing around the hallway, waiting for Bennett to come back. Treena was in class, and I forgot to get her key before leaving, so I stayed in the hall until I knew Bennett's class was over.

"Watson!" a voice shouts out, and I look down the hall to see Bennett walking toward me. He's smiling big, and he's waving both hands in the air at me as if I can't see him. On impulse I smile and walk toward him, closing the gap between us.

"Got your text. What's this new idea?" he asks.

"We might not be able to find my mother, Sherlock, but what about my grandmother?"

"Your grandmother . . . ?"

"Claire's mom. Jessica said Claire never knew her dad, but she lived with her mom. Who might still live in Tallahassee, possibly, maybe, right?"

He analyzes me, then says, "Definitely. I'm surprised we didn't think of this earlier."

"Yeah, well, like I told you, I've . . . tried before," I say, "with not-great results, so I kind of avoided it."

"That's right." He nods, recognition in his face.

"Yeah. I realize now how I approached it wasn't really smart. But I think it's time to try again."

Bennett looks at me and gives a half smile. "Definitely. It is definitely time to try again."

"I was also thinking . . . Jessica said Chad was a mechanic in town."

"You didn't mention that—okay, we can work with that. If you want to meet him, we can probably find his shop by looking it up."

"Right, it's a long shot . . ." I muse, "but I think it's also doable."

"Didn't you message him, too?"

"Yeah, but I haven't heard back from him. So, we should use our detective powers, or whatever."

He laughs, then looks thoughtfully at me. "Are you okay finding him? I mean, what if he *does* turn out to be your father?"

"Do you think he'd even know?" I ask. If what Jessica

said was true, my mother was secretive. It's entirely possible that even my father doesn't know he's my father.

"I have no idea. I mean, it's just a chance, but it *is* a chance."

"Yeah," I say. "It is." But for some reason, that doesn't scare me. In fact, it makes me more eager. "I mean, I always knew my biological father was out here somewhere," I say, gesturing around, "but he's never felt so, I don't know, so tangible."

"And now he might be."

"Yeah. Wow, this is weird," I say, my world feeling bigger and smaller all in one. My heart starts to race, but I don't let it. I can't, not yet.

"With Bee, too, I think we have a full schedule ahead of us," he says, swinging his keys around his finger. They drop to the floor with a clunk. We both lean down to pick them up, and when he grabs them first, my hand brushes his. I pull mine back and straighten up, feeling my face redden. He busies his hands and leans against his door. "Right, well, it looks like we have plans for tomorrow."

"I was hoping you'd come along."

The stairwell door suddenly opens, and Trey walks out, his shirt a bit twisted. "Oh, hey." He balks at us standing there in the hall, then nods.

"What's up?"

I still can't figure Trey out. One night he terrifies us in some sort of initiation, and the next he takes care of my drunk best friend—at least, I hope he took care of her. It seems like he cares, but I can't help but get frustrated with the sight of Treena trying to impress him, with her getting irritated about his other girls around. I want to like him, for her, but it's hard separating him from how I feel about her leaving me repeatedly. They're woven together, and I need to at least figure part of it out.

"Just hanging out," Bennett answers for me. "What's up with you?" he asks.

"Actually, I was looking for you. Homework question," he says, and Bennett gives me a look.

"I guess that's my cue," I say, raising my eyebrows.

"Good luck," he says, then in a taunting voice he adds, "You're gonna need it."

I nod, turn around, and then turn back. "Wait, did you just quote *Star Wars* to me?"

He shrugs and I shake my head, smiling to myself as I head down the stairs, and inhale deep as I open the door.

"Hey!" Treena says, sitting on her bed with a book in her lap. "What's up? I haven't seen you all day! Sorry I've been gone. I had this huge test in chem and, oh god, I think I did okay, but you know how I feel about chem right now. I hate that it's just tests over and over again right now."

Okay, she's acting normal. So I guess everything went okay last night. I guess she's not thinking about what happened.

"Cool. Hope you did okay," I say, because I'm not sure what to say.

"What about you? What have you been up to?"

"Um, not much, just . . . more investigation," I say, realizing that, aside from her being with Trey, the main reason I'm upset is because she hasn't been there for me, throughout this whole thing. She was supposed to be the one going to all the places with me, not Bennett.

"Cool! Go well? Get some more fascinating tidbits?" she asks, which I find funny because if she really understood what I was going through, what I was learning, she wouldn't be calling it "fascinating tidbits." It's so much more than that.

It makes me think that maybe there was something more in Bee and my mother's ex-friendship. Maybe Bee wasn't just pissed off at her because of the whole Chad thing; maybe she was feeling betrayed by a friend. Left behind by a friend. Maybe that feeling is still around because they were great friends, best friends, and you never really get over losing someone that close.

"Yeah, a lot. My mother was . . . quite the person," I say.

"Oh yeah? How so?" she asks, putting her book down and looking at me with expectant eyes. She wants to bond, after all this time. And I can do one of two things: 1) tell her how she's been. Or 2) just talk to her.

So I sit down with a sigh and tell her a bit of what I've learned. Not everything, but enough to get her up to speed, ending with my next few steps.

"*Wow*. Really? Oh my god. You have . . . wow." She looks down. "I can't believe it. I wish I could have been there with you," she says morosely.

"You could have. Or, at least, you still can be," I continue, giving her the option to stay with me, try again. "Tree, I really need you with me. This has been hard."

"I know, I know. I can only imagine what you're going through. . . ."

"I *know* you want this year to be different, and I know you want to change, but this whole thing is changing me, and I'm not sure how. It's crazy how much it's affecting me."

She looks at me and nods. There's emotion behind her eyes, and it's like she's conflicted, but I don't know why.

"You're really brave, you know?" she says. "Doing all of this. It's, like, it's amazing and you're doing it. And I'm so scared for you, that you'll learn something bad. . . ."

"I've already learned some things that didn't make me exactly thrilled . . . I have no idea who my mother is. I'm still trying to figure her out."

"I know, I know." She looks down. "It's just . . . I've seen you do this before, and I've seen you hurt over this before, and I don't want to see that again. I don't *like* seeing you upset."

So that's why she hasn't been around? She'd rather get the condensed version of the events, after I've had time to process, than actually be there for me? "Tree, I'm older now, I can handle this. You don't have to be worried."

"I know, I know," she says. "It's stupid, but I am."

"Then I'd rather you worried with me, than worried elsewhere," I say, and she gives me a half smile. I think maybe my journey here has forced her to figure herself out, too, and that's scary in general.

"Okay, okay," she says decidedly. "I'm in. I'm with you on your next step."

"Tree, you can help at any step," I say, smiling, then add, "Oh! I didn't tell you. My mother was an artist."

"Wait, really?" I tell her about the art, and her eyes light up like mine probably did. "I can't believe that! You totally inherited it from her!"

"Maybe!" I say excitedly. At least that—that I can hold on to when everything else doesn't make sense. That is something real.

She smiles sadly, then says, "I hate that I missed that. I'm sorry I've been busy with school and . . . I'm still trying to figure that whole thing out, if I want to change majors, or . . ."

"Yeah, I know," I say.

"And Trey . . . is new," she says.

"Yeah, about that," I say, and she jerks her head up expectantly. I can't ignore last night; I have to address it. "He was okay last night, right? After he brought you home?"

"*Oh god,*" she says. "Last night. Yes. Oh, I'm so embarrassed." She buries her face in her hands. "I kind of hoped we'd pass over it."

"There's no way I'm passing over a very drunk Treena."

"Ha," she says. "It was not my finest moment."

"You weren't awful. You were a happy, flirty drunk," I say, thinking of Bennett's descriptions.

"Well, at least I wasn't an angry drunk. We have that on the hall. It's not pretty."

"But really, everything okay?"

"Yes," she says. "Despite my efforts of having him come back to my dorm with me . . . ugh . . . Trey was a gentleman. I can't believe I did that. I can't believe I kicked you out of our room. What was I thinking?"

"I don't think you *were*," I say. "It's okay, I bunked with Bennett."

"I'm still not convinced nothing is going on there. I saw you two at the party, acting all cute and stuff."

"Yeah, yeah," I say, waving my hand. "We're just friends."

"Uh-huh. The more you deny—"

"*Anyway*," I say, wondering how this conversation turned onto me so quickly. "Let's do something fun tonight."

"Oh!" she exclaims. "There's a carnival in the union— we can get cotton candy and play games. It'll be like the Orlando fair we went to last year after graduation."

"The one with the scary roller coaster?" I ask.

"You mean the scary roller coaster you refused to ride because you're a baby when it comes to extreme things?" she laughs.

"You refused to ride it, too," I point out, smiling.

"Only because I was afraid my flip-flops would fall off," she says innocently.

"Yeah, uh-huh," I say, laughing now, too. At the memory. At us back then. "I miss us."

"Me too," she says. "It's still weird thinking of you in Orlando without me."

"It's weird thinking of you up here, even though I've seen it. Celine called last night and was very impressed by your newfound partying."

"Celine," she says, nodding. "It's still weird you have a friend I don't know. What'd she say about me?"

"It's weird you have a whole life I don't know about," I say, then, "She just said that college changes you into a partying animal, or the like. So when she called and I was at Jason's party, it was kind of fitting. She was hitting on some guy at Starbucks when she called, and I felt almost more daring than her. Which was weird."

"Maude. You're looking for your birth mother. You're a million times more daring. And weird. Sorry, I just had to add one more."

I smile and lean on her shoulder. She's right, I know. It's just a different type of daring, I think. She then adds, "Didn't you think someone was cute at Starbucks once, too?"

"No." I shake my head, then grin. "Okay, yeah, that super-pretentious guy with glasses."

"What made you think he was pretentious? The no-new-music-is-good attitude, or the ironic facial hair?"

"Don't remind me," I say. "Hey, you liked that guy Lincoln who sometimes, but not always, referred to himself in the third person."

"Ah yes." She nods. "'Lincoln wants to take German

next year,'" she says, imitating him. "We have great taste."

I sit up and say, "It's a good thing your parents didn't know about Lincoln. They would have hated him."

"What, he was half Indian, they would have half loved him."

"Do they know about Trey?" I ask, broaching the subject.

"Oh, god no. Not that he's bad or anything, but I'm not going to introduce them to someone I'm not serious about."

"You're not serious about him? You seem pretty..."

"You know what I mean. Like, after we've been dating for a few months, yeah, okay, I'll tell them." She shakes her head, then says, "Oh god, that sounds terrifying!"

"Well, I mean, he's your first boyfriend. Wait. Is he your boyfriend?"

"I don't know..." she muses. "I mean, right now we're still... figuring things out, I guess?"

"Is he hanging out with other girls like he is with you?"

"No," she says, shaking her head. "He said he wasn't. It's just me." She pauses, then adds, "You do like him, right?"

"I just..." I hesitate because I'm still not sure. "He's okay, yeah, I just don't know him well. I mean, I wasn't into that whole haunted house thing, but... You're just kind of... with him a lot, so..."

"I know, I know. I'm sorry. It's just, you know. To be honest, he's making me feel more included. Like I'm part of something. After my attempt at finding a club to join kind of bombed, I just wanted something, and knowing this guy likes me and is introducing me to people and places . . . I don't know, it's kind of cool. It feels like college."

I nod, because what can I say to that? I want her to be happy. I want her with someone who will make her feel good.

Maybe that's what college is about after all. Not just discovering yourself, but discovering what makes you happy—whatever it might be.

NINETEEN

We continue talking through the afternoon, then eat a quick dinner downstairs before going back upstairs to change for the on-campus carnival Treena heard about. Treena puts on her bangles and a short, cute dress that her parents would freak over. Her mom's thoughts on clothing were typically the more the better. Let's be honest—the same goes with my mom, too. "I thought we were going to a carnival?" I ask, looking down at my jeans and black Pepperpots T-shirt. They're a local band we used to see together a lot, so I thought she'd appreciate me wearing their shirt.

"Yeah, but it doesn't hurt to look cute, right? Wait, I have a skirt that goes with your shirt," she says, pulling out a very short, very tight skirt.

"I don't know," I say, trying it on.

"It's perfect! You have to wear it," she says, jumping up and down.

"Okay, okay." I shrug, pulling it down a bit, still wondering why there are outfits for just a girls' night. I look at myself in the mirror and see, well, myself, dressed up. Only with a lot of leg.

Treena gives me a giant thumbs-up and we leave her dorm for the carnival.

As we walk down the sidewalk, arm in arm, I can see the guys looking at her, and I realize it's not just at her, it's at us. And that's when I feel it. The attention, the looks, the thoughts. They think we're cute. It's not like I haven't tried to dress up before, but never in a skirt like this, and never with results like this. So when I see Treena with her chin a little higher, and a bit of a bounce in her step, I get it. She likes the attention. And I guess she wanted to give me some, too.

"Oh, did I tell you they played here last week?" Treena asks, pointing to my shirt.

"No! Did you go?"

"Of course! They were awesome."

"I haven't seen them in forever," I say. It's not the same without her. "Do other bands tour through here?" I ask, thinking of the pixie haircut girl who said all the good bands go to Orlando.

"Yeah! I mean, before the Pepperpots, we saw Wilco at

Club Downunder, the on-campus venue, who were awesome. Oh, the club also has trivia nights, which are fun. Not surprisingly, Bennett won for us last time."

"Ha, yeah, I'm not surprised. He told me about his *Star Wars* obsession."

"Yep. He killed at the *Doctor Who* round. I mean, he named us the Weeping Angels, which apparently is a reference? I don't know. No one else could touch our team." I wish I'd been there. I wish I were part of these memories, too.

We walk on, toward the union, and though we're quiet, the night is not. It seems like a lot of people are out, heading in the same direction we are. And while a lot of them are excitedly talking, I'm happy we're not. Because it means we're okay enough to be back at our comfortable silence. We have an understood quietness.

The union is pretty crowded by the time we get there. It's an enclosed courtyard, bordered by Club Downunder, a theater, the cafeteria, and offices. Right outside is a colorful bouncy slide with a long line wrapped around it. Beaming lights are casting shadows down on it.

This is exactly what I needed after today. I learned so much, saw too much, and just . . . needed time away from learning. I just want to be me and have Treena be Treena, and remember what it was like to be us.

"We have to go on that later," Treena says excitedly, and I nod, thinking that a slide and miniskirt do not mesh well together. "But let's see what's going on first." We walk toward the center of the action, and inside it's just as crowded, with different stations of games and snacks. There's a popcorn stand, a cotton candy stand, and a funnel cake stand. There are also games set up, like at a real carnival, and photo booths. "Oooh, but first, snack?" she asks, gesturing toward the food stands.

"Cotton candy, yes," I say, and we get the blue flavor, all piled and wound high. I bite down on it and promptly feel the sugar coating my teeth. My dentist dad would kill me if he were here. Mom warns against boys and drugs; Dad, sugar.

"Is my tongue blue?" I ask, opening my mouth.

"Yes!" Treena laughs, pointing at her electric-blue tongue. "Mine?"

"Definitely. We look like Smurfs." I take out my phone and she yells, "Buddy Shot," and we take a picture, tongues out and smiling. And I think it'll be a great addition to my blog, because this is a new step forward, happily. We walk away from the stands and I find myself in a maze of people, but for once I don't feel so alone within it. It feels like I'm part of the flow, and not against it, and I'm not sure why I suddenly feel so different. Like I can do or be anything. I look up at the sky, and see the stars shining down, calm against the swirls of energy surrounding us.

A guy stops in front of us and shouts "Hey!" to Treena.

"Oh," she says, less enthused. "Hey, Brad." Then she looks at me. "Maude, this is Brad, one of Trey's friends from the soccer team. He was at the party last night. Brad, Maude."

"Hey," he says, taking me in. He looks athletic, too, with short brown hair and a jersey on. In fact, he looks remarkably like Trey. "Are you guys going to the club tonight?"

"No, we're just hanging out," she says, and I smile, happy that she's ditching plans for me.

"Really? Oh man, you're missing out. It's some girl from Tri Delt's birthday, and it's going down," he says, pumping his fist in the air.

"You don't even know who the girl is?" she asks, putting her hands on her hips. I like how she's getting an attitude with him. I like how she's defending herself.

"Does it matter?" he laughs. "Party is a party. Hope to see you guys out there tonight," he says, then eyes me again before walking away.

"Ugh," Treena moans. "That guy annoys me."

"Tri Delt?" I ask.

"A sorority. Trey mentioned going to Colt's, this club that plays country music, but . . . he didn't say there was a sorority party going on."

"Not a fan of sorority parties?" I ask.

"They're fine, whatever. There are a bunch of girls in my English class, and I think I'm just too brown for them. Like, they're really blond."

"Sounds fun," I say.

"Yeah, and they're all just perfectly gorgeous," she says, picking at her arm self-consciously.

"Tree, you're beautiful," I say, defending her.

"They're, like, models. And Trey's friends with them."

243

I sigh, automatically knowing—and hating—what I'm going to ask next. "Do you want to go to the club?"

She looks at me, her eyes alight, then looks back down. "No, no, it's just us tonight. I can see Trey tomorrow. . . ."

"Tree . . ." I say.

"No, it's our night. I want to spend time with you."

"Tree . . ." I say again, because sometimes she needs a push to be honest. And while I want her to say no again, I know she won't.

"Maybe."

"All right. Let's go," I say, relenting for her sake. "Plus, I need to get the full college experience and I haven't been to a club yet."

"We should get someone to drive us," she says, already planning. "Girls drink free there, and even though we're not twenty-one, we can still get by. I wonder if . . ."

"I'm on it," I say, taking out my phone and texting the only other person I know here.

TWENTY

"Well, this isn't *exactly* how I planned to spend my Wednesday night," Bennett says when we get inside the club. It was free to get in, because we arrived before eleven, and instead of getting yellow bands like most people, our hands were marked with do-not-serve-them-because-they're-babies black Xs. But, according to Tree, that doesn't seem to matter much.

"Not a fan of country music?" I ask him as I watch Treena peer around for Trey.

"Dead tractors, broken hearts, and missing dogs? Not so much." Just as he says that, a song comes on about a sexy tractor, and I start laughing. The club is big and loud, with lights beaming down onto the dance area. We're on the outskirts right now, looking at the dancers. There are tables and a few bars around us, boxing in the dance area where, currently, everyone is doing a very choreographed line dance. I feel like I'm in a musical.

"Do you think people practice before they come?" I ask, pointing.

"I know I do," Bennett says, and I laugh. I notice a few people in the front, leading the line, so I guess they teach it as the songs play. It all seems so forced; how is this fun?

"Trey!" Treena shouts, and we turn around to see Trey walking toward us, with girls on both sides of him.

"Baby, what are you doing here?" Trey asks, reaching out to her. The backup girls look at each other, then eye Treena. I can see what she meant earlier—the girls are gorgeous.

"Your friend Brad said we should come," she says sweetly, reaching up to give him a kiss.

"Awesome," he says, and I'm not sure if it's sarcastic or if he's really pleased to see her. "Come on, let's get you a drink."

"This is going to be an interesting night," Bennett mumbles, and I nod.

A few minutes later, Treena is holding two red drinks and pulling me into the bathroom.

"What's up? And, um, why are we going into a stall?" I ask, as she closes the door behind me.

"Trey has a fake ID, so he was able to get us these." She hands me my cup. "But since we're underage, we can't, like, drink them out there. So. Drink," she says, and starts chugging.

I look at Treena, high school good girl Treena, never entertaining the thought of drinking, and shake the image out of my head. Because that's not her anymore at all. And as I raise the cup I realize it might not be me, either. I take a sip of the drink, and it's fruity and cold. I look at her, and then back at where I am. "This is a little extreme—we're in a bathroom stall, standing over a toilet, and secretly drinking. Something is wrong with this picture."

Treena shakes her head. "Yeah, what's wrong is you're not drinking."

I place the cup to my lips again, and drink.

Treena is laughing by the time she's done. "Ugh, brain freeze."

"Ugh," I say, finishing off my drink. I don't feel any different yet, but knowing I will in a little bit, like I did last night, is oddly . . . freeing.

"Okay, let's go back out," she says with another giggle.

Trey and Bennett are by the bar—Trey surrounded by more girls and Bennett standing next to him, also talking to the girls, with his hands in his pockets. Treena magnetically attaches herself to Trey's hip, and I find myself next to Bennett, of course.

"Have fun?" he asks with a grin.

"Loads. Trey has an ID, apparently."

"Oh, I know. And with great power comes great responsibility . . . which he does not have."

"Spider-Man?" I ask.

"Uncle Ben, but yeah, Spider-Man."

"You are such a dork," I say.

"Hey, you knew the reference."

I smile, and awkwardly look down. Behind me, I hear Treena laugh, and turn to see her trying to command attention among the other blond girls, who, at least to me, don't stand a chance. Treena is just so much more of everything. I notice Bennett looking, and ask, "So where's *your* flock of women?" I gesture toward the array standing around Trey and Treena.

"Left them at home. It's exhausting bringing them around, you know? Someone is always hungry, someone always has to use the bathroom; I mean, come on."

I laugh and start to feel the alcohol seeping into my body. My face feels lighter again, brighter. I'm getting used to the feeling. I look over at Treena again to see how she's doing, and she's lapping up the attention, basking in Trey's glow, and I shake my head. She's going to get hurt. I just know it. Then I look over at Bennett, who's staring at me, and I feel brave. I feel stronger. What was it Jessica said about my mother—why paint an orange when you can paint the sky? I want to paint the sky.

"Want to dance?" I ask him.

"I don't think I can," he says, looking at the still-choreographed routine.

"I can't, either. Let's look stupid together," I say, and he gives in.

"If you say so." He takes my hand and leads me to the dance floor. We stay toward the back, away from the group of good dancers. At first we try to keep up—three steps to the right, three to the left, turn, turn, clap, toe, heel—but after a while we give up, and as I feel a whirl around me, I know I'm feeling good. I'm feeling different. I'm feeling lighter.

I bump into him, and we both laugh. He takes my hand and twirls me in a circle, completely abandoning the routine, and I come in close, then back out again. I spin into his arm, so I'm wrapped up in him with my back to his chest. He puts his other arm around me and I close my eyes, moving in time with him, feeling his weight against mine. I turn around, still linked in his embrace, and stare up at him. He's so close, and his eyes are hesitant. But I'm not.

The song ends and another one comes on, but I don't care—I don't move. The world is spinning around us, but we're on solid ground. A force pushes into me, and I spin around as a guy trips by.

"Ouch," I say, rubbing my arm.

"You okay?" he asks, taking a step back from where we were and shaking his head.

"Yeah, fine," I say, and I want to ask, "Where were we?" but the words don't come out.

"Hey!" I look over and see Treena beckoning me.

"Oh, um, I should—"

"Yeah, I'll be right here," he says, pushing his hair back and leaning against the wall.

I walk over to Treena, upset with that guy for knocking me back, and frustrated with myself for not doing anything.

"Nothing between you guys, huh?" Treena asks, giggling.

"We're friends," I say again, this time joining in her laughing.

"Well, you should go for it," she says. "Kiss him! I dare you to kiss him. Trey!" she calls, looking toward him. "Maude's going to go make out with Bennett."

"Tree!" I yell.

"Good. Dude needs to get some action," Trey says, and I blush uncontrollably. "Here," he says, handing me another cup.

"Do I have to run to the bathroom again?" I ask.

"Nope, just soda," he says with a wink. I take a sip. Definitely not just soda.

"How much have you had to drink?" I ask Treena.

"Oh, you know," she laughs, and I know it's more than the one drink we had together. And I'm starting to wonder if she drank *more* than the one time she mentioned to me when I first arrived.

"And everything's okay?" I ask, glancing at Trey, then her.

"Everything is great," she says, smiling, looking at Trey, who's also looking at another girl. But maybe that's just them. Maybe he's only talking to that girl, and it's innocent.

"Okay," I say, nodding. "I'm going to go to the bathroom, cool?"

"See you in a bit," she says with a wink, and I leave. I finish my drink quickly, then, inside the restroom, stare at myself in the mirror. My eyes look deeper, my face seems paler, but it's probably the lights. The me in the mirror is spinning a little bit, but I feel good. I feel brave.

I can't help but think I look more like my mother here, and maybe it's just because I know more about her. She might have come here. No, she wouldn't have come to a country music club. But she would have gone to a club. To a party. She would be the one turning heads. She would have been confident and in control.

Maybe I do have a little bit of that in me.

I leave the bathroom with one destination in mind. I locate Bennett easily—right where he was earlier. But to my dismay, that same pixie-haired girl from the dorm party a few days ago is talking to him.

I straighten up and walk right toward them.

"Hey," I say, eyeing her, then glancing coyly at him.

"Hey," he says, automatically putting his hand around me, on the small of my back. Like I'm with him. My face heats up, and I can't suppress a smile.

"Hi, Maude," she says. "Was just stopping by to say hi—ugh, I was dragged here by my roommate."

"We were, too," Bennett says with an exaggerated eye roll, and I nod in agreement.

"Well, giddy-up, I'll talk to you guys later," she says with a quick wave. She walks away and I turn toward Bennett.

"Hey," I say, looking up to him.

"Hey," he says simply, earnestly. No joke, nothing.

"Having fun?" I ask, cocking my head to the side and letting my hair spill over my shoulder.

"Surprisingly, yes. Which I never thought I'd say at a place like this." He smiles, leaning against the wall. His hand drops from my back and I furrow my brow in frustration. So I move in closer, facing him, only a few inches away. "How is the couple doing?"

"We don't have to talk about them," I say, shaking my head and walking closer until we're basically touching. I put my hands on the wall, on both sides of his waist.

"Okay," he says nervously. "What do you want to talk about?"

"What's your . . . favorite comic?" I ask, going for his interest.

"That's like asking my favorite child, if I had children," he says, and I don't move, so he answers, "Probably *Blankets*, this graphic novel about growing up and falling in love and family and stuff. I read it last year, and it really felt . . . real, I guess." He's babbling; I'm making him nervous. I never knew I had the power to do that. It fills me up and pushes me forward.

"It sounds good." I lean closer to him. "I have a confession for you," I say, and he hesitantly asks, "What?"

"I read *Sailor Moon*." I smile.

"I *knew* you were holding out on me." He grins.

"There's more," I say. "I was a Sailor Scout for Halloween last year."

"NO!"

"Ask Treena," I say. Our school had a dance, and it was kind of lame, but we got to dress up. That was the best part.

"Which scout were you? Let me guess. Brown hair . . . Jupiter?"

"Correct!" I grin.

"You probably should have brought the costume. I'm just saying. . . ."

"I didn't know I'd meet you," I say, looking him right in the eyes. He looks at me like he's trying to figure me out, like he's debating what to do, so I take a leap and lean forward. I feel his hands rise to my shoulders, then slowly make their way down to my wrists.

"Maude," he says gently.

"Yes?" I ask, raising an eyebrow and leaning in.

"Maude," he says again, a little stronger, grabbing hold of my wrists. "Not . . . now."

I freeze in place. "What?"

"Not now," he sighs. "This isn't . . . this isn't the right time." His voice sounds strained.

I recoil, feeling my cheeks redden. I thought he wanted this, too. I thought he was hinting at it. He danced with me; he put his hand on my back. He was close all week. And now, when we have a chance, no?

"Then when is the right time?" I ask, crossing my arms

in front of me. "When I'm gone?"

"No, it's not like that," he says, rubbing his face with his hand.

"Then what is it like?" I ask, frustrated.

"This isn't you," he says.

"How do you know this isn't me?" I ask. "This could be me."

"But it's not."

"Then tell me—who *am* I? Because I'm *dying* to find out," I say sarcastically.

"Well, right now, you're drunk. And we aren't going to do anything when you're drunk."

"You liked me last night when I was drinking," I point out.

"And I didn't do anything then, either."

"And when I'm sober?"

"What, did you want me to just start making out with you right before you met Jessica? Because that might have been awkward," he says, biting back at me. I purse my lips and shake my head. Why is this so hard? Why can't I even do this right?

He sighs, and puts his hands on my arms again. I step back, away from his embrace. "I do like you, but not like this. You haven't acted like this all week, and now, after finding out about your mother, you start . . . changing? The short skirt, the pushiness? It's not you."

"Well, maybe it is."

"And maybe it's not," he says, and I shake my head again.

"You're just scared," I say, not sure what he might be scared of, but feeling it's the right thing to say.

"Yeah, I am, and you know that. I thought you got it."

"And I thought you got me," I say.

"I thought I did, too," he says, and I frown at him, squinting my eyes until he's merely a blur. What was I thinking, anyway? Who does he think he is, telling me who I am, or who I can be? I can be or do whatever I want.

I turn around and though I hear him call my name, I ignore his voice. I have a new destination in mind.

I'm shaking by the time I get to the bar. It's not the one where Trey and Treena are sitting. I don't want to talk to them right now, see them in their happiness.

I know the bartender won't serve me, but that doesn't mean they won't serve anyone else around. I spot a guy who has a wristband, and he looks at me appreciatively. He looks familiar, and I realize it's Trey's friend Brad. I stand up straight, chest out, and lean casually on the bar, hiding my one X-marked hand behind my back.

"Hello," he says, eyeing me up and down, and it feels different, getting this attention. He does look just like Trey, and it's annoying, but he's hot so whatever.

"Hello yourself," I say with my best forward voice.

"You're Treena's friend, right?" he asks, smiling at me.

"Maude, yes. And you're Trey's friend."

"Brad," he laughs. "Can I get you a drink?" he asks, and bingo.

"Sure." I smile.

"What are you drinking?"

"Whatever you're drinking," I say, realizing that I have no idea what we've been drinking all night.

"Coming right up," he says, turning back to the bar. I look back and Bennett's right behind me.

"What are you doing?" he asks.

"I'm having fun. What are *you* doing?" I ask him.

"Come on, let's go find the others and get out of here. I'm not going to just leave you by the bar."

"Why? I'll be perfectly fine," I say stoically.

"Maude, come on, I feel bad about what I said. Let's just go back, and—"

"Hey, I know you," Brad says. "You're in my class, right?" He hands me a drink. Bennett looks at him, then back to me, then back to him again.

"Yeah," he says. "Hey, Brad."

"OH! You did that homework for Trey and me when we had that game. Dude, thank you. You saved my ass."

I look at Bennett, and his ears redden. He does homework for Trey?

"It was just the one time," he says to Brad, but I know he's saying it for my benefit.

"Whatever," he says. "Hey, weren't you going to hook up with some chick tonight? I heard Trey saying something about that."

Bennett shoots me a look and I feel it in my heart.

Then he looks at Brad. "Turns out that 'chick' wasn't who I thought she was."

I breathe in deep and glare at him. Brad is clearly oblivious to what's going on, since he adds, "So? Have fun, then get rid of her."

"Fascinating suggestion," Bennett says, glaring at me. "Don't you think, Maude?"

"Yep," I say, staring right back at him.

"Am I missing something?" Brad asks, ever observant.

"No, Bennett was just leaving and he came to tell me. Bye, Bennett!"

"Maude, come on."

"Bye, Bennett!" I say again, sweetly, and he glares at me before turning around to leave. My heart thumps in my chest as I turn back to Brad. "So." I take a sip of the drink and get back to the buzz I had earlier, before it was crushed.

"So," he says, moving in close, just as I did to Bennett earlier. I feel him hovering around me, feel his breath on my neck. "Tell me about yourself."

"Not much to tell," I say as I feel his hand on my waist. The touch wakes me up. His glassy eyes look down on me not like I'm someone, but more like I'm something. A prop. A goal for the night. I shrug his hand off my waist and step back.

"What?" he asks, grabbing my waist again and pulling me against him. Body on body. His hand is strong, and I try to break free, but I can't. I put my hand on his chest to push back, but he takes it as an invitation, and starts brushing his lips against my collarbone. Images flash before my eyes of this happening, of what could happen next. And I think of Bennett, who would never have done something like this to me. And I'm mortified and scared as tears spring to my face. But my reflexes kick in, and when pushing against him doesn't work again, I bring my leg up and knee him as hard as I can.

"What the hell?" he gasps, grabbing his crotch. I run toward the bathroom, hear him yelling "bitch" behind me. When I get inside, I'm panting and crying. I look at the sinks and see Treena there, staring at herself in the mirror.

"Tree!" I yell. "I'm so stupid, I'm so stupid." I run over to her, and when she turns around, she has tears in her eyes and black mascara lines running down her cheeks. "What? What happened?"

"Trey," she hiccups. "I caught him kissing another girl."

"Oh my god," I say, hugging her. "Are you okay?"

"No! I shouldn't have come here," she exclaims. "If I didn't come, I wouldn't have known, then we would have been okay."

"Wait, what?" I ask, pulling away.

She shakes her head, but I make her talk. "I kind of thought he might have other girls, but I just . . . I didn't want to know if I was right . . ." she says.

"Why? WHY would that be okay?"

"Because look at him!" she nearly shouts, gesturing

toward the door. "I'm not dumb. All those lunches he had with girls? They weren't just friends."

"Then why are you with him?"

"I'm not from his universe!" she says, flailing her arms around dramatically, and she's insanely overreacting. "I know there are other girls, but there's also me. He *chose* me, too. And I don't want to lose him."

"Tree, that's ridiculous. You're so much better than him. If he's cheating, get rid of him. Find a guy who doesn't. Someone a million times better."

"No!" she says. "I want Trey. He's so . . . he's so good to me. I mean, it's not just his looks. He's nice and sweet," she sobs. "Like last night, he really was nice. He likes me. And I really like him. I don't want to lose him."

I get that he's her first boyfriend, and I get that she's into him, but I'm worried about how hard she's falling. Especially for someone like this. I knew something was off about Trey, I knew it. "He's not worth it," I say, trying to level with her. How can she see him as perfect, when he's clearly less than that? I thought he was crappy from the start, and I should have said something. "He's a shitty guy—why keep him around?"

"What do you know?" She turns on me. "You've never even had a boyfriend. You wouldn't know what it's like."

I balk and stare at her. "What? Tree . . ."

"I knew you didn't like him from the start. You were jealous that I had someone and you didn't. So that's why you went to Bennett, but you screwed that up, didn't you? I saw him out there pissed off."

"Tree—"

"No, if you didn't bring me to this club, I wouldn't have known."

"Me? You wanted to come! I wanted to stay at the carnival." I look down at my outfit and realize there was a reason for the skirt all along. She was always planning on going wherever Trey was, no matter if I wanted to or not.

"Of course you did, because that's your life. Safe. You don't take any chances."

"And what you're doing is so much better? Getting drunk every night just to please your awful boyfriend? Staying with a guy who doesn't want to be with just you? Why would I want to turn into that?"

"Because it's fun! I don't want to just go to carnivals and watch movies anymore. I want to stay out and party. I want to enjoy college. I'm not in high school anymore. I'm different. I don't *want* it to be like we were back then—I don't want to be that boring girl anymore."

"Boring girl like me?" I ask. I look at her standing there screaming at me in the bathroom, and I don't recognize her. I don't recognize the Treena I used to know and love. This is not her. This is a warped twin who took over her body. And I have no idea what to do with it. "Treena," I say, going closer to her. I won't give up on her. "*What* is all of this about? Talk to me."

She shakes her head and hits her tiny fist against the sink. "I'm trying, I'm trying so hard," she says.

"Trying what?"

"Everything! College! Fitting in! Do you think it's easy? It's terrifying. I'm just trying to be me, and I don't even know who I am. I just know I don't want to be that same girl who played it safe for her parents' sake back in high school."

"What was so bad about her?"

She shakes her head. "You'll see next year. Being the quiet, smart girl isn't enough anymore. And I don't know how to balance that girl with the one I want to be now. I don't know how to be her anymore for you."

"For me?" I ask. Did college change her so quickly? "You shouldn't have to be anyone for me."

"Then, please, just let me be the crazy girl who's upset that her guy is with another girl."

I look at her, and she's right. She's different, and she can't go back to the girl I remember, as much as I want her to. This is a new layer, a new version. So I shake my head and leave her to figure herself out right there. If we say anything more, we might regret it.

I open the door, and stumble right onto someone outside. "Oof," I say, looking up at Bennett. Of course.

"What?" I ask, not in the mood for anything or anyone.

"Jesus, Maude, I'm just looking for Treena. I heard what happened, so I'm trying to get her so I can take her home. Don't worry, I'm not trying to take you away from the fun you're so clearly having."

I look at him, and I want to cry for everything that happened, and everything that didn't. But the room starts spinning and the lights get brighter and the noise gets louder. It feels like everyone is looking at me, and yet no one knows I'm here. And suddenly I feel tired, really tired, from the weight of the day. So I throw my arms around his shoulders and everything turns black.

TWENTY-ONE

THURSDAY

I wake up and have no idea where I am. I know the smell, I know the feeling, but I don't know where I am, and I don't know how I got here. My heart starts racing as the reality sets in—I don't know how I got here. Terrified, I jerk up and flick my eyes open.

Bennett's room. Oh. Okay. My breathing is fast and furious and it's only when I calm it down that I realize how much my head hurts. "Shit," I whisper.

"You deserve that," I hear to my left. I look over and Bennett is lying on his roommate's bed, looking at the ceiling. He sounds so cold. I have no idea why, and I still have no idea why I'm here.

"What?" I ask, my voice scratchy. I stretch my legs and they feel bare against the sheets. I look quickly, fearing there might be another surprise waiting for me, and realize I'm not bottomless, just wearing a very short skirt that isn't mine. I look up and when I see Bennett again, everything starts flashing back.

"Oh my god," I say, bringing my knees to my chest and covering my face with my hands. All of that happened last night. All of it was my doing. I was acting instead of thinking. I was someone else. *Why* did I do all of that? Why did I let myself do it?

I think of Brad, and him making a pass at me. How scared I was. How much worse it could have been. I think of Treena yelling at me in the bathroom, and how awful she was. I remember the look of pain in Bennett's eyes when I walked away. My heart feels like it's breaking inside, and I'm crumbling. I feel the lump in my throat as I sniff back a tear.

"Hey," he says, but I can't answer. Everything is coming back, and I don't want it to. Everything hurts. I'm awful. "Hey," he says again, but I shake my head.

"I'm so sorry," I manage to get out before the tears start falling, both from emotional and physical pain. My head is throbbing.

I hear him get up, and then I feel his bed give and shift. I feel his hand on my shoulder.

"It's okay," he says.

"No, it's not," I say, sitting up, knowing I must look terrible between the tears and the snot and whatever makeup is left from last night, probably already running down my face. But I don't care. I don't deserve nice right now. "How could I?" I ask.

"You weren't yourself," he says soothingly.

"That's just it. How did I let myself change so much? How was I so . . . so mean?"

"You had a long day," he says. "And you drank a lot."

"I was terrible to you."

"True," he says.

"Then why am I here?"

He looks at me carefully. "You don't remember?"

I shake my head. "I remember yelling at you," I start, and he looks down and nods. "I remember talking to Brad, and kneeing him in the crotch."

"Wait—why did you knee Brad in the crotch?" he asks, looking up.

"He tried kissing me. He was . . . forceful."

"*What?*" I nod in response, and Bennett stands up and starts pacing. "I knew I hated that guy for a reason."

"Bennett," I say.

"No, seriously, he did that to you?"

"Yeah, it's okay; I mean, I took care of it."

"But what if it was worse? What if he does it to another girl who doesn't think to fight back?"

I shrug because I don't know. And I don't want to think

about that—or him right now. "We should tell Trey. Oh god, Trey," I say, and Bennett sits down next to me again. "He cheated on Treena, and she and I had a huge fight in the bathroom."

"So I heard. She was . . . emotional," he says.

"What did she say?"

"Um," he says, looking away. "Well, by the time she came out of the bathroom, you were passed out."

"Wait, what?" I ask.

"Yeah, you stormed out of the bathroom and then passed out. On me."

"On you," I repeat.

"Thank god you're light," he says, and I shake my head.

"I'm so sorry," I say again.

"It's okay," he repeats.

"I hate Trey," I say forcefully.

"Yeah, you made that known last night. A few times. When we walked from the club to my car. I think everyone surrounding us knew."

"Oh god." I cover my face again. "Treena was so pissed when I said I didn't approve of him. She must hate me. He must hate me. Well, I don't care if he hates me, actually."

"I don't know that I'd be worried about them if I were you."

"Wait, why?" I ask.

"Because they got you drunk. They kept giving you drinks. And then when you went to console Treena when she was crying about Trey, she got pissed at you."

"I think I remember some of that."

"It was dramatic," he says. "And that's when you passed out, and she went back to Trey, and it was last call, so I got to gather you all up."

"Because you were designated driver . . ." I remember.

"Yep, an honor and a duty." He half smiles.

"We all owe you."

"You have no idea," he says, shaking his head.

"So what happened next?"

"Um." He pauses. "You were mad at me for . . . reasons," he says, and though I don't remember exactly why, I know it had to do with him shooting me down. Oh god.

"I threw myself at you, didn't I," I moan.

"More or less," he says, looking away.

"I'm really, really sorry," I say, mortified.

"It was . . . educational?" he says as a question.

"Shut up." I chuckle.

"I mean, I know I'm extremely good-looking."

"Ha."

"No, really, you're not the first. There were five more at the door just this morning," he jokes, and I know he's saying this to cheer me up, which is wrong because I should be cheering him up after how I got last night. "Anyway," he continues, "you were fuming, and the two Ts were in the back making up."

"What?" I ask, crinkling my nose. "After he cheated on

her, she took him back?"

"So it seemed. I didn't watch, obviously, but let's just say there were noises."

"Gross," I whine. "Why would she do that? She deserves so much better."

"I agree. I told you I worried about him doing that. Why won't she leave him?"

I think about it, and then I remember a slice of our conversation. "She said she likes him, and she doesn't think she'll do better. She's okay with it, as long as she doesn't know. How sick is that?"

He shakes his head and looks angry. "That's not right. He can't do that to her. And she can't do that to herself."

"That's what I said. She didn't agree."

"I don't get it," he says. "When I found out about . . . well . . . as soon as I heard I was cheated on, I was gone. I didn't want to put up with that shit, you know?"

He shakes his head again, and then looks at me. There's an awkward silence, and then he continues. "Yeah, so when we got back here, they went to her room and shut the door before you could say a word. So, despite your struggles, I got you in here."

"I struggled?" I ask, honestly not remembering anything. Why would I not want to stay here? After everything he's done for me?

"You were still pissed at me."

I sigh, shaking my head. "I can't believe I don't remember

all of that. I can't believe I got that bad . . . it's just . . ."

"You were in a bad place. It's okay to go crazy every once in a while."

"But I don't do that."

"Okay, yeah, maybe you were bad, but you can't hate yourself for something you couldn't control."

"But I could have. I could have stopped drinking. I could have said no."

"Yeah, but you didn't. So some part of you must have wanted to."

I think about that. I guess so. "I wanted to see what it was like, this college lifestyle. I wanted to see how I'd do, knowing how my mother was."

"Yeah, you said that. And?"

"Parts were fun."

"The dancing was fun," he says.

"Yeah, and then parts sucked." I laugh. "I feel like you're going to give me a 'never drink again' speech now."

"That would be a bit hypocritical of me."

"So what now?" I ask.

"Now . . . we get breakfast. I'm starved."

I look over at him and he's smiling. "You sure you don't hate me?"

"Only a little." He grins and I reach over and hug him. Not a passionate hug, not a hug that's trying to be more than it is. Just a hug. And when I feel his arms go around me, I know he feels it, too.

TWENTY-TWO

Bennett and I get ready—Treena isn't in her room, so there's no awkward confrontation—and then eat breakfast at the cafeteria on campus, and it's normal. More than normal; it's comfortable. Like last night didn't happen. Like we're starting over. And it feels okay. I mean, minus the vomit-inducing headache.

I pull my phone out to see if there's anything from Treena, but not a word. I'm not sure who should call first. I'm not sure I want to go there yet. A flash passes through my mind, and I open up my phone's notes, remembering that I typed something out yesterday.

"Hey, what's Lichgate? Is it a club or something?" I ask.

"Lichgate? How do you know about it?" he asks, looking surprised.

"Jessica mentioned it. She said my mom loved it there."

"Huh," he says, nodding his head. "Let's go to it."

"What *is* it?" I ask.

"I think you'll like it." He smiles and leads me to the parking lot. Though we've traveled quite a bit together, it's never been by car, and for some reason I'm comforted by the sight of his tiny old blue Hyundai. It's not fancy; it's just him. When he starts the ignition and turns around to back out of his spot, our hands touch on the armrest. But instead of taking his away, he wraps it around mine. And I happily let him.

◇◇◇◇

After a few minutes of driving, we pull into a church's parking lot. "This is not what I had in mind at all. And I'm pretty sure my mom was Jewish."

"We're just parking here," Bennett says, letting go of my hand to get out of the car. I get out, too, and walk over to him. Our hands magnetically find each other again. But this time, instead of just holding on, our fingers lace up together, holding on tighter, more intimately. I inhale, aware of our touch and how my pulse is speeding up. My spirits magically lift, and I feel bright. And this time it's for real, and not an illusion brought on by alcohol.

Next to the church is a wooded area. A forest expands sky-high and we follow a sidewalk toward a small gap between two trees. "I assume you know where we're going, because, to me, it just looks like we're about to get lost in the woods."

He smiles. "Maybe that was my plan all along." We walk

a few steps in, following a small dirt path with trees surrounding us. A giant wooden board greets us, welcoming us to Lichgate, and when I open my mouth to ask, once again, what it is, he just raises his eyebrows and pulls me along.

We continue following the wooded path until we're completely hidden from view. And then, a light pokes through and the way opens up to an immense clearing. It's like all of the sunshine has been reserved for this one soft, green lawn. It's large and bright, and just rolling grass and an ancient oak tree in the middle.

"It's beautiful," I say, gazing up at the old tree that has to be hundreds of years old. It's huge and warped, wrinkles upon wrinkles decorating it. It's impossible to see the entire thing at once; I have to turn my head to view all of the branches reaching high up, and then dropping way down, touching the ground like fingers. Bennett leads me toward the base of the tree and I follow, feeling warm and comfortable. We stand in the shade, and I touch the bark, the leaves.

"*This* is Lichgate?" I ask, once again surprised by something my mother liked. She is full of surprises, it seems. But this—this is something, much like her art, that I appreciate, too.

"It's been here for years," Bennett explains. "Like, before Florida was really Florida, you know? We learned about it in one of my classes; we were assigned to do an art project on it. A while ago, an FSU environmental studies professor decided to preserve it. She bought the tree and built the cottage over there." He points to a small, fairy-tale-looking cottage in the corner that I didn't even notice.

I marvel at the tiny house. "It's so cute."

"Yeah. She lived there for years, and after she died, a charity was put together to keep it all up. It's really just here, not taken care of by anyone. I love it because no one messes with it. I mean, anyone could come here and totally vandalize the place, but you just know not to. It's like it belongs to everyone. I think it's really cool."

"It's because it's so pretty," I say.

"I come here sometimes to do schoolwork. It's quiet."

"I can't believe my mother used to come here, maybe even painted here."

"Yeah, it's cool you found that out. I prefer this to country music clubs." He nods and I agree.

I walk in a circle, taking it all in, and feel my feet against the grass. And the weirdest sensation comes over me. This is it—this is a part of her. She was here. I don't know when, and I don't know why, but I know she stood at least somewhere around here. And I swear, I can almost feel her touching me. I close my eyes and take in the moment. Then take out my camera to capture it all, wondering if she did the same.

"You know, once the story of the tree got out, people wanted to see it. So, I don't know, sometimes learning about something's history is a good thing," he says, and his words don't lose their meaning on me.

I stare at the branches nearly touching my feet, twisting

along the grassy ground. My hand grazes the rough texture. "Perhaps. Can we see the house?" I ask.

"Yeah, it's open," he says, and I push myself to walk away from the spot, because really, this entire place is a spot. Her spot. Our spot.

We walk out of the shade and toward the small, fenced-in house.

"This is amazing," I say as we pass a small garden full of vegetables and brightly colored flowers. Peppers, carrots, peas are all marked in a line.

We get to the gate out front, and Bennett stops.

"Okay, so this is her lichgate, thus the name of the park. Apparently it's, like, a fence that separates a church from a graveyard, so a place in between," he says, and I think about my in between right now. In between high school and college. In between the before and after of finding out about my mother. The in-between of who I was and who I'm slowly becoming. "She built it so she could go between rest and being alive and living."

"Kind of nice and creepy," I say, touching the gate.

"Yep. So we're, I guess, going to be alive when we cross it. Or dead. I'm not sure which way is which."

I think of my mother, and shake my head. She never really had a chance for an in-between. She moved so quickly from high school to college to me to death. There was no time for transition for her, and not for the first time I wonder what she could have become.

The house is an old cottage, with a stone foundation on the bottom, wooden walls, shuttered windows, and even a chimney atop it.

"Are you sure we can go in?" I ask when we approach the old front door.

"Yep, it's open for tours."

He opens the door.

Inside, it's just as I expected, and my heart soars with how adorable the little house is. Everything is wooden inside—wooden floors, walls, dressers, bookshelves. "It feels like Hansel and Gretel lived here," I say as we walk inside and take it in.

"Right? So, that's her kitchen," he says, pointing to a small room at the back. It's not completely outdated, as I thought it would be; it has just enough appliances to make a meal. We pass a tiny living room with a non-wooden couch, and then go up a rickety set of wooden stairs. At the top is her bedroom, with a small dresser and tiny bed. I turn around to look out the window and see the tree staring back at us, hugging us with its branches. I can see why she wanted to live here; I'd love to wake up to that view every morning. Everything is quiet. My mind is quiet. After last night, I needed this.

I turn around and see Bennett staring at me, his eyes soft and smiling. I walk to him and wrap my arms around his waist, pulling him toward me. "Thank you for taking me here. I needed it."

His arms come around my shoulders and I can feel his cheek pressed against the top of my head. I close my eyes and lean into him, knowing that hugs don't usually last this long, at least they never have for me, but not caring. Because right now, this is the only place I want to be.

He pulls away a little, and I feel a repeat of last night. I brace myself for him to push me back, but something about the way he looks at me says he won't. He rests his forehead against mine, and, this close, I'm able to see him, really see him. There's apprehension in his eyes, fear, and I want to tell him it's okay, that it'll be okay, just like he told me earlier. But when I open my mouth, his face changes to resolution, and he takes my chin in his hands and he kisses me.

I feel light, like I'm floating, like nothing can hold me down as I lean into him, into our kiss. He was right—those other moments weren't perfect, especially last night. This is what we needed. His arms hold me tight as our kiss deepens and I smile and I laugh because I can't help it. The house collectively sighs, as if it, too, had been on edge as we danced around our feelings and our pasts. It engulfs us in a hug as he kisses me again, brushing my hair off my face with his hand.

"Okay?" he asks, searching my eyes.

I smile up at him, and answer, "Yes, okay."

He grins back and pulls me in for another kiss, and this time he's the one smiling and laughing and I don't want it to end. We add another memory to the house, something that's very much alive.

The house is not full of death; it's full of life.

◇◇◇◇

We walk back outside, back to the tree's reaching grip. Bennett pulls me down with him onto the grass, and we collapse against the strong base.

"I think we definitely broke one of your parents' rules," Bennett jokes, playing with my hand, tracing the lines and ridges with his finger.

"They said no boys . . . they never said no kissing boys."

"I feel it might be implied." He smiles.

"Well, it's all your fault," I say, resting between the crux of his arm and body.

"Oh, is it?" he asks, leaning back against the tree. He looks at me again, and then says, "You were unexpected."

"Good unexpected, or bad unexpected?" I ask.

"Definitely good. No other girl has ever turned down any advances within moments of meeting me—despite me not even offering anything."

"Oh, yeah," I say, covering my face with my hands. That *is* the first thing I said to him, wasn't it? "That's embarrassing."

"Not embarrassing," he says, taking my hand away. "Cute. You're different, and I like that."

"Every girl loves being called 'different.'"

"You know what I mean," he says.

"You are, too," I admit, and he smiles. "And also quite unexpected."

"Didn't expect Treena to have awesome friends like me?"

"Ha, no, it's not that. I just wasn't planning on . . . becoming invested in someone while here."

"Yeah." He takes my hand in his again. "And it's Thursday, so you've only got . . ."

"Two more days here."

"Right," he says.

"Right."

"And, after last time, I can't—"

"Bennett," I interrupt him.

"Yeah?" he asks, looking at me, clearly thinking about what comes next and not what's happening now.

"Let's not think about the future. Or the past."

"It's hard not to," he says sullenly, and I turn around and face him, placing my hands on his waist.

"Hey, we walked through the lichgate," I say.

"Okay," he says, confused.

"So we're alive. We're alive and living."

"Wasn't that the other side? Aren't we supposed to be dead on this side? Or something like that?"

"You're killing my motivational talk," I deadpan. "You've been giving them to me all week. It's my turn."

"Oh, sorry, continue." He grins, sitting up straighter and pulling me onto his lap so I'm somewhat kneeling around his outstretched legs, somewhat straddling them.

"We're alive. Let's just be alive together, okay?"

"Okay," he says, kissing me again.

"Luke Skywalker would not be worried."

"Please, I'm clearly more Han Solo."

"Does every guy want to be Han Solo?"

He looks at me and answers, "Obviously. He's a pirate. And he flies the *Millennium Falcon*. And he gets the girl." He's completely serious, and I smile. Because there's nothing fake about him. Nothing at all. So I lean onto him and he circles his arms around me. We stay like that for a while, as the wind blows through the leaves and passes over us.

The tree is all around us, and it still feels so large, so vast. We are two branches rising up, and falling back down, finding and twisting around each other. We look into each other's eyes, and when he kisses me again, I'm only thinking of the present.

There may be no future for us; there's just now. And now is enough.

TWENTY-THREE

We walk out from the park and head back to Bennett's car. "Capitol?" I ask. "Bee seems probably the scariest."

"Scarier than your grandmother or Chad?" Bennett asks.

"Well, okay, maybe not. But I think I want to start there, with her, since we weren't able to yesterday."

"Capitol," he repeats, authoritatively nodding in agreement. We get into the car and I assume he knows the way, so I just sit back and let him drive. "Excited? Nervous?" he asks.

"More nervous, really. There's always a chance she'll refuse to talk to us."

"There is that," he says, "but who can resist such charming people?"

"Someone who hates the questions we're going to ask?"

"Maude."

"Yes, Bennett?"

"You are far too pessimistic for our super-awesome detective adventures." I shake my head and laugh. Our ride is quiet, mostly, as I figure out what I want to say, how to even introduce myself without consequences. I let my mind wander until we park on the second floor of a garage.

When we get outside, I finally see the capitol building.

"Wow, that is . . . um . . . suggestive," I say.

"Yeah, I don't know what they were thinking. The domed building in the front is where the museum is. It's the old capitol. The, uh, erection behind it is where all the government stuff happens now. Pun embarrassingly intended. I couldn't help it."

"Gotcha," I say as we climb the steps to the historic building in front that looks more stately than the rest of Tallahassee, as if it belongs in D.C. and not a college town.

Bennett stops before we get inside. "Do you want me to come? I can stay here, you know. It's cool."

"No," I say, shaking my head. "I think, with Bee, I need moral support."

"Then moral support I will be," he says, and follows me through the doors.

Inside, we come face-to-face with a grand staircase. There's a plaque nearby on the wall, and I read that the building was originally erected in 1845, but more recently restored to look like it did in 1902. We could go upstairs and see the history of Florida's government, visit the gift shop, or walk to the reception desk. With a nod, we go to the desk.

"Hi, um," I say, hoping I sound intelligent to the woman behind the desk. She's older, probably a volunteer who remembers when this building was the new capitol and not the old one. "We're here to see Bee Shrayer?"

"Who?" the woman asks in a shaky voice, and I'm not sure if she didn't hear me or we're wrong, and Bee doesn't work here.

"Bee. Shrayer," Bennett says, louder and more slowly, using her married name like I did.

"Oh! Bee. Yes, she's upstairs. I'll call her down."

I steal a glance at Bennett while the woman places the call. He crosses his fingers, and I do the same, when she hangs up the phone.

"She'll be right down."

"Thanks," I say, and we walk over to an exhibit describing how most governors are sworn in on the very steps we just walked up. I get out my camera and take a picture of the staircase, the plaque, the old documents stored in glass cases.

"Can I help you two?" a woman—Bee—asks us. "Are you here for the school paper interview?"

I straighten up and instantly get nervous. This woman is the exact opposite of Jessica. She's dressed smartly, in a dark suit and matching glasses. But unlike Jessica, this woman ostensibly hates my mother. This is Bee, who refused to talk to me. And I'm here, in front of her. Not taking no for an answer, but also terrified. "Oh, no," I say, stumbling a bit. She's even more intimidating than I imagined. If Jessica was a carefree butterfly, Bee is concrete and stone. "Um, we are, I mean, I am . . . I'm Maude," I finally conclude.

"Maude," she muses. Then her eyes go from cloudy to bright as she realizes who I am. "Maude," she says again, turning my name into a reprimand. "How did you . . . why did you?"

"I'm sorry, we're sorry, for visiting you at work like this," I say quickly, hoping not to lose her while surreptitiously looking for guards. "I know you don't want to see me, and don't want to talk to me about my mother, but I had to find you. I'm only in town for another day, and I want to learn everything I can about my mother, and if that meant I had to track you down at work, I did it. I'm really, really sorry, but I have to know. If you don't want to talk to me, I'll leave, but I had to . . . try," I finish, taking a breath and letting the nervous energy out of my body.

She stares at me hard, crossing her arms in front of her body, and then moves her eyes to Bennett. "And you are?"

"A friend, ma'am," he says, looking as nervous as I feel.

She looks back at me, takes a breath, then says, "Come with me," motioning for us to follow her past the staircase and out a back door to a concrete courtyard that separates this building from the new one. We keep walking behind her, following the clicking of her heels, down another set of stairs so we're back to street level. She gestures to a black table with a yellow umbrella over it, and we all sit down. A part of me is relieved, while the other part is still on edge.

"This is where I oftentimes eat lunch," she says, breathing deep and not looking up to meet our eyes. "I thought it would be best to speak out here, away from my colleagues."

"Thank you," I say breathlessly.

"Don't thank me yet," she says, shaking her head and finally looking up. "I *told* you that I didn't want to get into this."

"I know, and I'm really sorry, but—"

"I told you that I wanted to leave it behind, but you came here anyway. You tracked me down at my job."

"It's just—" I start, cheeks heating up.

"I can have you escorted out, you know that, right?"

"I really just want to—"

"Want to what?" she demands.

"Talk," I finally get out, embarrassed. "I really just want to talk to you. If you don't want to answer, that's perfectly fine, I just needed to see you."

"But why me?"

"Because I only found a few people my mother knew, from an old high school photo, and I'd hate myself for not following up on all of them."

She assesses me and I stop blinking. "I admire your tenacity. But you still went about it the wrong way." She hesitates, then asks, "Why me?"

"I have nothing on her," I admit. "Just a few old photographs and some old stories from Jessica. I still don't know who my mother really was. And I don't want to leave until I get every story I can. So I can have something to hold on to, and inform me about . . ."

"About you?" she asks warily.

"Yeah," I admit.

"Right. Okay, well," she says, rubbing her hands together. "I still don't think I can help you."

"You can try?" I push, knowing this is the last time I'll ask. If she says no, we'll leave.

After what feels like an hour, she nods. "What do you know so far?"

So I tell her everything. Her eyebrows raise when I mention Key Club, and when I mention Jessica again, she lowers her head. All of this means something to her—I just don't know what.

"You have done a lot." She hesitates again, then says, "Claire and I were good friends in high school. Best friends. We met in a history class during our freshman year, and simply clicked. She was more outspoken than me, quite a bit, but she was, I suppose, the yin to my yang. Opposites attract and all that."

"What was she like back then?"

"She was smart and caring, and spirited, that's for sure. Always speaking her mind. She wasn't the kind of person who lied to you just to make you feel better. Though painful at times, it was also refreshing. It wasn't until later, when she became Clarabelle, that things changed."

"Her nickname," I say.

"Right. That stupid nickname." She shakes her head. "Have you ever seen a person act one way, and then completely change into another person a second later? To me, she was Claire, this amazing friend—this best friend—I had. But then when she met Jessica and fell into her other crowd, she became Clarabelle. And people loved Clarabelle so much, Claire rarely ever came back out."

I feel things clicking together and starting to make sense. How she could be one thing, and how she could be another. My mind flashes to Treena.

"So is that why you stopped being friends?" I ask.

Bee shakes her head. Under the table, I feel Bennett's hand on my knee, palm up. I place my hand in his for comfort. I like that he's here, but not interrupting, not making it about him. He's just *here*. "I was dating this guy Chad senior year. It was the first guy I really liked, and Claire knew that. She actually set us up. I'd liked him for a while, and . . . wow, I haven't thought of this in years."

She looks down at her long, thin fingers, and taps them gently. "As I'm sure you've guessed, he cheated on me with her."

My heart drops. For her, for me.

"I know it sounds absurd that I'm still upset about it

years later, but he was my first love. And she was my best friend. And worse, she knew how much it would affect me—not just being cheated on, but the similarity of it all," she says, then explains, "The same thing had happened to my mother—my father had an affair with her best friend. I cried to Claire dozens of times about it; she was there for me. At least I thought she was. But then . . . anyway, after that, we didn't talk. I just . . . I didn't understand how someone could change so quickly, and so completely."

"I'm so sorry." I look over at Bennett and he, too, is looking down. He's been there; he understands.

"Yes, well, it's okay now, obviously. But at the time, it felt like the end of the world." She pauses. "And high school is hard enough as it is."

"What happened after?" I ask, having to know. This story does have a happy ending, right? She's here now.

"Oh, a lot of things, but that's not important. I graduated school, went to college, and am here now. I never really spoke with her again, and it killed me. It still does, in a way." We're quiet for a second, letting her words settle among us. "I've only told one other person about all of this, my husband, and even he doesn't know the whole story."

"You shouldn't have had to go through that," I say, shaking my head.

"It's okay," Bee says, and she's strong, stronger than I would be. I probably would have kicked us out if I were her. She had reason to keep us away; I can't believe I pushed so hard. "I just didn't want to relive it. It's not just talking about it; it's you."

"Me?" I ask, confused.

She shakes her head. "I was scared of what I'd see. And I was right to be. You look just like her. You're her."

"Oh . . ." I say.

"It reminds me of all the things we said and did and shouldn't have. It reminds me that I hated her for what happened, but I hate myself, too, because I never got to . . . we never cleared things up before she . . ."

"Died," I say, and she puts her head in her hands and nods.

"She left, and I never said good-bye. We were best friends," she says again, sniffling. I put my hand on her shoulder and can't believe how different she is from Jessica, how strong she is. Her biggest regret is not forgiving my mother, for something that didn't need forgiving.

"I'm so sorry we brought all of this up."

"It's okay, it's okay," she says, shaking her head. "I just wish I was able to talk to her, just one more time. I've forgiven her now; maybe I would have, then."

"I'm sure she knew you didn't hate her."

"I just wonder what was going on in her mind that whole time. And I wish I could have been there for her . . . through it all."

I look at her carefully, and say, "You're a good friend. You really are."

"Thank you." She smiles gently, then furrows her

brow. "Can I ask you something?"

"Of course," I say.

"You came here looking for information about your mother. . . . What about your father?"

I balk. "I don't know who my father is," I admit. "Do you . . . ?"

"Oh, no. Like I said, we weren't talking then. I just wonder . . ."

"If it was Chad?" I answer her thought.

"Yes . . ."

"I don't know." I shake my head again. "And I don't know if I'll ever know."

"Are you going to see him while you're here?"

"I'm going to try," I say. "I'm curious."

She nods, then says, "Despite all that I've said, he's a good guy. At least he was."

Good, I think. "Good." I look back at her and see her glancing at the building, perhaps needing to leave. So I ask one more question. "Her art—did you know anything about her art?"

"Yes, I remember. I didn't get it, really, but I loved it. It was different . . . like her."

"I'm a photographer, and I just, you know, it's something we have in common."

She looks at me and nods, saying, "It's a good thing to have in common." She looks back at the building again, and I get it.

"We should leave you alone, let you get back to work."

"Yes, right," she says, almost in a daze. "I'm sorry I was not open to talking prior to today, but as you can tell, this was all a bit hard. But thank you for coming by. I think I needed to revisit Claire."

"Thank you for talking to us," I answer, getting up. Bennett stands next to me, his hand on my lower back.

Bee looks up at me and adds, "Your mother was wonderful. You should know that. She was crazy, and we didn't end on good terms, but she really was wonderful. She was my lifeline."

"Thank you," I say, meaning it. Because I needed to hear that. More than she knew.

◇◇◇◇

We leave Bee at the table, after I take her picture, and head back toward the car. We're walking through an alleyway bordering a restaurant that has beautiful graffiti on both sides—spray-painted images of a woman crying, the sun rising, an abstract stacking of squares. You wouldn't know this art was down here if you didn't step inside.

"So what now?" Bennett asks tentatively.

"Stopping would be so easy right now," I say, processing it all. It seemed so petty, but it wasn't. My mother wasn't the person I thought she was; she was hardly a person I would have been friends with, and certainly not a mom. Which makes sense—she was nearly my age. But still—it's hard realizing the mother I once had is someone I can't see myself in at all. Whenever I felt different, I always felt comforted by the fact that I might be a perfect replica of someone else. But I'm not really. Not at all. It's unsettling, and part of me wishes I never started this in the first place. "Okay, how about this—we leave it to fate," I say.

"Fate? That's so unlike you. Don't you like concrete answers?"

"Yes, but I don't know how many more concrete answers I can put up with," I admit, pulling my hair back. "There's Chad and my possible grandmother."

"Right, which to find first?"

"I'm . . . I'm scared of calling my possible grandmother again. I think . . . I don't want to be let down by her again."

"So, Chad?" he asks.

"Yeah, let's find Chad. If we do, great, but if we can't find his shop . . ."

"We stop," Bennett says, opening his car door for me.

"Yes, we stop."

In the car I steady myself, then type "Chad Glickman mechanic Tallahassee" on my phone, assuming that Jessica was right, and Chad is a mechanic here. And that his shop has a website, or at least contact information. I scroll through the results and find a few mechanics, but none that have Chad's name attached to them. Maybe the shops don't list their mechanics. My heart speeds up as I scroll some more, and I'm still not sure if I'm hoping to find him or hoping I won't. Because he might bring up a whole other round of questions. I change my search and just look for his name, but nothing appears that's promising. I change the search again and just look for mechanics in Tallahassee.

"Okay," I say. "There are ten results. Should we just . . . call them?"

"Better than visiting all of them," he says. "I just wish we knew what part of Tallahassee he worked in—that would narrow it down."

"Let's start over by the high school. Maybe he never moved out of that area," I decide, seeing two shops around there. Bennett gets out his phone and dials one number, while I click on the other.

As the phone rings, I realize I have no idea what to say. Just ask for him? Ask if he works there?

"Hello," a man says before I can decide on anything.

"Hi, um, I'm looking for Chad Glickman?"

"No Chad here."

"Oh, okay, thanks," I say, feeling dejected.

"No luck," Bennett says, putting his phone down.

"Same here," I say. Then I pick up my phone, and we both try again. And again. I'm not sure what to feel, as each call brings me excitement and dread and fear and hope.

"Hello?"

"Hi, I'm looking for Chad Glickman," I say, for the fourth time.

"Hold on, I'll get him," the voice says, and I freeze. It

worked. Chad Glickman works at this mechanic shop. And I have no idea which one it is, which one I called. I grab Bennett's arm and point to the phone. He hangs his up quickly, turning to me.

"What do I do?" I whisper frantically. Bennett shakes his head and I quickly drop my phone, ending the call.

"You hung up," he says, pointing out the obvious.

"I wasn't ready," I admit. "I mean, this is a guy my mother dated. Around the time I was born. There's a small chance he's my father. Probably not, but you never know. What do I say to that?"

"It's okay," he says, taking my hand in his. "Would you rather go visit him? We know where he is now, at least."

I think about it. I want to see him, definitely, but also I'm terrified. Of what he'll say. Of what he won't say. "I think . . . yeah . . . okay . . ." I say, noting the number I called, and which shop it's attached to. "This is so weird."

"This whole experience is weird," Bennett says, and I smile. "Do you want to go now, get it over with, or wait? We can go tomorrow if you'd rather, or—"

"Now," I say quickly. "Let's just go now."

He turns the car on. "Okay, let's go."

"I'm kind of scared," I admit, feeling adrenaline coursing through my veins as he starts to drive.

"I'm here," he says. "It'll be okay. And if it's not, we can leave."

I nod, reminding myself that leaving is always an

option. I look at Bennett and am happy he's here with me, but part of me still wishes it was Treena. Despite everything. I think back to what Bee said about my mom, and how her biggest regret is not making things right. I know, no matter what, I'll go back to Treena and we'll work things out. We won't ever lose each other, despite what we do, and knowing that comforts me, in a way. I don't want us to grow apart—I know we'll grow, but I want us to grow together.

She and I used to joke about who my dad could be—a celebrity, the president, anyone, really. And though I don't know about Chad, it's upsetting she's not going through this with me. "I wish I could tell Treena . . ."

"About this?"

"About everything. This. You."

"I think she knows who I am," he says, pulling back onto the road.

"You know what I mean," I say.

"So I get to be the topic of girl talk?"

"You wish." I shake my head. "There are some things you just really want to tell your best friend when they happen."

"She'll come around," he says.

"I know," I answer.

◇◇◇◇

We pull up to an old, weathered building with an open garage door. An equally weathered billboard in blue and white towers above us, reading CARL'S CARS.

"Looks like we're here," Bennett says, and I nod, looking up.

"So what now?" Before us, there are two cars in the open garage, both elevated, with a mechanic working underneath each one. There are stains on the floor, towels tossed around, and giant red toolboxes next to them. There's also a lot of noise.

"Well," he says, looking at me, "you can either go in there and ask for him, or we can turn around and go back to my dorm to make out."

I start laughing despite my nerves. "Tempting," I say.

"You can do it," he says, taking my hand. "The talking to him, that is. The making out we already know you can do."

"Thank you for the affirmation," I say. I look at the shop and think my whole unknown past could be through that door. And all I have to do is open it.

I turn to Bennett, but he cuts me off. "I know—I'll stay here."

I smile. "Thank you."

I get out of the car and open the front door of the building. A little bell rings, signaling that I'm here, and I look around. It's a small room with a few empty plastic chairs lining the wall. There's a TV playing the local news, and before me is a desk with one man standing behind it, scribbling something into a notebook. The room smells like gasoline, oil, and burnt coffee.

I look over the guy behind the counter. He's tall, taller

than Bennett at least, with dark brown frizzy hair. Hair like mine. He's wearing a red plaid shirt and has a few days' worth of scruff on his face.

Something tells me this is it. I walk toward him.

"Excuse me," I say, and he looks up at me. He has a pink scar on his cheek, I notice, right under his eye. "I was wondering if a Chad Glickman worked here?"

"Yeah," he says, standing up straight. "Did you call earlier?" I recognize a slight southern accent in his speech.

"Um, yes, sorry, dropped my phone," I say, blushing. "Um, is he here? Working today?"

"It depends." He rests one arm on the counter and leans to the side. "Who wants to know?" he asks with a grin, and that's when I know it's him. And I'm not sure if he's being nice or flirting with me, and that makes it all very uncomfortable.

So I answer simply, "Claire Fullman."

He jerks back, removing his arm from the counter, and drops his mouth open. He furrows his brow and stares at me, takes me in. Then he remembers to breathe—as I do—and drums his fingers on the counter. "Claire Fullman?" he asks. "I haven't heard that name in years. How do you know her?"

"I'm her daughter," I admit.

His face goes white, ashen, and his fingers stop moving. "Daughter?"

"Yes. Um, she gave birth to me before she . . ."

"Yeah, yeah," he says, looking down. He rubs the back of his neck with his right hand, and I can see wrinkles stretching his face. "I know, I remember."

I can see this is hurting him, surprising him. I need to backtrack. "Sorry for throwing all of that at you . . . so quickly. Chad, I'm assuming?"

"Yeah, I'm Chad," he says, nodding. "And you are?"

"Maude," I say.

"Nice to . . . nice to meet you," Chad says. "Why don't we . . . um . . . okay, hold on. I'll be right back," he says, then walks through a door behind the desk.

As soon as he's gone, I let out a long breath. I can't shake the sight of him being surprised to see me. I can't deny that it might mean something else—that I might mean something else to him.

The door opens again, and he's back, looking less flustered. "Okay, sorry, let's go outside. I'm taking a break," he says, and walks out from behind the counter. I follow him out to the side of the building, where there is a pile of tires and a wooden picnic table with an ashtray atop it. He signals for me to sit down, then gets out a package of cigarettes. "Mind if I . . . ?"

"No," I say, and he lights his cigarette, the embers burning deep orange as he breathes in.

"So," he says. "You're Claire's daughter."

"I am," I say, and when he doesn't answer, I add, "Again, I'm sorry for coming here like this. I'm only in Tallahassee for a few days. Um . . . I never knew Claire, obviously, so I wanted to meet some of her friends from school, see what she was like, learn some things about her," I admit.

He nods, blows smoke away from us, then starts pacing. "How'd you find me?" he asks—not briskly; more curiously.

"I saw her high school yearbook, and saw you were in Key Club with her," I say. "I tried messaging you on Facebook, but—"

"What? Oh, I never check that thing," he says.

"Right," I say. "So I saw Jessica Cally yesterday, and she said you were a mechanic—"

"Jessica? How's she?"

"She's good," I say. "A painter. Still here in Tallahassee."

"Wow." He chucks the rest of his cigarette on the grass, steps on it, then sits at the table.

"And Bee Trenton said you used to date Claire, so—"

"Bee? You talked to her, too? I'm sure she had plenty of nice things to say about me," he says, shaking his head.

"She didn't say much," I say, hiding the rest of it. It seems like he doesn't need reminding. "Anyway," I continue. "Um, I was hoping you could tell me a bit about her."

He nods, then says, "What do you want to know?"

"Anything," I practically beg.

He exhales gruffly, then wipes his mouth with the back of his hand. "She was a real firecracker, your mother. Didn't take crap from anyone. She just did what she wanted, whenever she wanted. And I loved that about her."

"Like what? What'd she do?" I ask.

"I'm sure you heard about her nickname already," he says, and I nod. "So, that. She stood up to teachers, argued about her grades and usually got her way. She convinced people to do things for her, for free. She just had this amazing charm that people couldn't resist."

"Why were people so drawn in by her?"

"She was . . . magnetic," he says. "Her personality, everything. And she was beautiful. Guys would do anything to be with her." He laughs. "I mean, even me."

"So you dated?" I ask, already kind of knowing the answer.

"Ahhh," he says, rubbing his head again. "Claire and me, we weren't relationship people. We had fun, but we always knew there was more fun to have. She had other guys; I had other girls. We were eighteen."

It's strange to think that all of the stories and information I've collected continue to pile up and create a picture of a woman I don't know. And will never know. But the biggest realization comes from them thinking I'm like her. I'm not. Being a high school student is the only similarity we have, and that's just it. She was *just* a high school student—not a mother at all. It makes sense, but it's still crushing.

"Do you have any other memories of her?"

"Hmmm," he says, scratching his chin. "Me and her and Jessica used to play this game where we'd go into a store and see what we could leave with. Small things, you know, like toothpicks or bookmarks. Just put them in our pockets and walk out. Jessica was caught once, but never us. We always got away with it. It was such a crazy game. That girl, she got me to do anything."

I know now that not only am I not like her, but also if I knew her, I wouldn't have been friends with her. Which is bizarre to admit. How can we be so different? She might have been one of the girls who laughed at me, and I feel like each story Chad shares brings her farther and farther away from me.

When I don't answer, he says, "But all that ended, you know?" He leans back. "I didn't go to college, but she did. She was so smart. And then she dropped out when she found out about her— Well, you, I guess," he says, nodding toward me. "And then . . ." He pauses again, then looks down. "It was real sad when she died. Real sad."

"Did you go to the funeral?" I find myself asking shakily.

"Yeah, I went. You were already gone," he says, nodding toward me again. "Heard you were adopted right away. Everyone went; we all saw her off."

"So you really liked her?"

"Hell yeah, she was amazing," he says quickly, smiling this time. "Not your average gal. She would have gone on to do something really great, I know it. You know," he says, turning to me, "you do look a lot like her. You're more serious, but have her hair. And her, you know, look. It's kind of freaking me out."

He brought up the similarity, so I have to ask. "I never knew who my father was. Do you have any . . ." I trail off, because I can't finish the question. It's too hard. Because what if it's him? And what if it isn't—then the man is still out there?

"Clue?" he finishes. "If you're thinking it's me, you're wrong." I sigh, and I'm not sure if it's from joy or sorrow.

"Yeah, me and Claire were together, but she had a lot of guys. Like I said, she didn't stick to just one." I'm not sure what to say to that. It makes me sad and frustrated all in one.

"So you have no idea who it might be?" I ask.

"No," he says, then gets up and stalks around. "I know what you're thinking—you're judging me, and her. You're not your momma, but I knew her, I knew what she was like." His aggression and candor startle me. "But I was there. I don't want you thinking I was just a guy she dated, who left her. I'm sure you heard all about me from Bee, that I left her for your mom. Yeah, that happened, but it was only 'cause I always liked Claire. I wasn't being a bad guy, I was just getting the girl I wanted. And yeah, we might not have been serious, but I was there." He stops walking and turns to me. "I was there when she found out about you."

I breathe in. "What did she say? What did you say?"

"She wasn't happy, of course. No offense." I shrug because I'm used to that. "But I told her I was there for her, you know? Those other guys, they ran off when they found out, left her alone. She was all alone, but with me."

His need for telling me this startles me. It makes me appreciate him more, for what he did for her. For how they were. "What about her mom?" I ask.

"Honey, you don't know what that girl went through. Her mom wasn't around a lot, and her dad up and left before she was born. She was left a lot, and she was left again once she was pregnant with you. But she had me and Jessica and we were there for her."

I shake my head at this thought. She was crazy, she acted out, she was a person who wanted people, who wanted to feel loved. And she didn't have love, not really. Maybe from friends, but not from her mother. And that pains me, because I *do* have that with my mom. And Claire gave it to me. By giving me up, she gave me the life she didn't have.

"So, no, I don't know who your daddy is. But whoever he is, he's not worth it."

"You sound like you were protective of her . . ." I muse, because it didn't come off that way at first. Not at all. It's interesting he changed.

"Yeah, we had each other's backs. She was a good person. Don't judge her by stupid things, like cheating with me. Know she was a good person. She loved. She loved with everything."

"Thank you," I say, knowing I got enough. She wasn't perfect, but neither am I. Neither is Chad or Treena or anyone. I'll never be like her, but she had someone, at least, who was. And like with Bee, I feel the need to ask about her art. "I heard she was a painter."

"She was an artist," he says. "That shit was her life. She lived and breathed it. Always carrying around that sketchbook."

I nod, comforted by the information. There's that.

I don't want to bring the memories back for him anymore, so I thank him again, and then turn to go. "Hey," he calls when I'm a few feet away. "850-555-6548."

"Huh?" I ask.

"It's her phone number," Chad says. "Susan, her mom's."

"How do you know?" I ask.

"We didn't have cell phones back in high school; we had to memorize numbers."

"And you still know hers?" I ask, doubtful.

"Some people you just don't forget," he answers, and after a second I nod. That's quite enough.

After seeing my face, Bennett takes me back to the dorm. He doesn't ask questions, doesn't press me for details, and I appreciate that. Because I don't know what to say. We park in the lot behind the building, and when we get out of the car, Bennett takes my hand and leads me to the gazebo. I follow wordlessly.

"How're you feeling?" he asks as we sit down, and I lean my head on his shoulder.

"Numb," I manage to get out. "Just . . . numb." He rubs

my hand, and though I know he's doing it, I don't feel it. I don't want to be comforted, so I take my hand away and let my head fall into my hands. My thoughts are overwhelming and I want them to leave.

I hear Bennett rustle around and then feel him tap my shoulder. I look up and he's holding my camera.

"Go on," he says. I stare at him, and then look down at my camera. I take it in my hands, feeling the weight shift. My fingers automatically go to the right place and I feel better. No, not better, more in control. I can't control the past, but I can manage this.

I force a smile, then get up and follow the path toward the green. I'm grateful that he already gets me, already knows that I need to be alone right now, losing myself in my photos.

I take a seat on the grass in the shade of a tree and hold the viewfinder up to my eye. This is how I like to see things, compact and contained in a small window. Here I can see the full picture, because the full picture is chosen and can be changed easily. There's no past, no future, just what's seen. I quickly snap, taking a picture of two girls laughing, of a squirrel reaching for a nut, of a Frisbee flying high in the air.

I turn around and see a woman holding hands with a little boy. The boy is trying to run ahead and kick a rock, and it reminds me of the little girl on the slide at the park near my house, before this whole journey started. Back then

I was ready to take the plunge, but now I wish someone had held me back like this mother. And I think back to my mom, my real mom, telling me I might be disappointed.

I sigh and lean on the tree. I didn't think it was a bad idea because, back then, I still had this pure, unadulterated image of Claire. That she was this person who knew what was best. Who made one small mistake and sought a way to make it better. I allowed myself to believe that.

But in truth, she wasn't the person I wanted her to be, and she never could be. I let my mind autofocus on an image I wanted, and didn't adjust the settings, didn't account for the light or the shutter. I never autofocus on photos, so why would I do that on my life?

Yes, she was a girl who slept around and stole and didn't care about anything. But she was also smart and charming and passionate about so many things. She stood up for what she believed in. She was a bad friend, but also a good friend. Part of me wants to dislike her for the things she did—especially to Bee, because it hits so close to home—but part of me knows that it was all part of her figuring herself out. It was part of her in-between time. It would be easy to hate her, but I don't. She might have been someone I wouldn't have liked, but she was just a teenager. She could never be like my mom, because she was never really a mom. And I have to be okay with that. I can't just focus in on the old image I had—I have to let it develop into this one, and be proud of the final look.

I wanted this all to *mean* something, but in the end, I think it just means I have to move on.

I stand up and walk back to the gazebo.

"You okay?" Bennett asks once he sees me.

"I will be," I admit. "I think . . . I wanted this all to mean more. Like—I thought that if I came here and found out about her, I'd learn more about myself. About where I should go and what I should be. But all I learned is that I don't really want to be like her. Which is okay, you know; she wasn't much older than me. But it's unsettling not having an image anymore of someone I think I'm secretly like. Of someone I want to impress."

"Well, if you think about it, she gave you up, and that must have been a hard thing to do. My mom's told me about it so many times, working with foster children. Claire was brave in giving you up, and you got the life you deserved because of that."

"I know, you're right," I muse.

"Do you think Chad was lying? That he is your father?" he asks. I've been thinking the same thing.

"I don't know. It's possible. He was with Claire for a while," I say, and though I didn't necessarily like him much, it wouldn't be the worst thing in the world. He was there for her. He cared.

"You called her Claire," he points out. "Your mother. At the start of this, you kept calling her your mother, but today she's Claire."

"I know," I say. At one point I took solace in the fact that I was part of something else, and that there was a story there. And though I still do, in a way, I think I realized the point to all of this. Yes, she was my birth mother, but she was never really my parent. My mom is—she's the one who raised me, and who I'm more like, in so many ways. Even when I don't want to admit it. "I think my parents are my real parents. I mean, not by blood, but by . . . everything else."

"I get that," Bennett says, and I turn to him. "Claire might have had you, but your parents raised you into who you are. It doesn't matter who gave birth to you, it's who raised you. And who you decide to be."

I lean back and think about it. Despite feeling done, I still feel like there's more. "Well. I think I'm okay for now." I look at him, grateful for his company, and realize I don't want to sit here and mope. I want to make the most of this day that started out much more magical. "Come on, let's go do something else," I say.

He smiles and says, "I've got an idea."

TWENTY-FOUR

In an effort to cheer me up, Bennett's promised more movie watching, which I'm pretty sure translates to making the most of an empty dorm room. "You know what's cool?" he asks as we walk down the hallway toward his room. I've walked up and down this hallway all week, but all of a sudden I'm nervous. As if the destination is completely different. I guess, in a way, it is.

"What's that?" I ask.

"The fact that my roommate's never around."

"Don't get your hopes up," I say, jabbing him in the waist.

"Kidding," he says, throwing his arm over my shoulder. "I still promise to not get into your pants." He puts one hand on his heart, and one in the air, as if he's taking an oath.

"Har har har," I say, and he kisses me gently.

"Ahem."

We break apart quickly, realizing that Trey is in front of us.

"Trey," Bennett says, brushing his hair forward. I self-consciously pull down on my shirt, and avoid eye contact.

"Hey yourself," he says, and I can hear an untold joke in his voice.

"Isn't this your Treena time?"

"Um, no . . . actually, Maude, you might want to go see her . . ." he says, and I look up at him.

"Why? What's going on?" I ask, worried.

"She's . . . angry."

My eyes widen, but in truth I'm not that surprised. "Does this have to do with last night?" I ask.

"Um, sort of," he says, looking down. "I, uh, didn't think we were exclusive, and she did."

I squeeze my fists in anger. Of course he didn't realize it; of course he didn't commit to her. I didn't trust him from the start, and he's only proven himself to be unreliable since. I clench my teeth and turn to Bennett.

"I'm gonna go," I say, not meeting Trey's eyes. Despite what's going on between Treena and me, I have to go. Some things are more powerful than fights.

"Yeah, okay, let me know if I can do anything," Bennett says, squeezing my hand before I walk down the hall to the stairwell.

"Hey, Maude?" Trey asks. I turn around, bracing myself

for what he's going to say. "Make sure she's okay. I feel really bad. I just—I feel like a jerk."

"You are one," I say before turning to walk out. I could add so much more, and the words come to me with each step, and I hate myself for not thinking of them quickly enough. But they don't matter; he doesn't matter.

Before the door to the stairs shuts, I overhear one more thing.

"So that's what you've been doing all week, huh?" Trey asks.

"Shut up," Bennett answers.

When I get to Treena's room, it's silent. Eerily silent. I walk toward her bed and see her, facedown, pillow over her head. It's worse than I thought.

"Tree?" I ask, sitting next to her. She shakes her head. At least, I think she shakes her head, as the pillow moves. I take it off her and put my hand on her back. She turns around and her eyes are red and puffy, her sheets drenched in tears.

"He. Broke. Up. With. Me."

"I heard," I say, trying to sound as sympathetic as possible.

"I. Hate. Him."

"I do, too. You know I do," I say, holding on to her hand. "What happened? Or do you not want to talk about it?"

"No, it's okay," she says, wiping her eyes. "He was dating another girl. Actually, a few other girls. He thought he was able to do that."

"I thought you knew he . . ." I start, but then realize it's not time to correct her.

"I thought he might, you know, whatever with other girls . . . but not actually date them," she sniffs.

"What's the difference? They're both awful," I say.

"I know, I know. I guess . . . I was okay with whatever because I didn't know about it. But when I realized he actually *liked* these other girls, and saw them as much as he saw me . . ."

"It was worse because he cared," I say, shaking my head.

"Yeah. He said it was because we never 'defined the relationship,'" she says, using air quotes. "But, hello, he comes here every day. I thought we were pretty defined."

"I'd say so. It's ridiculous. I wonder if the other girls know. . . ."

"I don't know." She shrugs.

"Do you know their names?" I ask.

"No. Why?"

"No reason. We could have found them. Told them."

"Ha. He would have loved that," she says, pushing herself up a little. She twists her hands and looks down. "About last night . . ."

The night comes back to me in full color. Her anger, the way she blamed me for everything. Her complete turnaround since I've been here, from excited to see me, to me being a nuisance. All over some guy. Who left her.

"I was . . . really drunk," she starts, and I wait for more.

I'm not taking the bait. "And I said some awful things."

"Yeah," I say. "It wasn't your finest moment."

"I'm different here," she admits. "I don't know; I came here and it felt okay to be a new me. And I didn't realize it would be strange when you came. Like two worlds colliding."

"I really like the back-home you," I say.

"She was great and all, but . . . she wouldn't have gotten Trey."

"Why is Trey so important?" I finally ask. "Yeah, he's cute, but what is it about him?"

"I don't know," she says. "He just seems so important, like a huge step for me. And not just the boyfriend-ness. He is what all the girls want. And for some reason he wanted me. I got the most desirable guy. How insane is that?"

"Yeah, but he turned out to be awful."

"I just liked where I was, beside him. And he *liked me*."

"But you weren't *you*," I protest.

"I know, but I didn't care. Part of me still doesn't," she says, falling back on her bed. "I mean, despite everything, I'd probably take him back if he came back in here."

"Tree."

"I know, I know. You don't need to lecture me," she says, and I shake my head. She's so much more than this. She's too devoted, and sometimes that's good, but sometimes . . . And I have no idea what to say or do to make her see things differently.

"Tree, you're gonna find plenty of guys who like you. You're beautiful and smart and fun and sweet. You don't need to change to be someone you're not."

"But I have to change just a little," she says. "It would be strange not to. I just want you to change with me. And not judge me for being different."

"Tree, I don't judge you."

"You did," she says.

I pause, because maybe she's right. I had this preconceived notion of who she was, and when I realized she wasn't the same person, I freaked. "Maybe I did. A little."

"I didn't like being judged by you."

"I didn't like being left behind!" I say. "I still don't like it. I'm at school with people I don't care about."

"And Celine," she says, and I sense a hint of jealousy in her voice.

"Celine? Yeah, she's there, but she's not, like, you."

"You just talk about her a lot . . . and she's really cool, and . . ."

"Tree. You have *college*. Celine does not live up to that."

"I just don't want to lose my best friend."

"I don't either!" I argue, and we realize, I think at the same time, that we're fighting for the same thing. We're suddenly on the same side instead of against each other. So we laugh.

"I'm really sorry about everything. Like, this whole week. And the past few nights."

"You did yell at me in a public bathroom."

"Oh my god," she moans, covering her eyes with her hands. "And you were right, too. Like, *everything* you said was right. I was just too stupid to hear it."

"You're not stupid."

"Maude. I am. I know it."

"I can't believe you got back with him after last night."

"Yeah, you let me know that was a bad idea. Bennett, too."

"Bennett?" I ask, my ears perking up.

"You don't remember? After you told me I was insane for getting back with him—which I was—I think Bennett almost punched him. He's not one to tolerate cheating."

"That sounds about right." I smile to myself.

"Wait, whatever happened with you guys last night? You looked like you wanted to kiss him one second, and kill him the next."

"Oh, um, long story," I say, waving her away. Not the time to get into this.

"No, tell me. I need something to distract me from . . . everything."

I think about earlier, how after he kissed me she was the first person I wanted to tell. But now it feels so different, so new. She's not the same Treena I knew back at home, and I have to accept that. I have to grow and change with her, and we'll figure out the new versions as we go. "It's nothing. I also drank too much last night."

"You *did*. I was impressed."

"Well, you were doing it, so . . ."

"Yeah," she says, looking down again.

"I'm here for you, I am, and I want you to feel better, but I just . . ." I stop, planning my words. "I've been really pissed at you all week," I say, and she cringes. "I was so excited to come up here and hang out with you, and you just blew me off every night. I mean, I couldn't even sleep here. . . ."

"I know, you're right."

"And yeah, Bennett's great, but I had to stay with a guy I barely knew. And it really . . . it really hurt me." I finally let it out, feeling everything wash out of me. Everything I've wanted to tell her, everything I've felt. She needs to hear this before we move on. Before I do. I don't want to regret not talking, like Bee does.

"I know. I know. I'm so sorry," she says. "I didn't realize how hard it would be, combining my two lives. Like, have them see what I was like back home. But, I don't know, I shouldn't be embarrassed of that girl, you know? I'm still her. I like her."

"I know you are. I like her, too."

"And," she keeps going, unloading it all, "I shouldn't have had to choose between you and him; I should have been able to hang out with you both. Or, just say no to him for a bit and see you. I was just so scared that he'd leave me if I went a day without him. Which is stupid, I know, but it was how I felt. I was an idiot. And I'm sorry. I'm really, really sorry."

She stops, and there are tears in her eyes, and I want to hug her.

A knock at the door interrupts us.

"I'll go get it," I say, standing up, "in case it's Trey."

"If it's Trey, make him come in."

"Not yet," I say, shaking my head.

I open the door and it's Bennett. I smile, step out into the hall, and shut the door behind me.

"How is she?" he asks.

"She'll be okay. It's just . . . not a good time."

"Yeah. Trey is kind of an ass."

"Yep," I admit. "Speaking of, did you almost punch him last night?"

"Oh, ha, um," he says, reddening. "Not really. I mean, I've never hit anyone, if that's what you're asking. I was just really pissed about the cheating."

"Uh-huh," I say, crossing my arms in front of my chest and smiling at him.

"Unless you like guys who fight, in which case I totally Rocky-ed him."

"Did you scream 'Adrian!' after?"

"Obviously," he says. "No, but I might have pushed him, but that was it. Why? Did Treena say something?"

"The same thing, really. I'm just surprised you left it out of your assessment of the night."

"Would it have made me more attractive? More like Han Solo?" he asks, taking my hands.

"Something like that." I shake my head.

"I just," he says, looking down at his feet, and then back up to me, "I don't want you to think I'm like that—like him. I wouldn't—"

"Hey." I cut him off, putting my hand on his shoulder. "It's okay. You're nothing like Trey," I say, knowing how true it really is.

"Okay, good." He smiles. "And I'm glad she's okay. I feel bad."

"You don't have to. Anyway, I should probably get back in there. We're . . . talking."

"Oh, okay, good. Wait, does that mean I don't get you as a roommate again tonight? Because that's terrible timing."

I laugh. "I think I'm going to stay here. But I'll stop by."

"Okay," he says, kissing me gently. I go back inside and she's sitting on her bed now, looking miserable. Her hands and hair are covering her face.

"That was Bennett," I say. "Checking in."

"Why's he checking in?" she asks, looking up at me. And I see the pain in her eyes, the realization that everything she's decided has been wrong.

Because, much like I did with Claire, I was autofocusing on Treena, too. I was assuming she'd be the same person that I remembered, but of course she isn't. She changed, just like I will when I move away. And I can't hate her for experimenting as someone else for a while to figure out who she really is. Just like I did last night. It's our time to try, right?

I need to open my aperture to let some light in, see her for who she is now, and who she will become. I know she'll be okay, just as I know I will be, too.

So I sit on the bed with her and answer her question from earlier.

"I like Bennett. And he likes me, too," I say, and she perks up. "He helped me through a lot this week, with my mother, and . . . other things." She looks down, knowing "other things" means her. "He's a really good guy."

"So, are you, like, dating?" she asks curiously.

"I think we're figuring things out. We only somewhat know each other."

"So, wait, hold on," she says, grabbing my arm. "Did you guys, like, kiss?"

As I open my mouth, I realize that, just as I wanted, she is going to be the first person I tell. Maybe this will all be okay after all.

TWENTY-FIVE

FRIDAY

The next morning, I wake up in Treena's room. For once. I look over and she's leaving for class.

"I left out some no-milk chai for you. I'll be back in an hour, okay?" she asks.

"Sounds good," I murmur sleepily.

"Oh, your mom called your phone, by the way. It flashed a few times this morning."

I pick up my phone and see the missed call. There's also a text saying my relatives are coming to town tomorrow, so I shouldn't be too late. Which reminds me of something. . . .

"See you!" she says, heading out, and I wave. When the door shuts, I pick up my phone and know what I have to do. It's just extremely hard.

I pace around the room, heart beating in my chest. This is the last call, the one person I have left.

I have the number Chad gave me. And it matches the one I called years ago looking for answers. The same number where the woman hung up on me. She was a disappointment then, and I don't know if I can be disappointed again. But I was fourteen then. I'm older now. I'm stronger. I can do this.

I dial the number.

"Hello?"

"Hi . . . Can I speak with Susan Fullman?" I ask the woman who answered the phone. She has a husky voice, one made by ten-too-many late nights and ten-thousand-too-many late cigarettes.

"I'm Susan."

"Oh, hi, Susan, um." I stop because this is her—this is it. I'm talking to my biological grandmother for the second—and possibly, if this doesn't go well, last—time. I can never repeat this moment, and I'm so nervous, I can't even take it all in.

"Well, spit it out." She hurries me, so I panic.

"I'm Claire Fullman's daughter."

There's silence. Then the strike of a match, a deep inhale. "What did you say?"

I go slower this time. "My name is Maude, and my birth mother was Claire Fullman . . . your daughter, right?"

More terrifying silence. "How'd you get this number?"

I breathe in and say, "Chad Glickman." Silence. With all the power I have in me, I push myself to continue. "I know this is strange, and I don't mean to make you uncomfortable. I just . . . I never knew my mother. And I'm trying to. That's . . . what I'm doing."

"Where are you?" she asks with a cough.

"In Tallahassee. I'm here looking at FSU, and decided to look her up while I was here. I mean, I know she's not here, but I just . . . I met a few of her old friends, like Chad." I falter, and there's nothing. "I understand if you'd rather not talk, but I just thought I'd . . . try."

Another deep breath. "I had a feeling this day would come. How old are you now? Sixteen?"

"Seventeen," I say, knowing the past years don't just count my age.

"It's been seventeen years. . . . I don't know what you want me to say."

"Just . . . anything. About her. About you. I mean, you're my—"

She cuts me off. "Claire was . . . Claire had problems."

"Right, the heart condition," I answer.

"Oh, she had problems before that," she says with a sigh. "Listen, hon, this isn't a good time."

"Excuse me?" I balk.

"I can't talk about this right now. I'm not ready to be a grandmother, if that's what you're looking for. I'm not grandmother material. And, as your mother used to say, I'm not mother material, either."

"I'm *not* looking for that," I say. "I just wanted to talk to you...."

"About what? You don't want to know about me after seventeen years. You want to know about her. And what can I say? She lived, and then she didn't. Is that good enough?" This time it's my turn to be silent. She's being awful, and I don't know why. We're related. I'm part of her, and she doesn't see that, or doesn't want to see it. She just wants to push me away.

"No, wait, I—" I start, but I don't know what to say.

"I don't know what else you want, but I have to go. You have my number; call again and maybe I'll be ready to talk then."

"Oh..." I say, feeling my heart break and tear and open. "That's it?"

"What more do you want?"

"Anything," I say. "Literally, anything."

There's a gruff sigh, and then, "Claire and me didn't get along much. We did our own thing, and then she was gone and I blamed myself for a while. But I'm good now. It's been seventeen years and I'm good now. Is that it? Is that what you wanted to hear?"

"Oh, I'm so—"

"Don't sorry me. I've heard it enough. Like I said, I'm not ready to be a grandmother, so you figure this one out."

"Okay," I say, feeling the tears start to gather in my eyes

and fall down, each with a touch of disappointment.

"I'm sorry, but not now," she says, then hangs up. I keep the phone next to my ear, as if thinking she didn't really say good-bye, and maybe she's still there. Maybe she's playing a joke on me.

Or maybe I'm the joke.

Couldn't she have spoken to me longer? Really, what could have been more important than talking to me? I mean, she said we could talk another time, but I want to talk now. If my long-lost granddaughter called me, I'd keep her on the phone for hours. I'd want to hear all about her life. I'd want to tell her about mine.

But I'm not her, and maybe she doesn't like surprises. She's never reached out to me—maybe there's a reason there.

I finally put down the phone, and sit on the bed. I remember that there's one more message out there, to Lisa, but I don't care anymore. The search is over, I've exhausted my sources, and I'm okay with it. Susan gave me answers she didn't even know she was offering.

And I think I found all the answers I really need.

After a few minutes of staring at nothing in particular, I realize I need to get out. I decide to discover the campus again. Only this time on my own.

I leave Treena a note, then grab the key for her bike.

Downstairs, I hop on and feel my legs push against the

pedals. Push by push, I'm moving forward, going faster and farther than I knew I could go.

My mother went here. I don't know where she lived, or what she did. I barely know what she liked, but she was here, on this campus. And it feels surreal and wonderful all in one to be in the same place as her.

I bike off the green and to the union. I pass the club where Treena and the guys did trivia, and think my mother probably saw a gig there. Long, loose skirt; I can picture her dancing and feeling the music. So I stop and take a picture.

I go past a bookstore and some more buildings. Past an observatory and a statue of three people standing tall. I pass a baseball field and the football field where I started out this entire journey. I turn around and head back up, toward the English building, and get a bit lost on the sidewalks and side streets. And I find myself in the middle of a garden.

It's small, but it includes rosebushes and a reflection pond. I get off the bike and sit on the grass. I focus on the pond, but not the water; instead, my reflection. I see myself in ripples and waves and every version of me colliding into one.

Like Treena, there are a few me's, too. There's the me who's perfectly behaved in school, who doesn't want to cause a problem. There's the me who jokes around with my parents and calls my mom out on her lameness. There's the me who's home when I'm with Treena, acting like a family of two. And there's that empty space that's just filling up with memories that aren't mine. That space is reserved for my mother. That's the me I'll never fully know, but am trying to piece together.

The thing is, I'm happy she gave me up. She was my age—she was hardly a mother. She wasn't ready for that. And I love my parents so much. So for all of that, I'm grateful.

I think, in the end, I lost the image of someone I'd admire and look up to. Instead I just found . . . a person. And that person doesn't bring me any closer to figuring out who I am, and where I should go next. What I should do. Perhaps that's the biggest disappointment of them all.

Despite wanting to, I'll never be like my parents. But I'm not like Claire, either. I'm different. And because of that, I can be whoever I want.

I just need to decide who that person is.

◇◇◇◇

I get back to the dorm and see Trey in the main lobby.

"Oh, hey," he says, a bit surprised.

"Hi," I say, trying to pass him.

"Um . . . how is she?" he asks, gesturing up toward Treena's room.

"She's great," I say briskly, not wanting him to know how hurt she is.

"Good. Good. I . . ." He brushes his hair out of his face. "I feel shitty. She was good, you know? I just feel shitty."

I look up at him and wonder what he was like in high school. Did he get all the girls then, too? Or was he just as

dorky as us? I wonder if this is who he is, or if he's transition-
ing, too. "You should tell her."

"I don't think she wants to see me," he says.

"She does. But later."

"Okay." He nods. "Later."

He walks down the hall, hiking a bag over his shoulder.
I don't know what's going to happen there, but if I can get
some closure for Treena, at least that's something. I think,
in a way, he's trying to figure himself out, too.

I feel a buzz in my pocket.

Awake?

I smile and head to Bennett's room.

"Bennett?" I ask, peeking my head inside the door.

"Hey!" he says, looking up from his computer. He's still
in his pajamas.

"Am I interrupting . . . ?" I ask.

"No, come in," he says, grabbing for my hands and pulling me down for a kiss. I sit on his bed behind him and he
gestures to the screen. "Just animating," he says. I look at the
little green alien spinning in circles.

"You made that?" I ask, amazed.

"Yeah, it's not much. I designed him last week—I'm seeing how he moves now. I think he's a bit spastic, really."

"How so?" I ask, running my fingers through his hair.

"I don't know—see his mouth? How it's a huge grin? I

figure he's just always happy, you know? Always amusing himself. So right now he's spinning in circles because he likes to feel the world spin."

"How do you feel the world spin?" I ask.

He turns and faces me. "Wait. Have you never spun in a circle and then fallen to the ground?"

"Oh! That. Yes."

"I was going to say. First bike, then spinning . . ." He smiles.

"Yeah, yeah," I say. "I like him. He kind of reminds me of you."

"Because I'm a spastic green alien?"

"Obviously." I smile, and he starts tickling my sides. "Okay, okay, you're not a spastic green alien!" I laugh, pushing at him. He stops, and wraps his arms around me. "He's happy and alive. Like you."

Bennett stares at me, and then kisses me again, and it's cute, and he's cute, and I know we're not forever, but I'd like to remember this moment forever.

I walk back downstairs and find Treena sitting on her bed, reading.

"And where were you?" she asks, grinning.

"Bike ride." I throw her bike key at her. "And then upstairs," I admit, smiling.

"Oooohhhh." She fake swoons, and I jump on her bed, covering her mouth with my hand.

"You hush," I say, removing my hand. "What have you been up to?"

"Actually," she says, putting down her book, "Trey stopped by."

"He did?" I ask. I didn't think he'd stop by so soon. "How'd that go?"

"Okay." She shrugs. "Not awful."

"So . . . ?" I ask, sitting on the bed next to her.

"We're not back together, if that's what you're asking. And that's good. He wants to have fun; I want to be a bit more serious. And that's okay. It's good we know it now," she says.

"You sound very mature about all of this," I say, seeing a hint of the Treena I remember, the one who logically explained *why* it was better that she skip prom, because why spend all that money on something that only lasts one night?

She shrugs and smiles. "I've thought it over. I don't really want to be with a guy who wants to be with other girls, you know?"

"*Finally*," I say, exasperated, and she laughs. "You need someone better."

"Yeah. I mean, I guess I want a guy who just wants me."

"Good."

"I only wish it hurt a bit less, you know?"

"You're still allowed to be sad."

She sighs. "I'm actually impressed with you. You've

accomplished so much, and aren't really showing it."

I think about how Bennett was in on so much with me this week, and remember how I always wanted it to be Treena. So I tell her about the last step I took.

"I talked to my grandmother today."

"Wait, hold up," she says, kneeling on her bed. "Your grandmother? How? When? What?"

"I know, crazy, right?"

"No, monumental. Didn't you think you talked to her the one time?"

"Yes," I say, because she remembers. "And it was the same person. I was right." I explain how Chad gave me the number, and how the call went. "She kind of doesn't want anything to do with me."

"How can that be?" Treena asks, outraged. "You're her *granddaughter*. How can she just not care?"

"It's been a while, I guess. I've never been part of her life, and for all she knew, I never would be."

"No, I don't believe that. She had to have assumed you'd come around one day. That you'd want to know."

She's right, and Susan mentioned something along those lines. But still, she didn't seem to care. It's like her assumption was fulfilled, so she was done. "She doesn't seem to care about that."

"You have to do something about it."

"Tree, it's over, there's nothing I can do. I've dug up the past enough."

She stares at me, then opens her laptop. "Susan Fullman, right?"

"Yes . . ." I say warily.

"Phone number?"

I tell her and she nods. She writes something down, turns around, and then starts to pull me out the door. I get what she's doing, and shake my head in protest.

"No, Tree, we can't just visit her. I've dropped in on enough people this week."

"We can and we will. She doesn't just say no to you like that. It's not right."

"I appreciate the commitment, I do, but this is all—" I start, and wonder, all so . . . what? So sudden? Not really; I've wondered about her for years. And I'll continue wondering some more. So, really, what's one more stop? If it's bad news, then it can't change anything I don't already know. "Okay." I nod, convinced. "Okay, let's go."

We jump into my car—Treena doesn't have one up here—and she directs the way. We drive off campus and past downtown, where Bee might be at work, thinking about yesterday. And we pass the school that was my mother's, and I tell Treena so, wondering what Mr. Wayne is up to now. And then we drive down a road nearby that's just as dilapidated as the roads by the school. I know this wasn't where my mother lived—our letters were all returned to sender—but I still can't help feeling we're not far. That she grew up among the loose tires, broken cars, overgrown yards, and tossed bottles.

We pull up to a house I assume to be hers, and it's just like the others, only smaller. A tiny shack of a place with one flowerpot outside, and a car resting in the driveway. There's no garage, just an overhang, under which boxes are stored.

"We're here," I say, stopping the car and breathing hard. I've done this before, I've approached the stranger, but this time it's so much more personal. Because this person didn't just know my mother, she was a part of her. She's a part of me.

I came here so quickly, without having time to think, that everything crashes on me now. I shake my head no, because I can't believe I'm doing this. I can't believe she's just behind that door. How did I get here?

"You've got this," Treena says, probably sensing my discomfort. I look at her wide-eyed and she gives me a reassuring stare back.

"I don't know how to do this," I say.

So she gets out of the car and meets me at my side. I open the door and she says, "Just like this." I hug her, glad she's here with me. I need her with me.

I knock on the door and there's motion inside, a grumble, a cat's cry. Shuffling tells me she's on the other side, looking out the peephole.

"What do you want?"

"It's me," I say, steadying my voice. "Maude."

"Maude," she says in a gruff voice, and I'm surprised

with how I'm not scared, how I'm standing taller. "Didn't we talk already?"

"Yes, but I wanted to come see you. In person."

There are more shuffling sounds, and a bolt clicks. She's opening the door. *Be brave, Maude, be brave.*

"What do you want?" she asks, and I see her for the first time. My biological grandmother. She's short and stout with frizzy brown/gray hair and wrinkles lining her face. She has a cigarette in one hand, and looks much older than I assume she is. She can't be more than mid to late fifties.

"I just . . ." I start, because what do I want? I got it all, didn't I? "I just wanted to see you."

"Well, you saw me, you happy?" she asks, and my heart drops. I knew she wouldn't be nice, but I didn't think . . .

"My friend drove a long way to be here," Treena interrupts. "She just wants to talk to you, that's it. Can't you give her at least that?"

Susan stares at her, then looks at me. "I like her."

"I do, too," I say.

Susan sighs, then asks, "What do you want to know?" She crosses her arms and leans against the doorframe, not inviting us in or allowing us to see anything beyond her.

"Just . . . anything about her. Anything at all."

She looks down, then back at me. "I wasn't meant to be a mom, just like she wasn't meant to be a mom. I didn't do a good job, so you can see why I don't want to talk about this."

I blush, because I can see it. That must be hard to admit.

Just as it must have been hard for my mother to give me away.

"Claire was spirited and very single-minded. She did what she wanted, whether I liked it or not. In that way, she was a lot like me, but she was also very secretive and in her head. I never knew what was going on in there. Not even when she was a kid."

I nod again. These are things I've heard before, but they're more than that. They're from her.

"I'm sorry, I can't talk about this," she says, shaking her head. "It should be easy for me to bring up thoughts about my one daughter, but I don't want to go back there. I can't."

"I'm sorry," I say instinctively, uncomfortably. How weird it must be to feel strange talking about your own daughter. I can see the reservations in her eyes, the desire for me to leave. But I don't want to. "I'm sorry this hurts. I just . . . I really wanted to know."

"There was only one way to really know that girl. Wait, hold on." Susan goes back into her house.

I look at Treena and she shrugs. We wait a few seconds, and then Susan comes back holding a book.

"You deserve this." She hands me a small black notebook and I open it up. It's full of drawings. It's Claire's sketchbook.

"Oh wow," I say, about to cry.

"You'll learn more about her in there than through me."

"I don't know what to say." I shake my head. "Thank you."

"Yeah, well," she says, then, "Good luck."

"Thank you, thank you," I say again.

She nods and then says, "I can't offer more. Maybe later. But right now . . . that's it. I can't think of her any more."

I shake my head and still don't understand. Why would you not want to remember your own daughter? Maybe because there's more. She wasn't a mother to her, not really, from what I heard. Maybe, like Bee, she lives with regrets. Ones she doesn't want to face. Maybe she needs to keep part of Claire inside her, so that she never disappears. Not fully. It's sad and painful.

Susan shuts the door, and I tuck the notebook under my arm as I walk back to the car. When we get in, I look at Treena and start to cry. From meeting Susan. From holding the sketchbook. For seeing the life Claire was a part of. For understanding, at least a little.

"I know," Treena says. "I know." She puts her arms around me, and in the moment I know this is it. This is the end of my journey. It's what I was looking for all along. I just didn't know it.

TWENTY-SIX

We go back to the dorm and I tuck the notebook away.

"Don't you want to look through it?" Treena asks.

"In time," I say, and she momentarily looks disappointed, but I think she gets it. It's something only my mother knew about, and now it's mine. It's a secret we can share.

To fill the time, we walk around campus again and just talk. She shows me some sites I've already seen, and others that are more personal to her. A building she thinks is pretty. A statue that amuses her. We go to dinner in the cafeteria, and while leaving, we bump into Bennett outside. I look at Treena, but she avoids my eyes and just stares right ahead at him, a grin on her face. Which means something.

"What's up?" I ask.

"NOW!" Treena yells, and within seconds, I feel my

body being lifted and cradled like a baby.

"WHAT IS GOING ON?" I yell as Bennett holds tight and Treena tapes my hands together.

"Initiation." Bennett laughs and starts walking away from the cafeteria. I kick my legs, but Treena grabs them.

"I told you about the fountain . . ." Bennett says, looking at me apologetically.

"But it's not my birthday!" I protest.

"Doesn't matter—you're one of us now, you're going in," Treena says, and I audibly sigh with frustration.

"I'm assuming there's nothing I can do to change this?" I beg.

"Nope!" Treena squeaks gleefully, and I lower my head dejectedly. But as we walk through campus, toward the fountain, I'm kind of secretly excited.

Thankfully, we're not too far, but by the time we get there, Bennett is struggling to breathe.

"I'm not *that* heavy," I joke.

"I'm not *that* strong," he counters, and I laugh. "You can always get revenge," he whispers in my ear, too low for Treena to hear.

With the fountain in view, I'm reminded that it's not that big, and not that deep, just a round concrete structure with a spout in the middle. But it's definitely big enough to put someone in, and I guess that someone, tonight, will be me.

"READY!" Treena yells, and Bennett dips down tauntingly. She cuts the tape from my hands and I wince as it rips off my skin. "ONE!"

"Ahhhh," I start to yell, heart pounding in fear of the drop, the water, the cold.

"TWO!" Treena counts down. "AND THREE!"

On three, I feel myself being lightly placed into the water, and getting dunked under. The water crashes all over me, and it's cold, freezing. I jump up, gasping, my heart in my throat. They're watching, laughing, and high-fiving as the droplets roll down my face and my clothes start sticking to my body. I gasp, standing up. And despite how I feel, how cold and wet I am, I start laughing, because here I am, at a college, getting thrown into a fountain. And for some reason, it feels right.

"Fun?" Treena giggles, and I nod, and then quickly reach for her arm and pull.

"NO NO NO NO!" she yells, but Bennett doesn't miss a beat. He picks her up by her waist and puts her in with me. "AHH!" she yells as she drops into the water.

I laugh, helping her up, and watching as her hair sticks to her face. She scowls at Bennett and me, and then I grab her and hug her. She hugs back, whispering, "I'm glad you're here."

"Me too," I say back, over the roar of the water spouting out. "Revenge?" I then ask, and she nods. We turn around toward Bennett. He raises his eyebrows, then runs.

I jump out and chase after him around the fountain. He sidesteps me a few times, but eventually I grab his fingers and he skids to a stop.

"Wait, wait, wait," he protests, and instead of dragging

him in, I hug him, getting the fountain water on his clothes.

"Ughhh," he yells, and I laugh. "I said revenge on *her*, not *me*!" I look up and pull him in anyway. He doesn't resist, instead jumps in with me, water hitting at our knees.

"So this is college?" I ask.

"Not bad, right?" he asks, before kissing me under the falling fountain water. We get water in our eyes, our noses, our mouths, but we laugh the entire time. I focus only on his touch, and know that this moment would be the perfect picture.

TWENTY-SEVEN

The drive home to Orlando is different than the drive to Tallahassee. Instead of questions and insecurities floating through my mind, I'm full of answers and resolutions. And though there are still mysteries left, ones that might forever go unsolved, I'm okay not answering them. For now, at least. With the breeze blowing through the windows, I let those thoughts leave me and drift out on the highway, scattered among the discarded cups and roadkill.

My parents are out when I get home, so I carry my bag to my room and plop it on my bed. With nothing, but everything, on my mind, I pick up my camera and phone and flip through the photos I took. There's Lichgate in all its glory. The girls laughing on the green. The stained glass on the building. And then there's Treena and me doing a Buddy

Shot. Bennett kissing my cheek.

Then there's the photo of the yearbook, there's Jessica painting, there's the mechanic shop, and the capitol. Those are parts of my journey, too, and although not as happy as a dunk in the fountain, they're more important.

I sit down at my desk and open my laptop for the first time in a week. Instinctively I check my email, as if I'm still waiting for another person to let me in on a history I wasn't part of. Instead there's an email from Bennett with an attachment. I open the file and it's an animated penguin saying hello. I laugh, because of course that would be how he tells me he misses me. I miss him already, too.

I have a text from Treena, too, saying hi. Saying she misses me. Saying she's not happy that I'm gone.

I go back to the assignment that started this entire journey.

Family.

I attach my camera to my laptop and load the files, watching them rewind through my entire trip. Once they're done, I organize them into a folder. And I realize the important ones are already used; they're on my blog. I flip to it and see my entire trip played out in reverse, and I get what Ms. Webber wanted me to do. In the series, I'm documenting my journey, but also my path. Every piece of it, even the bad. I didn't know how it would all end as I posted, so each addition feels real and not forced. I didn't create something in reflection, I created it as it happened.

That is my story. This blog is my project.

I do like the process, after all.

I plan on turning that in to her, but still, I want something that represents my mother for the project. Along with photos I'll eventually take of my parents, I want something that connects to Claire. So I pull up a picture of my feet at Lichgate. That's us. That's me, standing where she was. That's the part of her that's in me.

Then I load the photo of my reflection in the pond. It came out slightly fuzzy because I wasn't focusing well, but it works. I'm a blur. I'm not clear and crisp like some people; instead I'm messy on the edges and not quite formed. I'm many pieces all put into one, and one day I'll figure them all out. But right now, I'm happy being a blur. I'm happy being every part of me, every image of me, even if they don't *feel* like me.

The pictures tell the story—my story. I've heard Claire's from so many different voices that I want this essay to showcase my story. Maybe I like being behind the viewfinder so much because it's my way of telling my truth.

I edit the photos, correcting the color and the saturation, for over an hour, until I hear the door open.

"Honey?" my mom calls.

"In here," I call back. "Coming!" I hit Save and run out to say hi.

"You're home!" my mom shrieks, and pulls me in for a hug. I roll my eyes dramatically at my dad, but he's smiling, too. He gives me a hug and asks about the logistics—the car, the drive.

"Car rode smoothly, no accidents, not too much traffic."

Mom asks the more obvious questions: How's Treena? What did I think of the campus?

"Treena is good, she's really happy there and it was great seeing her. The campus is beautiful, really beautiful, and it has a great photo lab."

"And how was . . ." my mom starts, but doesn't finish.

"It was okay," I admit. "I'd really like to tell you all about it later, if you don't mind."

"I never mind," she says, smiling.

I help them get ready for dinner, and it feels normal, like nothing changed, even though everything did.

And after dinner, as promised, I tell my mom about what I learned. I leave some parts out; some parts are just for me.

"I can't believe you found out so much."

"Yeah," I say. "I hope that's okay. . . ."

"More than okay. I'm so proud of you . . . for all of this," she says, and I smile. I open my computer and show her some of the photos I took, and describe the ones I plan to take.

"So now I just need you and Dad to complete it. Because, you know, family," I say, and a look of love and gratitude crosses her face, and for a second I thank my teacher for this project. Because, to me, it was so much more than that.

Before going to bed, I pull out the box that has the photo of my mother in it. It'll now hold the sketchbook, too.

If there's one thing I learned on my journey, it's this: family is more than just the person who gave birth to you. Yes, it's my mother, but it's also my mom and dad, for allowing me to decide who I want to be; it's Treena, for making me a friend; it's everyone who's helped me figure out which version of myself is right. And though I still might not be entirely sure, I'm on my way.

When I think of my future, I focus on what it might be. Not the imagined, ideal version, but the real, gritty future of someone who doesn't know what she wants, and all of the good and bad that might come of that. And that's okay.

And when I focus on that, only that, I know that what happened before me doesn't matter; it doesn't dictate my future. Only I can do that.

And, with the sketchbook in hand, I'm ready.

Acknowledgments

◇◇◇◇

To Karen Chaplin, who pushed me to make this story more than I could have imagined. Thank you for your faith and encouragement. To the entire team at HarperCollins Childrens Books, including Olivia Swomley, Bethany Reis, Christina MacDonald, Kate Engbring, Olivia Russo, Kim VandeWater, and, of course, Rosemary Brosnan. You're all terrific, and I'm constantly amazed by the work you do.

To Michelle Andelman, thank you endlessly for helping me flesh out this story. I'm so happy I was able to have you on my side for so long. To Claire Anderson-Wheeler, thank you for championing the book from our first phone call. You're wonderful. And to the entire team at Regal Hoffman & Associates—thank you for your support.

To my original readers: Joe Chandler, who's quite honestly one of the best writers I know; Misty White, for helping me put Maude in the driver's seat; and Michelle Carroll, for an insane amount of support and love. To the many loves of my life: Megan Donnelly, who inspires me daily; Colure Caulfield, who I text probably too often; Shannon Calloway, who I can't text nearly enough; Katie Harding, my like-minded twin; and Gina Elia, my cousin whom I adore.

As always, to everyone at Alafaya Library. To Danielle King (for your patience with my craziness), Breanna Ramos (for listening as I babble about ideas), and David Smith (for answering my probably too-personal research questions). Speaking of research, to Allison Miehl for answering all my high school questions and for friendship bracelets. To Anu Mathur for being a great sister and answering emails entitled "Treena's Indian-ness." And to my O-Hall 3N friends—the skateboarding scene is for you.

To my amazing writer friends Jenny Torres Sanchez and Jessica Martinez—I couldn't have survived my debut year without you. I love our writer triangle. And to Jennifer Chen and Melissa Sarno for being agent sisters for life. And to the Fifteeners—thank you for a crazy-supportive debut year.

To all of my friends and family who read *TNWSY*—your support means the world to me. I'm seriously so lucky to have you. And to all the readers, writers, bloggers, booksellers, and, of course, librarians who supported my first book: thank you, thank you, thank you.

This book is about family, so of course to my wonderful parents, Paul and Tami Gibaldi, who also freaked out the first time I drove to Tallahassee alone. I love you. To Justin Gibaldi. How I have a brother who doesn't like to read is beyond me, but I'm still happy to have you. And to Jetta, still.

To Samir Mathur for being the most patient, supportive, wonderful husband. For taking over baby duty so I could write and edit. For everything and anything. And to Leila, my love, always.

LOVE PICTURE-PERFECT ROMANCE?
READ MORE FROM
LAUREN GIBALDI!

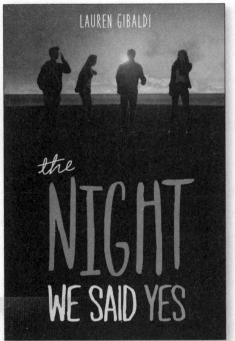

And don't miss *Matt's Story,*
a Night We Said Yes e-novella

HARPER TEEN

An Imprint of HarperCollinsPublishers

WWW.EPICREADS.COM